"My feelings for you are not in the least brotherly, Maggie.

"I would have thought that kiss in your trailer earlier proved that."

At that reminder, the air seemed to vibrate suddenly with charged tension. Maggie cleared her throat. "I, ah, I've been meaning to talk to you about that."

"What about it?" Colt asked.

"Well, obviously, it was a—mistake."

"A mistake?"

"Of course," Maggie answered. "It was a chemical reaction...stimulated by the fact that we were in such close proximity, alone there in the trailer."

"Well, Doc, I hate to point this out, but we're in even closer proximity right now. And we're alone. Feeling any chemical reactions?"

"No," Maggie answered, as primly as a schoolmarm. "It must have been a...one-time occurrence, and now it's completely out of our systems."

This time Colt laughed. "A chemical reaction. Right. You keep telling yourself that, Doc. Maybe sooner or later you'll even believe it."

Dear Reader,

Welcome to another month of fabulous reading from Silhouette Intimate Moments, the line that brings you excitement along with your romance every month. As I'm sure you've already noticed, the month begins with a return to CONARD COUNTY, in *Involuntary Daddy,* by bestselling author Rachel Lee. As always, her hero and heroine will live in your heart long after you've turned the last page, along with an irresistible baby boy nicknamed Peanut. You'll wish you could take him home yourself.

Award winner Marie Ferrarella completes her CHILDFINDERS, INC. trilogy with *Hero in the Nick of Time,* about a fake marriage that's destined to become real, and not one, but *two,* safely recovered children. Marilyn Pappano offers the second installment of her HEARTBREAK CANYON miniseries, *The Horseman's Bride.* This Oklahoma native certainly has a way with a Western man! After too long away, Doreen Owens Malek returns with our MEN IN BLUE title, *An Officer and a Gentle Woman,* about a cop falling in love with his prime suspect. Kylie Brant brings us the third of THE SULLIVAN BROTHERS in *Falling Hard and Fast,* a steamy read that will have your heart racing. Finally, welcome RaeAnne Thayne, whose debut book for the line, *The Wrangler and the Runaway Mom,* is also a WAY OUT WEST title. You'll be happy to know that her second book is already scheduled.

Enjoy them all—and then come back again next month, when once again Silhouette Intimate Moments brings you six of the best and most exciting romances around.

Yours,

Leslie J. Wainger
Executive Senior Editor

Please address questions and book requests to:
Silhouette Reader Service
U.S.: 3010 Walden Ave., P.O. Box 1325, Buffalo, NY 14269
Canadian: P.O. Box 609, Fort Erie, Ont. L2A 5X3

THE WRANGLER AND THE RUNAWAY MOM

RaeAnne Thayne

Published by Silhouette Books

America's Publisher of Contemporary Romance

SILHOUETTE BOOKS

ISBN 0-373-07960-5

THE WRANGLER AND THE RUNAWAY MOM

RAEANNE THAYNE

lives in a crumbling old Victorian in northern Utah with her husband and two young children. She loves being able to write where she is surrounded by rugged mountains and real cowboys.

For Kjersten Thayne,
the best daughter a mother could ask for,
and for Avery Thayne, who deserves coauthor status,
since he insisted on sitting on his mother's lap
through nearly every page.

Prologue

Margaret Prescott choked back a scream and watched her husband topple to the thick carpet of his office like a marionette whose strings had been severed. Only the blood seeping from the neat round hole in the middle of his forehead shattered the illusion.

The two figures standing over the crumpled form of the man she'd once thought she loved didn't even turn in her direction. Michael's heavy oak washroom door, ajar just enough to allow her a distorted view into the room, must have muffled the tiny cry that rasped from her throat.

"What the hell you do that for, Carlo?" The tall one with the droopy eyes and beak of a nose that gave him a morose expression stared at the other man.

Carlo, thin and wiry, with short-cropped hair so blond it was nearly white, lifted a shoulder negligently and slid the sleek chrome revolver inside his tailored suit coat. "I lost my temper. He should never have baited me like that."

His blue eyes were dead, Maggie thought, fighting to hold

on to lucidity through the panic that clawed through her. Cold
and flat and dead, like a cobra's.

"How we supposed to find the merchandise now?"
Droopy Man snarled. "What's DeMarranville gonna say?"

"I imagine he'll say good riddance."

"Only problem is, you killed the stupid bastard before he
could tell us where he hid the stuff."

"Ah, but he did tell us."

"You mean that bit about his wife carrying the secret or
whatever the hell he said? That was just bull, to get us off
his back."

"You think so?" Carlo looked impassively at Michael's
body—at the blood that had begun to pool under his head,
at the sprawl of lifeless limbs—then back at the other man.
"I believe you're wrong. I think the good lady doctor knows
exactly where our merchandise is. I have no doubt she'll be
more than happy to lead us right to it."

"You're screwed in the head. Why would she do that?"

"You don't give me nearly enough credit, Franky."
Carlo's mouth twisted into a small smile that sent chills rip-
pling down Maggie's spine. "I've been told my powers of
persuasion are quite extraordinary."

Without a backward look at the man whose life he'd just
taken, he turned and walked out of Michael's office.

When the other man followed him, Maggie swayed in the
washroom, her breathing coming shallow and fast. Several
moments passed before she worked up the courage to push
the door open.

Michael's vacant eyes stared at her from the floor in familiar accusation. As if it were her fault, all of it. If only she
had been able to call for help somehow when she had heard
them all come into the office. If only she'd been able to
provide a distraction by coming out instead of choosing to
remain in the washroom when she heard their raised voices
and accusations against Michael.

If only she had been smarter or faster or stronger.

No. She jerked her head up. Unlike her failure of a marriage, she had nothing to do with any of this. It was just another one of Michael's dirty little secrets.

Embezzlement, they'd said. *The boss frowns on his people stealing from him. But turn over the stuff and he'll go easy on you.*

They'd lied. She stared at Michael's body and felt the panic bubble up inside her again. She couldn't have stopped this. If she had somehow made her presence known tonight, she had no doubts she would be just as dead as Michael. And then where would Nicky be?

Nicky! She had to get to Nicky before they did. Somehow she had no doubt Carlo-of-the-dead-eyes would have no compunction about hurting her child to force her cooperation, to compel her to lead them to these mysterious books.

What irony, that she'd come to Michael's office concerned for her son's emotional well-being only to find his physical safety now jeopardized. She had planned to plead with him to call off his lawyer, the nasty little man who had informed her this afternoon that Michael planned to seek custody of Nicky in the divorce.

Michael didn't want Nicky. Hadn't wanted Nicky, she corrected herself, on the verge of hysteria. He barely acknowledged his son's existence unless it was to snap at him for some infraction. He only wanted custody to hurt her for leaving him—for finally seeing the gaping cracks in their facade of a marriage, the lies and the infidelities—by taking away the one thing that mattered to her.

And now it looked like he was reaching out even after death to destroy the life she had begun to rebuild so carefully.

She wouldn't let him! She could run away, take Nicky somewhere safe, where the ugliness of his father's life couldn't hurt him.

She fumbled with the door handle and rushed out into the hall, then punched the elevator button.

Nicky loved the two elevators up to his father's eighth-

floor office in one of San Francisco's graceful older buildings. When they used to visit Michael here, back when she
was still pretending they could salvage their marriage, Nicky
would beg to ride them again and again until he was dizzy
with it.

Now, as she waited, the creaky elevators seemed to move
with excruciating slowness. She felt as if each moment lasted
aeons until finally one jolted open and she stumbled inside.

The other elevator suddenly pinged before the ponderous
doors could creep shut, and her pulse scrambled frantically.
Had they somehow discovered she was here? Were they returning to finish off any witnesses? Maggie shrank into the
corner near the buttons and willed the doors to close.

She held her breath, waiting for them to spot her, for the
gunfire that would end her life. The only sound, though, was
heavy footsteps as two unfamiliar men in dark suits hurried
toward Michael's office.

"I know she's in here somewhere. I saw her go in," she
heard one of them say. "She can't have gone far."

"Dammit. We have to find her," the older one said, an
angry frown slashing across his distinguished face. "We
can't have her running around loose with what she knows.
She's a loose end, Dunbar, and you know how much I hate
loose ends."

The rest of what he said was lost as the doors finally slid
shut with a quiet whoosh. The car lurched into motion, carrying her away from the immediate danger.

Suddenly exhausted, wrung out from the aftermath of the
adrenaline overload, she rested her forehead against the metal
of the elevator door. It was as cold as death against her skin,
and Maggie wondered if she would ever feel warm again.

Chapter 1

"Go to hell, Beckstead," Colt McKendrick growled into the phone. "I'm on vacation. I have six weeks coming to me and I'm not about to let you screw me out of it this time. Joe, hand me that hoof pick, will you?"

His foreman—and closest friend—obeyed with a knowing smirk. "When are you leaving this time?" Joe Redhawk asked. Colt glared and chose to ignore him.

"Sane people don't take vacations wading around in cow manure and playing around with hoof picks, whatever those nasty-sounding things might be," Special Agent in Charge Lane Beckstead responded on the phone.

Cradling the cellular phone in the crook of his shoulder, he worked the pick to pry a rock out of Scout's front left shoe. He grunted in frustration as his bandaged hand slipped on the hoof pick. It had been two weeks since he was injured during an arrest, and still the damn thing was about as useful as teats on a bull.

"If I were sane," he muttered, tightening his grip despite

the pain, "I wouldn't be working for the Bureau in the first place—"

"Amen," Joe piped up.

Again Colt ignored him. "—which means we wouldn't be having this conversation and I wouldn't be taking the first vacation I've had in eight years. Besides, maybe I like wading through cow manure."

"Exactly my point. You're the only person I know who would choose to spend your vacation on a cattle ranch in Montana. What's the difference between whatever you're doing there and taking up this little job for me on the rodeo circuit?"

"The difference is, I deserve this vacation. I've been on the Spider Militia case for nearly a year. I'm tired, Lane, and the last time I spent longer than a weekend at my ranch was two directors ago."

Tired? That was an understatement if he ever heard one. Burned out, more like. Sick of the lying and the intrigues and the bureaucracy. Eleven months of working to infiltrate a hate group in the Northwest had left him exhausted, disillusioned about whatever shreds of humanity might be left in the world.

He needed the peace he found only here at the ranch where he had been raised, where he had the clean, pure scent of pine surrounding him instead of the stink of hatred and violence, and only a few ghosts to disturb his sleep instead of the legion that haunted him in the field.

"Twenty bucks says you're not going to be getting your vacation," Joe murmured.

"McKendrick," Beckstead replied, "you're the only agent in the Bureau who knows the business end of a cow from a rump roast. We need you on this case. Now we've traced our witness, a Dr. Margaret Prescott, to a rodeo in Durango last week. She's using the alias Maggie Rawlings and has taken a job providing medical care to injured performers on the rodeo circuit. We know where she is and where she's going but we don't have any way to get an agent close to her."

The "royal we" the FBI was so fond of grated on his nerves, as it always did. Damn, he was tired of it all. Colt let Scout's foreleg drop to the ground and gave him a slap that sent the gelding cantering off through the corral, his newly cleaned hooves kicking up little clouds of dust.

He pinched at the headache beginning to brew between his eyes. "And you think I could manage to get close to this Maggie Rawlings?"

"You have to admit, you're the logical choice. Besides the fact that you're a damn good agent, you're the only cowboy we've got. The lone ranger, so to speak. You have any idea how hard it is to find another special agent who's ever even seen a rodeo, much less competed in one?"

Colt snorted. "I rodeoed in college. I was twenty-two years old last time I was stupid enough to ride into the ring. Twenty-two and a hell of a lot more reckless."

"This is a big case, McKendrick. Huge. Michael Prescott embezzled millions from at least two dozen clients over the years. He gambled most of it away but some is still hidden away somewhere, and we owe it to those clients to try to find it, to those people who trusted him to invest their life savings." He paused, then poured it on. "To those little old ladies who lost everything."

"Like the little old ladies who whacked him?" Colt said dryly.

Beckstead gave up the motherhood and apple pie routine. "Okay, so he ran with a bad crowd, too. Look Colt, I won't lie to you. We're after somebody bigger than our dirty accountant ever dreamed about being. For at least one of his clients, Prescott offered a nice extra service. He prepared a set of phony books for somebody we've been after for a long time. Lucky for us, though, we discovered the accountant kept a copy of the real records. Insurance, maybe, or extortion. Who knows. We think it's on a computer disk in the same place he hid the money. We figure if we can find it, we can nail his client.''

Colt didn't want to be curious. If not for this damned inquisitiveness, he never would have joined the Bureau in the first place, after his stint as an MP in the Marines, back when he had nowhere else to go.

''How big?'' he finally said. ''Who was Prescott in with?''

''Big. Damian DeMarranville.''

The string of epithets Colt bit out at the name didn't seem to surprise his boss. ''Yeah, that's what I figured you'd say,'' Beckstead drawled. ''You and DeMarranville go way back, don't you?''

''Far enough.'' Colt thought of lost innocence and broken trust. The face of his former partner formed in his mind, and he frowned. The decent, decorated agent who had trained him had just been a front; he'd been hiding insides as rotten and worm eaten as a whole tree full of bad apples.

''Prescott was dumb enough to think he could steal from the big dog himself and get away with it,'' Beckstead went on. ''Skim a little off the top and think nobody will notice.''

He jerked his mind from the past. ''Stupid and slimy. A bad combination.''

''A deadly combination.''

Colt leaned on the split-rail fence and stared at the hard blue of the Montana sky, at a pair of magpies darting across the air, at the mountains bursting with color. He wanted to stay right here, dammit. Just for a little while, until the ghosts became too loud.

But he wanted DeMarranville more.

''How does the wife fit in?'' he finally asked.

''We're not sure, other than that she witnessed the hit by two of DeMarranville's associates. Carlo Santori and Franky Kostas. You know either of them?''

''Yeah. Not the nicest crowd. Is she clean?''

''We don't know. I doubt anybody could be married to

Prescott for six years and keep out of his business, but you never know. That's what we want you to figure out.''

Nobody was innocent. If he'd learned one indisputable lesson in the last ten years, it was that.

''Why don't you just haul her in for questioning?''

Beckstead paused. ''Frankly, she's safer where she's at.''

''If the Bureau can find her, DeMarranville sure as hell can. Seems to be the smartest thing would be to put her into protective custody.''

''It's not that easy right now.''

The SAC was hedging. Colt had worked with him long enough to read the signs. ''What aren't you telling me?''

''We think Damian still has contacts on the inside. How else could he have escaped prosecution all these years?''

He'd often thought the same thing. DeMarranville seemed to know every move the Bureau planned against him long before they made it. It was one of the most frustrating things about him.

''You'd be working deep undercover so we can keep her whereabouts a secret,'' Beckstead went on. ''Only Dunbar and I would know you're not just taking an extended vacation.''

''Who would be my contact?''

''Does that mean you'll do it?'' Beckstead didn't bother to conceal his satisfaction. Like a fisherman who knew he'd just hooked his sucker, Colt thought. The analogy was an apt one. He couldn't think of any other bait but DeMarranville enticing enough to make him give up the chance to spend time on his ranch in exchange for a summer wearing his rear out traveling to every two-bit town with a rodeo across the West.

He gave the mountains one more regretful look then pinched at the bridge of his nose again. ''Looks like I don't have much of a choice.''

He hung up the phone and glared at Joe Redhawk. ''Don't say a word. Not one damn word.''

"Who me?" the Shoshone's mouth twisted into the closest he ever came to a grin. "Looks like you owe me twenty bucks, brother."

"You got another one comin' in. Busted-up shoulder."

At the shout from the doorway, Maggie jumped at least a foot. The bandage roll in her hand flew across the little trailer, unraveling into a gauzy mess as it sailed into the corner behind the examination table.

"Sorry, hon." Peg's eyes shimmered with sympathy inside their fringe of thick black mascara. "I keep forgettin' I'm not supposed to sneak up on you that way."

Maggie fought to control her breathing, the panic that spurted out of nowhere these days at loud noises or sudden movements. Would she ever stop jumping at shadows or would the fear always be lurking there, just under her skin?

She forced a smile that quickly turned genuine as she caught sight of Peg's ensemble for the evening—skintight hot pink jeans with a glittery western-cut shirt and matching pink tooled-leather cowboy boots. With her bleached hair and her smile as big as Texas, Peg looked like an older, less-favorably endowed Dolly Parton.

"It's not your fault. I'm just a little jumpy tonight." She retrieved the now-contaminated bandage roll from the floor and tossed it in the garbage. "Too much caffeine on the road this afternoon, I think."

"If you say so, darlin'."

She looked away from Peg's worried frown. She knew her father's second wife—and widow—was brimming with curiosity about why she had abandoned her new apartment and her job at the clinic so soon after Michael's death. But to her relief, Peg hadn't pushed for an explanation, either when a desperate Maggie called her in the middle of the night three weeks earlier or in the intervening time they had traveled the rodeo circuit together.

Instead of answering the unspoken questions, Maggie busied herself gathering the supplies she would need to treat a cowboy with a bum shoulder.

"How's Nicholas?"

"Last I checked, he was runnin' Cheyenne ragged, and that granddaughter of mine was lovin' every minute of it."

"She's the best baby-sitter that rascal has ever had. I don't know what we would have done without the two of you."

"You know I'd do anythin' for you, darlin'. And not just for your daddy's sake, either. God rest him."

The two wives of Billy Joe Rawlings couldn't have been more different, Maggie thought, not for the first time. Her mother had been pearls and imported lace. A cultured debutante, the worst possible choice of wife for a cowboy trying to be a rodeo star. Helen had run off with Billy Joe when she was seventeen, more to spite her parents than for any grand passion, and had spent the rest of her life bitterly regretting it.

It had been a disastrous marriage, and their divorce when Maggie was three had been a relief to everyone involved.

Peg, on the other hand, had been perfect for her father. Even though she seemed flighty, with her flamboyant wardrobe and her ever-changing hair colors and her gaudy jewelry, Peg was the most grounded person Maggie knew. She had turned Billy Joe's dream of being a star into something more realistic, the creation of a world-class rodeo stock company that provided animals to events across the West.

Peg was warmhearted and generous and had been more of a mother to Maggie in the six weeks each year she spent with her father than Helen had ever been.

Feeling guilty for the thought, she jerked her mind back to her job. "So where's my patient?"

"He should be comin' anytime now. Wouldn't let 'em bring him in on the stretcher. You'd have thought the damn thing was a coffin the way he carried on."

She sighed. "There's nothing like a stubborn cowboy."

"Nothin' like a gorgeous one, either, and I'm telling you,

this one's a Grade A prime cut. Haven't seen him around before and, believe me, I never forget a good-lookin' man. I'd let this one leave his boots under my bed anytime.''

"Thank you, ma'am.''

At the slow drawl, Maggie turned to find a dusty, hatless man filling the doorway, his arm pressed across his stomach at an awkward angle. Peg hadn't exaggerated about his looks. The contrast of black hair and eyes as blue as a mountain lake was arresting, as was the cowboy's firm jaw and thick, cry-on-me shoulders.

If she were the sort of woman who went weak-kneed over the rugged Marlboro Man type, she would have collapsed into a boneless heap on the floor by now.

Lucky for her, she wasn't that sort of woman.

Peg winked at the cowboy. "You ever get lonely," she said on her way out of the trailer, "mine's the green-and-white rig with Rawlings Stock written on it in big pink letters.''

"I'll keep that in mind.'' He managed a grin but Maggie recognized the lines of pain slashing the edges of the stranger's mouth.

"If you'll climb up here, I can take a look at that shoulder.'' She gestured to the examination table.

"It's just dislocated. You only need to pop it in and then I can be on my way.''

"Why don't you let me make my own diagnosis?''

He shrugged and slid a Wrangler-covered hip to the table. "Whatever you say, Doc.''

She carefully unbuttoned his colorful cotton shirt then slid his arm out of the sleeve. "I'm afraid I haven't been paying attention to the announcer. What event were you riding? It's too early in the evening for the bull riders, which is where I get most of my business. Does that make you a bronc buster, then?''

He gave a gruff laugh. "Bronc buster? Do I look crazy to you?''

She glanced at him under her eyelashes, then instantly wished she hadn't. He looked tough as hardened steel, with that tanned skin stretching taut over hard muscle.

She had patched up dozens of cowboys since she'd been hired. Broken wrists, pulled muscles, cuts and bruises mostly. None of the wounded glory boys had made her feel as odd as this one did—jittery, as if she really *had* overdosed on caffeine.

Nerves, she tried to tell herself. That's all it was. She was on edge, anyway, and he was just so…big. She didn't like big men. Never had. Was it any wonder he made her uncomfortable?

The completely inappropriate—and unwanted—tingle of awareness that slid over her out of nowhere made her speak more curtly than she normally would with a patient. "You're here, aren't you? I haven't treated too many physicists on the rodeo circuit."

He laughed again, then winced as the movement jarred his injury. "Well, I guess I'm no physicist, but at least I'm smart enough to stick with the little guys, the ones that don't fight back. I'm a calf roper. Wrenched my shoulder with a bad throw."

"Any rodeo event can be dangerous, Mr.…." she stopped at the realization she'd just insulted a man whose name she didn't even know.

"McKendrick. Colt McKendrick. Call me mister and I don't figure I'll answer."

"McKendrick. As I was saying, any event can be dangerous. Even deadly, as I'm sure you know."

"That's what keeps the crowds coming back," he replied. "What does the *M* stand for?"

The abrupt change of subject left her floundering. "Excuse me?"

He glanced pointedly at her chest and she felt heat soak her cheeks. It took her several beats to realize he was referring to the silver name tag emblazoned with M. Rawlings, M.D.

"Medical. As in medical doctor," she replied, knowing perfectly well that wasn't what he meant.

He rolled his eyes. "The other one."

"Maggie," she said shortly.

"Nice to meet you, Dr. Maggie Rawlings."

She finished her examination in silence, aware of him watching her movements with interest. "You're right," she finally said. "It's dislocated, Mr. McKendrick."

"Colt."

"Right. Colt." She glanced at the shoulder. "I can readjust it, pop it back into the joint, but I'm afraid it's going to be painful."

"I know," he said glumly. "Go ahead."

With true cowboy machismo, he barely winced when she stood to his side and extended his arm out. It took several attempts before the joint worked back into place but he didn't complain.

When she was done, he immediately rotated the shoulder. "Much better."

"It's going to be inflamed and painful for a day or two. I'd advise you to take it easy."

"Does that mean I can't ride tomorrow?"

"I'm afraid not."

He didn't appear devastated by the news as he shrugged into his shirt and began to work the buttons one-handed. "Well, thanks, Doc. What do I owe you?"

"Nothing. Sponsors and the rodeo association take care of my salary. It pays to keep the cowboys healthy."

"Makes sense to—"

Before he could complete the sentence, the door crashed open and bounced against the wall with a bang as loud as a shotgun blast. Maggie had barely yanked her heart from her throat when a voice boomed through the trailer. "This is a stick-up, lady. Put your hands where I can see 'em and nobody gets hurt.''

Instead of obeying, she took a deep, calming breath and frowned at the little dynamo standing in the doorway in sheepskin chaps, a denim vest and a cowboy hat two sizes too big for his blond head. Her big, bad hombre of a five-year-old had a wooden pistol aimed right at her stomach.

''Nicholas. You know you're not supposed to come in here when I'm working.''

''I'm Nicky the Kid, the meanest bandito in the land.''

''Where's Cheyenne? And where did you get that gun?''

He grinned, showing off the tooth he'd lost just the day before. ''Grandma Peg gave it to me. She says a bandito ain't no good to nobody unless he's packin' heat.''

''Isn't any good.'' How had his grammar managed to completely degenerate in the three weeks since they had been on the circuit? He was picking up all sorts of bad habits. The next thing she knew, he'd start chewing tobacco.

''Where's Cheyenne?'' she repeated.

''Right here.'' Peg's fifteen-year-old granddaughter poked her head through the doorway. ''Sorry, Maggie. He got away from me.''

''I'm sure it's not your fault. Nicky, stick with Cheyenne. No more running off. I mean it, young man.''

''Okeydokey, Mom.'' He planted a sloppy kiss on her cheek, then hopped out the door. With another apologetic smile, Cheyenne set off in hot pursuit.

''My son,'' Maggie said, when the dust cleared.

The injured cowboy grinned. ''So the doctor has a criminal hiding out on the family tree.''

She stiffened and thought of Michael embezzling millions from his criminal clients. The cowboy was more right than he knew. After a few uncomfortable beats, she forced a smile. ''That's right. So watch your step.''

"I'll be sure to do that," he said.

Only after he had left and she was alone once again did she realize that for the first time in nearly a month she had forgotten to be afraid.

Chapter 2

The sunrise edged the mountains east of Cody, Wyoming, with lavender and pale coral and just a sliver of gold. From his perch on the top step of the broken-down camper the Bureau had somehow managed to round up for him, Colt sipped at his coffee and savored the cool, clean morning air as the gold began to swallow the other colors.

Maybe this whole rodeo thing wouldn't be such a bad gig after all. There was definitely something to be said for enjoying the morning, content with the knowledge that he would be catching the sunrise from a different place in just a few days.

He hadn't even minded competing the night before, right up until the moment he dislocated his shoulder.

Last time he had been inside a rodeo arena, he'd been twenty-two years old, cocky as hell, and sure he could rope and ride anything that moved. In the intervening fourteen years, he had forgotten that hefty jolt of adrenaline that always hit right before the gate opened. He'd forgotten everything—the confusion in the chutes, the smells of leather and manure thick in the air, the heady cheers of the crowd.

He grimaced. The crowd hadn't cheered too long after he'd wrenched his shoulder, although he doubted anybody else but him could tell it had been deliberate.

He had discovered that particular ability—to dislocate his shoulder on demand—when he'd been a kid. He'd used it a few times to get out of work on the Broken Spur, until he wised up and discovered it was less painful just doing the work.

In this case the results had been worth every second of pain. He had found the perfect chance to meet Dr. Maggie Rawlings, of the sexy voice and the cool, competent hands, to begin the process of gaining her trust.

After meeting her, he had no doubt he faced a chore as tough as roping the wind.

Colt's gaze darted to the trailer he had purposely parked beside the night before, in the little campground adjacent to the rodeo grounds. She probably had no idea the scruffy cowboy she had just fixed up had slept only a few feet away from her.

If you could call it sleep. He rubbed his bum shoulder. The narrow bed—with its mattress that felt about as thick as a paper towel—had combined with his aching muscles to keep him tossing and turning most of the night.

He'd still been awake long after the rodeo announcer called the last event, when she finally came in with her kid's blond head snuggled in the curve of her shoulder as he slept.

Colt had watched as she carried the boy inside her trailer, hooked to a rickety old pickup that had definitely seen better days. A few minutes later she came out alone. He had watched her open the door to the trailer and gaze up at the stars, tiny scattered pinpricks of light against the black sky.

She looked small and vulnerable standing there, with her shoulders bowed as if they could hardly bear the weight of her head anymore.

He'd watched her for a long time until she'd finally gone back inside her trailer, leaving him unsettled, restless.

Beckstead never mentioned the dirty accountant's widow had the kind of beauty that could bring a man to his knees. Delicate, fragile, with soft, translucent skin, a lush, kissable mouth and huge dark eyes. She had pulled her hair—the exact shade of a Montana wheat field in July—back into a tight, efficient braid, but stray tendrils had escaped to wisp alluringly around her face.

The minor fact that she was the first woman he'd been attracted to in longer than he cared to remember shouldn't make any difference in his investigation. He couldn't *let* it make a difference.

He had been on assignments involving beautiful women before. Dozens of them. But this odd protectiveness clogging his chest was definitely something new. For a minute there the night before, as her smooth, slim hands had fussed over his injury and her clean scent of peaches and vanilla had drifted past him, he had caught the dark smudges of fear under her eyes, and he had battled a completely irrational desire to do everything he could to wipe that fear away.

She was the subject of an investigation, he reminded himself sternly. He had a job to do and he couldn't let himself be distracted by a beautiful woman with big needy eyes, even if she did smell like heaven.

A small whisper of sound drew his attention back to her trailer in time to see the door open just a crack and a little figure sneak out. Her kid—what was his name? Nicholas, that was it—crept down the steps dressed in the same desperado attire he'd been wearing the evening before. With one foot on the ground, he paused and looked around furtively, as if he were preparing to rob the local bank.

"Your mom know where you're goin', partner?" he asked softly.

The kid whirled toward him, his eyes wide like he expected to find Wyatt Earp himself staring him down. When he spied Colt, his bony shoulders slumped in relief. "Uh, sure she does."

"Honest?"

A flush stole over the boy's cheeks, making the freckles stand out like dots on a ladybug, and Nicholas looked down at the flattened grass. "Well, she's still asleep. I figured I'd be back before she even woke up."

"Where you headin' this early in the morning?"

"To see the horses." The boy walked closer, his dark eyes that were so like his mother's bright with renewed excitement. "I'm gonna be a cowboy when I grow up. You a cowboy, mister?"

"Sometimes," Colt answered, truthfully enough.

"You got your own horse and everything?"

He fought the beginnings of a smile. "Yeah. His name is Scout. He's stabled over at the rodeo grounds."

"Can I ride him sometime?"

Colt studied the boy's eager little face. He didn't know much about kids, but encouraging the boy's budding hero worship might be the perfect way to find out more information about the mother.

A five-year-old probably wouldn't exactly be bubbling over with information about embezzled money and phony books, but the boy might be able to provide him with a little bit of insight into their financial status, if nothing else.

It was exactly the kind of lead he should follow up on. He'd be a fool not to—a good undercover man capitalized on every advantage he could find. So why did the idea of using the kid make him feel so sleazy?

"Maybe later," he finally said. "I think you ought to just stick around here for now. Your mom might worry if you're not here when she gets up. Moms can be funny that way, you know."

The boy nodded solemnly, glumly. "Yeah, I know. I'm supposed to stay with my mom or with Cheyenne all the time. Stupid, huh? I'm not a baby. Heck, I'll be six in fifty-three days. Old enough to go plenty of places by myself.''

The impassioned speech was punctuated by a loud, man-size grumbling from the vicinity of the little boy's stomach that had Colt biting the inside of his cheek.

"You take time for breakfast before you headed out this morning, partner?"

Nicholas shook his head. "Nope. We got nothin' but bran muffins over there. Bran muffins stink."

"I'd have to agree with you there." He paused for only a moment, knowing he had no choice but to try to befriend the boy. The quicker he finished this job, the quicker he could return to the ranch to salvage what was left of his vacation.

It still left a sour taste in his mouth, but he ignored it.

"I bought some doughnuts yesterday. Think you might be able to do me a favor and help me out by eating one or two?"

"What kind?"

"Powdered with raspberry filling."

Clearly tempted, the boy looked first at his own trailer then back at him, chewing on his lip. Colt could just imagine the internal debate whirring through his head. Dr. Rawlings probably had a typical maternal—and medical—prejudice against the kind of sugary treats that lacked any nutritional value. Powdered doughnuts likely placed pretty high up on that taboo food list, which should make them damn near irresistible to a boy who would be six in just fifty-three days.

"Sure," he finally said. "Raspberry filling's my favorite."

Ignoring the twinges of a conscience he thought had withered away from disuse years ago, Colt walked inside the camper and grabbed the box off the table, then as an afterthought, poured a glass of milk from the little refrigerator. Maybe the calcium in the milk would redeem him in Dr. Rawlings's eyes for the doughnut.

Yeah, and just maybe before they rode tonight, Scout might up and decide to recite the Declaration of Independence.

Colt handed the plate and cup to the boy. "Here you go."

"Thanks, mister."

"You can call me Colt. I figure a guy ought to be on a first-name basis with somebody he shares a jelly doughnut with, don't you?"

"Sure. I guess so."

"What do folks call you?"

"My mom calls me Nicky, 'cept when she's mad," the boy said around a mouthful of doughnut. "When she's mad, she calls me Nicholas Michael Prescott."

Prescott, not Rawlings, the alias the embezzler's widow was using on the rodeo circuit. Either she hadn't explained to her son that they needed to use a different last name for a while or he was too young to grasp the concept. If the boy chattered this freely with everyone, DeMarranville and his crew would have no trouble tracking her down.

Maybe they already had.

A vague sense of unease scratched between his shoulder blades and he scanned the cluster of campers and horse trailers. No one else was out this early in the morning, but that still didn't make him feel any better.

He turned back to the boy, shaking off the disquiet. "So you want to be a cowboy, do you?"

"Yep. My mom says maybe someday I can get my very own horse. Not back in San Fra'cisco, but somewhere else."

"You lived in San Francisco? That's quite a ways from here. You miss it much?"

Nicky nodded and bit off another chunk of doughnut. "I had a race car bed and a great big tree house, with a trapdoor and a treasure box. My mom helped me build it. She says maybe we can build another one at our new house."

"Where are you moving to?"

His thin shoulders lifted in a shrug. "Don't know. My mom says we'll know when we get there. We're playin' gypsies this summer, she said." He paused for a moment. "Hey, what's a gypsy?"

"Somebody who travels around a lot."

"That's what we're bein', all right."

"What about your dad? Did he help you build the tree house, too?"

A sad look crossed the little boy's face. "No. I asked him to, but he never had time. He died."

Before Colt could answer, the door to the trailer across the way banged open, hitting the aluminum skin, then ricocheting closed. It was instantly shoved open again and a frantic voice resounded in the morning air.

"Nicky? *Nicky!*"

Maggie stood barefoot in the doorway in an oversize T-shirt that just skimmed her knees. Her wheat-colored hair looked soft and crumpled, in direct contrast to her terrified gaze scouring the surroundings in every direction and her chest heaving in panic like she'd just outrun the meanest bull on the circuit.

Colt could tell exactly when she spied them, because a vast relief poured into those deep brown eyes, followed quickly by the beginnings of anger.

"Nicholas Michael Pres—" she faltered for just a moment "—Rawlings. What are you doing out here?"

"Eatin' breakfast with my pal Colt." The boy mumbled, taking another bite.

She sent a scathing look in Colt's direction, whether at him or at the box of doughnuts in his hand he didn't want to hazard a guess.

He nodded politely, deciding an aw-shucks demeanor might be the best course of action. "Mornin', Doc."

"Good morning," she snapped, then turned back to her son. "We have talked about this, young man. You know the rules. I have to know where you are all the time."

Nicky, in the middle of a swallow of milk that left a white mustache on his upper lip, sent her a bewildered look. "You know 'xactly where I am. Right here."

"I didn't know where you were when I woke up. All kinds of terrible things went through my head."

A mischievous gleam appeared in his eyes. "Like that big ugly aliens came down in a UFO and grabbed me and took me back to their planet so I could be their slave and wash their dirty socks and stuff?"

"Something like that. A little less dramatic, maybe." Her stern expression softened, and she pushed a lock of hair out of her son's eyes. "You really scared me, bud. Don't do that again, okay? Wake me up before you go outside next time."

"Okay. Can I finish breakfast with Colt? He said maybe sometime he'd let me ride his horse. His name's Scout."

"I'm sure Mr. McKendrick has things to do this morning," she said, her voice coated with a thin, crackly layer of frost.

"Not really. If the boy wants to see the horse, I'd be glad to take him down to the pens."

"Please, Mom? I'll come right back, I promise."

"Not right now. Maybe I can find time to take you down to see the horses later."

"But Mom… "

"Later, Nicholas. You're still in trouble for breaking the rules. Now go inside and wash your hands and face."

The boy opened his mouth to argue, but closed it again at the implacable look on his mother's face, a look even Colt could recognize. *Smart kid,* he thought, then grinned when Nicky trudged up the three metal steps of their trailer with his bottom lip jutting out in a pout a rock star would have envied.

As soon as her son was out of sight, Maggie turned back to Colt. She looked about eighteen years old in that T-shirt, he thought. That didn't stop him from being curious about what was beneath it.

"How is it?"

He blinked at her. "How's what?"

She looked at him like he'd taken a hard spill from a horse and landed on his head. "Your shoulder. I asked how your shoulder is feeling this morning."

"Oh. Good. It's good. I was thinking maybe I'd ride tonight after all, since I'm feeling just fine this morning. What do you think?"

"I think it would be extremely foolish, unless you want to reinjure your shoulder."

"Maybe I'll see how I'm feeling later."

"That's your decision, of course." She paused for a moment, as if weighing her words, then spoke stiffly. "Look, Mr. McKendrick. Colt. I don't want you to take this wrong, but I would appreciate it very much if you would stay away from my son."

He stared at her. Where the hell did *that* come from? "I just gave him a jelly doughnut and told him he could take a ride on my horse some time, Doc. It's not like I offered him a fifth of Jack Daniels and some smokes."

She frowned. "I realize that. It's just that he's at a vulnerable stage right now. He—he lost his father recently."

"I'm sorry." What emotion triggered those shadows in her eyes, those lines around her mouth? Grief for the husband she had lost or fear of the men who had killed him?

He was willing to bet it was the latter. According to the dossier Lane had provided him with, she and the late accountant had been at the starting gate of what had been shaping up to be a nasty divorce.

She looked away for a moment, and when she turned back, the clouds were gone. With a cool nod she acknowledged his condolences. "Even though his father wasn't very…involved in his upbringing, Nicky has taken his death hard. I'm afraid he's looking for a male role model."

"Lots of boys dream about being cowboys. I don't see that there's any harm in that."

"I'm afraid I do. He's an impressionable little boy and he doesn't need a—a saddle bum filling his head with all sorts of nonsense about the Code of the West and a cowboy's honor.''

So much for trying to ingratiate himself with her through a friendship with her son. He opened his mouth to defend himself but she went on as if she didn't notice.

"He's been through enough. Please don't compound a little boy's pain by encouraging a friendship that will only end in heartbreak when you move on to the next rodeo.''

With that she turned and walked into her trailer, leaving him frowning behind her.

She had sounded like an absolute idiot.

Later that night—after she'd taped a couple of bruised ribs, set a broken arm and bandaged a nasty gash from the wrong end of a bull on the final night of the rodeo—Maggie lay in her narrow bed in the trailer and replayed her conversation with Colt McKendrick.

Please don't compound a little boy's pain by encouraging a friendship that will only end in heartbreak when you move on to the next rodeo.

Okay, so she'd overreacted when all he had done was show a little kindness to a lonely little boy. He'd offered to let Nicky ride his horse, that's all, not move in with him.

He was probably exactly as he appeared—a down-on-his-luck cowboy searching for glory in the arena. Older than most of the wranglers she treated, true, with a maturity in those lines around his eyes, in the confident set of his shoulders, most of them lacked.

So he was older than the norm. That didn't mean anything. Maybe he was escaping a bad relationship, or, God forbid, the law.

He was certainly attractive, in a raw, wild sort of way. Maybe it was that dark brushy mustache that made him look like one of those outlaws Nicky had become so enamored of. Butch Cassidy, maybe, or Jesse James. Dangerous and fascinating at the same time.

Maggie rolled her eyes at herself. Didn't she have enough to worry about without her hormones suddenly waking up from whatever internal cave they'd been hibernating in for the past few years? It was all she could do to take care of her son and perform her job each day without giving in to the panic always lurking around the edges of her mind. She didn't have energy left to indulge in even a harmless flirtation.

He *had* been awfully sweet with Nicky, though. She smiled at the picture the two of them had made this morning, sprawled out on the back step of McKendrick's old camper: two satisfied males eating their empty-calorie breakfast in the morning sun.

Nicky needed that in his life. Maybe not the empty calories, but the guiding influences of an older man. Even before she left Michael and moved them to their little apartment, he had been starved for male companionship. Michael had been too busy with his deals and his clients—and his other women, she later discovered—to pay much heed to his son.

If Colt McKendrick wanted to give Nicky a little of the attention he needed so desperately, was she wrong to stop him? No. She wasn't wrong. She didn't even know the man. Until she did, she couldn't trust him. Couldn't *afford* to trust him.

It was up to her to keep her son safe until she could earn enough money to help them settle somewhere.

Once she could be certain the men who killed Michael had given up searching for her, she could find a job somewhere, get an apartment for them. With her medical experience, she should be able to find work anywhere. Maybe by fall, before the new school year began.

Maggie gazed up at the dingy, water-stained ceiling of the trailer, suddenly struck by a powerful craving for her old life back. For the safety, the security she'd always taken for granted.

She hadn't been happy, married to Michael. Oh, she had

loved him once. Or thought she did, anyway. She had been vulnerable when she'd married him, she now admitted—had been in her last year of residency when her mother introduced them, just a few months before Helen died after a long battle with cancer.

Throughout her last days her mother had dropped not-so-subtle hints about what a fine young man he was—wealthy, successful, handsome—until Maggie agreed to go out with him more to make her mother happy than because she was interested in dating him.

After Helen died, Michael had been a constant, supportive presence. He had been charming and attentive, and she had soaked it in like a flower starved for rain.

She had known almost from the first that she had made a grave mistake, but by then she was pregnant with Nicky, so she'd done her best to make the marriage work.

For all the good it did her. All that had changed six months ago when she'd found out about the lies, the women. And the safety of her life had been destroyed forever when she had watched Michael topple to the floor of his office with a bullet hole in his forehead three weeks ago.

She didn't want to think about that night, the night when everything she thought she could count on had crumbled to ashes. She had rushed to the house of Rosie Vallejo, her former housekeeper and Nicky's long-time care provider, and her first thought had been to call the police to report the murder.

She remembered waiting, shivering in delayed reaction, in Rosie's humble living room, for the officer to arrive. But when the car pulled up, some latent survival instinct prompted her to look out through the curtain. To her horror, the men climbing out of an unmarked late-model sedan in the driveway were the two she had seen from the elevator after the murder.

The only explanation she could come up with for their

presence at Rosie's house was that they must have found out where she was from her call to the police.

She's a loose end. You know how much I hate loose ends, the older man had said in that cold voice.

She had barely managed to grab Nicky and flee out the back door. Maggie frowned now, remembering the terror. She still didn't know who the two men were. Maybe this DeMarranville person the two killers had talked about had sent them as some sort of backup to Carlo and Franky. A grim contingency plan.

Regardless, she had rushed back to her apartment to grab some belongings and had discovered a message from Peg on the answering machine. Rawlings Stock was providing the animals for a show a few hours away from San Francisco, and Peg wanted to come to visit.

The call had seemed heaven sent. Peg wielded a great deal of influence in the rodeo world, and Maggie had no doubt she could help her find work on the circuit, even mucking out stalls.

She hadn't had to resort to that, fortunately. Peg had known of an opening in one of the rodeo sponsor's sports medicine program, and her years of experience working at the clinic had qualified her for the position.

She had jumped at the chance. It was the perfect opportunity for her and Nicky to hide from DeMarranville's men until she could earn enough money to make a new start somewhere safe. Amid the transient life of the rodeo circuit, she could become anonymous, with a new assignment in a different town every week.

She hoped it would be the last place anyone would think to look for her, since Michael had insisted she keep that part of her past—the summers she spent on the road with her rough-and-tumble father—a secret. It didn't gel with the image he wanted his wife to portray, of quiet, wealthy elegance.

He didn't even like to talk about her work at the clinic, preferring instead to focus on her mother's world of country clubs and society teas. The world where Maggie had never belonged.

She shifted in the narrow bed as familiar shame pinched at her. She allowed Michael to completely dominate her present when she was married to him. How could she have let him so completely take over her past, as well, rewriting it to meet his own expectations?

She had loved those times with her father. Maybe she had turned to the rodeo circuit as an escape now because it represented the best part of her childhood. A safe haven, even then. She had looked forward to her summers with Billy Joe with as much excitement as a prisoner handed a three-day pass to the outside. It was worlds away from the coldness, the studied politeness, of her life with her mother.

She rolled over and punched at her pillow. The reasons weren't important. The only thing that mattered was Nicky's safety. If it meant keeping him safe, she would dress up like a rodeo clown and go head-to-head with Corkscrew, Peg's nastiest bull.

She yawned and glanced at her little travel alarm clock. Nearly 1:00 a.m. and they would be leaving early in the morning for the long drive to Butte, Montana.

She needed sleep. Needed it and feared it at the same time. During the day she could forget, could block from her mind the memory of Michael's death. But in sleep she was powerless against the terrors that stalked her subconscious.

She fought it as long as she could, but finally her exhaustion won out. The nightmare crept up on her, more terrible because it was all so real. Michael falling again, the blood oozing from his wound like wine trickling from a spilled bottle. Those agonizing moments when she had cowered in the washroom while the men who killed him talked casually over his body, as if they were discussing stock prices or baseball scores.

And then running, running.

In her dream it was as if she were stuck on an out-of-control treadmill, always running and never making any progress, while Carlo with the dead eyes pursued her. He moved inexorably closer to her and, try as she might, she could do nothing to escape.

When he had nearly reached her, he veered away, and she thought she had escaped but suddenly Nicky was there in his arms, kicking and struggling, his little fists pounding against the stranger who held him. Terror and fury and raw fear erupted inside her, and she screamed her son's name just as Michael's killer reached into his pocket and pulled out a wooden pistol like Nicky's.

Even though it looked like a toy, she knew it would be as deadly as the real thing. She cried out and grabbed for it, just as a terrible clanging noise erupted from the pistol.

She awoke in a rush, her heart pounding and the blood rushing in her ears. It was so real! She could still hear the echoes of her cries, still taste the fear in her mouth.

What had awakened her? For long seconds she lay in the darkness and listened to the stillness of the night, forcing her muscles to relax, her breathing to slow.

Thunder rumbled in the distance, long and low, like a slow, steady drumroll played by ghostly hands. That was it. She must have heard the warnings of the impending storm.

Lightning flashed outside the window, and the sky immediately growled again. This time it was joined by something much closer, a clang very much like what she'd heard in her dream, followed by muffled cursing.

It wasn't the storm that had awakened her, she realized as all the fear came surging back.

Someone was out there!

Chapter 3

Lingering visions from her nightmare chased themselves through her mind. Could Michael's killers have found her? Panic exploded in her chest, and she thrust the light quilt aside to scramble out of bed, consumed with a wild, frantic urge to gather Nicky and flee into the night.

After an instant she forced herself to breathe deeply and try to think through it all rationally. How could they possibly have found her? She had been excruciatingly careful to leave no clue about her whereabouts. She hadn't tapped into any of her bank accounts. She hadn't told anyone at the clinic where she was going. She hadn't even told Rosie.

It was probably just some drunk cowboy. A bronc buster or bull rider who celebrated the rodeo's end with one too many beers at a honky-tonk somewhere and now was simply trying to find his way back to his bed.

Maggie stared at the ceiling. Though she dearly wanted to stay here and hide in her bed—to pretend she hadn't heard anything but the gathering storm—she knew she had to check out the commotion.

It was the responsible thing to do, and Margaret Elizabeth Rawlings Prescott always did the responsible thing.

She slipped from her bed and crept through the darkness to the window at the front of the trailer, underneath the loft where Nicky slept noisily, making sweet little huffing breaths in his sleep.

Although swollen black-edged clouds hid the moon, far-off lightning arced across the sky just long enough for her to make out a dark, hulking shape crouched by the passenger side of her pickup.

Great. The drunk cowboy was throwing up on her truck.

Again she had the completely childish urge to crawl into her bed and pull the covers over her head. But what if it wasn't a drunk cowboy? What if it was somebody trying to break into her truck? She didn't have much of value inside it, but she was damned if she would let somebody take what little they had left.

She needed a weapon, if only to scare the intruder away. A quick scan of the trailer turned up a cast-iron frying pan in the dish drainer. A frying pan. What a cliché. She only needed a headful of curlers to look just like Alice Kramden from *The Honeymooners,* taking on Ralph after he stayed out too late with the boys. Still, it would probably make any drunk cowboy think twice before tangling with her.

Before she could talk herself out of it, Maggie grabbed the pan by the handle, rummaged through a drawer for a flash-light, then opened the door quietly. She sidled along the length of the trailer until she reached the truck's bumper.

"If you leave right now," she called out softly, "I won't phone the police." She clicked the flashlight beam on and aimed it right into the would-be thief's eyes, then gasped when Colt McKendrick's baby blues blinked back at her. "You!"

"Yeah. Me." He sounded disgruntled. "Who'd you think it was?"

"I don't know. A drunk cowboy, maybe, being sick on

my truck.'' She squinted at him. ''You're not throwing up, are you?''

''Don't think so. Thanks for asking, though.''

''What are you doing, then?''

''You mind moving the flashlight a little? You're blinding me here.''

She shifted the beam to the ground. ''Sorry. What are you doing?'' she repeated.

She sensed, rather than saw, his shrug. ''I was on my way to bed and noticed you had a flat. Figured I'd fix it so you wouldn't have to deal with it in the morning.''

She stared at him. ''You just took it upon yourself to start fixing it without talking to me first?''

''Um, could you move that flashlight again?''

Maggie flushed when she realized she had instinctively aimed it into his eyes once more. She pointed the light to the ground again, where it now illuminated a jack propped next to a tire that sagged forlornly. ''Why are you doing this?'' she asked.

''It seemed the neighborly thing to do.''

He wasn't breaking into her truck, he was going out of his way to fix her flat tire. She couldn't remember the last time anyone had done something so genuinely kind for her. A burst of warmth flooded through her, trickling over her shoulders and down her back.

Her opinion of Colt McKendrick suddenly seemed to shift and slide around inside her. She didn't *want* to soften toward him, though. She didn't dare.

''You really don't have to do this,'' she mumbled. ''I'm perfectly capable of changing a flat tire.''

''I'm just saving you the trouble. Just look at it as my way of paying you back for patching up my shoulder yesterday. Nice frying pan, by the way. Odd time of the night for making pancakes, if you don't mind me saying.''

Embarrassed heat soaked her skin at the flash of his grin in the darkness. She dropped the frying pan to her side. ''You never know what sort of riffraff you could run into in the middle of the night.''

''True enough.''

Lightning suddenly seared across the night again, and the air smelled of ozone and that peculiar musty smell of a summer storm about to be unleashed.

McKendrick glanced up at the sky. ''Looks like I'd better get a move on if I'm going to beat that. You know, I could probably make better time if you'd shine that flashlight over here.''

''Oh. Of course.'' She clicked it on and watched him jack up the truck and quickly, efficiently, replace the flat tire with her spare.

When the last lug nut had been tightened, he hefted the flat into the bed of the pickup. ''You'll want to get this tire repaired before you go too much farther. I wouldn't want you to be stranded on the road somewhere without a spare.''

''I'll do that.'' She frowned. ''I wonder what happened to it. It wasn't flat earlier this evening.''

He busied himself gathering up the tools. ''Maybe you picked up a nail or something. Had a slow leak for a couple days that finally finished the thing off. Or you could have— Damn!''

''What is it?'' She aimed the flashlight at him and saw him cradling one hand with the other.

''Blasted jack cut my hand.''

''Let me see.''

He wiggled it as if he could shake off the pain and picked up the crowbar. ''It's okay. Nothing that hasn't happened to me dozens of times on the ranch.''

She gazed at him, momentarily diverted. ''You have a ranch?''

He looked away as if he were too embarrassed to meet her gaze. ''Uh, I used to.''

Compassion swept through her. He must have fallen on hard times and lost his ranch, the same fate suffered by countless other ranchers during the recent run of lousy beef prices and high feed costs. Maybe that's why he was on the circuit. For a good cowboy, a summer spent rodeoing could be a quick route to ready cash to help rebuild a ranch.

She swallowed her words of sympathy, somehow knowing they wouldn't be welcome. "Still," she said quietly, "I would feel better if you allowed me to take a look at that hand."

Before he could argue, she dropped the frying pan into the dirt and grabbed his fingers. As her hand met his skin, hardened and rough from hard work, heat raced between them every bit as powerful as the lightning sizzling across the sky.

Unnerved, Maggie cleared her throat and dropped his hand. "That looks deep. You should put some disinfectant and an antibiotic on it."

He shoved the injured hand into the back pocket of his jeans. "I'll be all right."

"I insist, especially since it was my tire you were fixing. Come on. I've got some iodine in the trailer."

"I wouldn't want you to wake up your kid. I've probably got something I can use at my place."

She frowned at him. "You might as well accept my help. I'm not going to be able to sleep until I know you've put something on that."

"Fine, Doc. Whatever you say. Since you're so set on it, you can come and watch to make sure I stick the Band-Aid on right side up."

As he led the way to his camper, the skies finally opened and began to spit huge drops that plowed into the dusty ground like bullets. They made it inside just as the storm began in earnest.

"Welcome to the McKendrick hacienda," he said, flipping on a light above the little stove. Maggie instantly realized she had made a mistake by following him.

A huge mistake.

The camper was no more than eight feet wide and a dozen

feet long, small and compact and intimate, especially with the storm playing a symphony on the thin aluminum skin of the roof.

Her nerves were in entirely too much turmoil for her to be comfortable in such close quarters with Colt McKendrick. She couldn't breathe without brushing against him, but she inched as far away as she could manage. ''Um, where's your disinfectant?''

''It's in here somewhere. Why don't you sit down, and I'll see if I can rustle it up?''

He bent to rummage through a drawer, highlighting thin spots where his jeans had worn almost white from all the time he spent in the saddle. She caught herself staring and jerked her gaze away.

What on earth was the matter with her, gawking at the man like she was some kind of buckle bunny on the make for a good-looking cowboy? Embarrassed, she slid onto one of the vinyl bench seats around a little gray-speckled Formica table.

To distract herself she studied the interior of the camper, looking for some clue into McKendrick's personality. It appeared to be about the same general era as the trailer she had bought with the proceeds from selling her Volvo. The decor was straight out of the 1970s, all orange, yellow and dark green tones. A well-used rope, coiled neatly, hung on the back of the door. A pair of worn boots, an older twin to the pair he was wearing, waited by the bed.

Earlier in the day she had noticed that the pickup and horse trailer both looked fairly new and in much better condition than the camper. Wasn't that just like a cowboy? Worry about his horse and his truck but not about where he laid his own head at night.

The only somewhat jarring note that kept the inside of the camper from being completely stereotypical was a stack of books on the window ledge. She studied their authors. Larry McMurtry, Louis L'Amour, a couple of mysteries. Just what she might have expected. But she suddenly did a double take at the slim volume at the bottom of the stack. Descartes? A cowboy who reads philosophy?

Before she could ask him about it, he emerged from the cupboard with a battered first aid kit lifted victoriously in his hand. "Here we go. I knew this was in here somewhere."

He slid into the seat across from her and thrust out his hand. "Okay, Dr. Rawlings. Do your worst."

She eyed his hand with trepidation. After what had happened outside when she touched him—that odd, silvery shower of sparks—she was reluctant to make contact again.

This is ridiculous, she thought, and forced herself to take a deep breath. She was a professional. She could handle putting antiseptic on a man's hand without getting all fluttery over it. Couldn't she?

Her nerves firmly in check, she picked through the first aid kit until she found a small dark bottle of iodine, then reached for his hand. The sparks threatened to return, but she sternly suppressed them and examined the injury. His hand was a testament to years of hard work, with a varied collection of nicks and scars.

Instead of a new injury, as she had assumed, it looked as if the jack had ripped open an existing wound, a jagged, ugly cut that traced the curve of his lifeline. "What did you do here? Before tonight, I mean."

He looked at it for a moment and she could swear he was being evasive again. "Uh, a cowboy's curse. I was putting up fence line and snagged it on some barbwire."

"Looks like it was painful."

He grunted in response and she managed not to smile. "Oh, I forgot. You macho cowboys don't feel pain like the rest of us. Now if you weren't a cowboy, I'd tell you this is going to sting a little. But since you are, I won't waste my breath."

Cowboy or not, he stiffened as she poured the iodine on,

and Maggie winced. "Sorry. I shouldn't have teased you." She instinctively blew on his palm to cool the burning.

He grinned. "Now there's a mother for you, thinking you can make it all better by blowing on it. My mother used to do the same thing when I was a kid."

She couldn't stop her smile, intrigued by the idea of him as anything other than the completely adult, completely masculine person in front of her. "Sorry. It's a habit I picked up with Nicky. You're lucky I didn't kiss it to make it feel better."

"Am I?" he murmured.

Was he flirting with her? She'd been out of the man-woman scene so long she simply couldn't tell. She shot him a glance under her lashes, but his strong, chiseled features remained impassive.

Unsure how to respond, she cleared her throat and opted to change the subject, even though the one she picked didn't make her any more comfortable. "Speaking of Nicky," she began, "I wanted to apologize for this morning. About calling you a saddle bum and all. I overreacted. It's just that I panicked when I woke up and he wasn't there. I'm afraid you bore the brunt of that lingering fear."

"No harm done."

"No, I shouldn't have lashed out at you like that. It's just…I tend to be a little overprotective of Nicky." She forced her gaze away from his to the bandage she was wrapping around his hand. "It's too bad today was the last day of the rodeo and we're moving on tomorrow. If we had more time, I would have let you take Nicky up on your horse. If you were serious about your offer, that is."

"Would I lie to a big, bad outlaw like Nicky the Kid?"

She couldn't help her laugh, one of the few genuine ones she'd enjoyed in quite a while, then instantly regretted it when he gave her an odd look that sent her pulse skittering.

"Where's your next assignment?" he finally asked. "Maybe we'll run into each other down the road."

"Butte, Montana. The Butte Vigilante Rodeo."

"Now there's a coincidence. I just sent in my entry fee for the same show this morning. They have a nice calf-roping purse I've got my eye on, so I'll be heading into Montana 'round about Wednesday. I'd be happy to take your little guy up on Scout one day next week."

She shouldn't have this little hitch in her stomach at the idea of seeing him again. Darn it, she knew perfectly well she shouldn't. "I'm sure Nicky will look forward to it."

"Maybe you and I could get together, too, before the show one night. I know a great steak place in town."

He was definitely flirting with her. Oh mercy. What was she supposed to do now? "I don't... That is, I haven't..."

"Relax, Doc. You don't have to decide tonight." He twisted his bandaged hand and rubbed a rough thumb over her knuckle. She felt hypnotized by his grin, like a rabbit caught in the hard, killing glare of headlights. "Just think about it."

She carefully gathered her composure around her and tugged her hand away. "We'll see," she managed to say, then slipped from the seat and headed for the door. "Thank you again for fixing my tire. It was a very nice thing to do."

To her confusion, he scowled. "Niceness has nothing to do with it, Doc. Not one damn thing."

She gave him a puzzled look, but he didn't seem inclined to explain. If the man wanted to keep his secrets, who was she to argue? Lord knows, she had enough of her own. "Well, good night, then. I suppose I'll see you in Butte."

He was still scowling when she walked out into the rain. He swore under his breath and lifted the moth eaten curtains to watch her hurry into her own trailer. A light switched on inside, but the trailer went dark again after only a few moments.

Colt let the curtain fall. What the hell was he supposed to do now? Any degree of objectivity he might have claimed going into this assignment had just died a quick and painful death when Maggie Rawlings laughed back there, sweet and unaffected.

Unless she was the world's greatest actress, the woman was about as innocent as a newborn calf. No way could she be a party to the illegal activity of her husband. Nobody with that much vulnerability in her eyes could be involved in the ugliness of Michael Prescott's world. He would be willing to bet the entire Broken Spur she didn't know what her husband had been involved with, that she was just running scared from the men who had killed him.

He thought of the stunned amazement in her dark eyes when she had found him changing the flat tire on her truck—the tire he'd purposely punctured himself.

His plan was to quietly fix the tire and leave a note about it for her to discover in the morning, in another attempt to insinuate himself into her life. Instead, she'd awakened and come out armed with a cast-iron skillet and a flashlight, ready to take on a drunk cowboy.

His mouth twisted in a wry grin. The woman had grit, he'd give her that much. Another few seconds and she would have beaned him.

Instead, she had been pathetically grateful when she discovered he was repairing the flat tire. His scheme couldn't have worked better. So why did he feel no satisfaction, just this guilt churning around in his gut for deceiving her?

Maybe because he was inexplicably drawn to the woman, in a way he hadn't been to anyone since his wife walked out five years ago.

With another oath at the thought of his ex-wife, he dug through the briefcase carefully hidden in a cabinet under the bench where Maggie Rawlings had been sitting. He picked up his slim cellular phone and quickly punched one of the preprogrammed numbers.

Beckstead sounded tired when he answered—it was after midnight, California time—and wasted no time on pleasantries. "How is the assignment progressing? Are you any closer to Maggie Rawlings?"

"I want out."

He could practically hear his boss's frown over the phone. "What happened?"

Maggie Rawlings, and her big eyes, happened. He couldn't very well voice the thought, though. "Nothing's happened. I just don't think I'm making any progress gaining the woman's trust," he lied.

"You've been on the job less than a week. Give it some time."

"I don't want to give it time. I just want out. I'm too damn old to rodeo." That, at least, was the truth.

His boss laughed. "You're thirty-six, McKendrick. I think you have a few good rides left in you."

"I'd rather be taking them on my ranch than in the arena against a bunch of twenty-year-olds."

"Haven't we had this conversation already? Look, the net is tightening on DeMarranville. I know you want to put him away every bit as much as I do, and all my instincts are telling me Dr. Rawlings is the one person who can help us do that."

"Let me go at DeMarranville another way. Maybe I can work on a couple of his men who might be ready to cut a deal against him. Last I talked to Joey Perone, he sounded like he could be bought."

"No dice. I need you there. Right where you are." Beckstead paused. "You realize there's more at stake here than just the disk, don't you?"

"What do you mean?"

"We both know it's only a matter of time until DeMarranville tracks her down."

"If he hasn't already."

"He hasn't. Our sources inside his organization are quite clear on that. Not for lack of trying, though. His people are looking everywhere."

"Damian is nothing if not efficient."

"He doesn't know she witnessed the hit on her husband—if he did, she never would have made it this far—but he wants the disk more than we do. He's going to be very unhappy if she doesn't give it up."

"What if she doesn't have it?"

"Do you think he's going to play nice if he thinks she's holding out on him? If she really doesn't know what her husband was involved with, I'd hate to see her or the kid get caught in the crossfire."

Son of a bitch. Colt stared out through the rain streaking down the window like tears. He hated to think of Maggie or her son in DeMarranville's hands.

"I'd feel better knowing one of our agents was close to her, to offer some degree of protection," Beckstead went on.

What would his boss say if he knew exactly how close Colt wanted to be to the accountant's widow? "Okay," he growled, pushing the thought away. "But the stakes just went up. I want three months away from the Bureau when I'm done here."

"We bring down DeMarranville and you can have as much time as you want."

But would it be enough to make him forget Maggie Rawlings, with her big eyes and her outlaw son?

Somehow he doubted it.

Chapter 4

Her kingdom for a decent shower.

With apologies to William Shakespeare, Maggie fought shivers as she turned off the trickling little spray that was all the Butte, Montana, campground facilities offered and reached for the thin towel she had hung over the stall door just a few moments before.

A month ago, if someone had told her the idea of a pounding hot shower would come to symbolize the height of luxury to her, she would have laughed hysterically.

Funny how she had taken so many things for granted before her life degenerated into chaos a month ago. A decent shower topped her list—with all the hot water she could dream of and complete, heavenly privacy instead of these flimsy shower stall doors between her and the rest of the world, this thin barrier that left her feeling entirely too vulnerable.

She could barely remember what it had been like to shower as long as she wanted, without this constant, nagging worry at leaving Nicky sleeping in their locked trailer for even these few stolen moments. What would she do if she had time to do more than just scrape her hair back into a wet braid and apply only the bare minimum of makeup?

Might as well wish for the moon while you're dreaming, she scolded herself and slipped quickly into the clean clothing she had brought over from the trailer. This wasn't so bad, anyway. It could be much, much worse. She and Nicky had clean, warm clothing to wear, food in their stomachs and a roof over their heads—even if it *was* a thin aluminum roof with a tendency to leak when it rained.

Besides, in a big city, what were the chances of your neighbor stopping to fix a flat tire in the middle of the night so you wouldn't have to deal with an unpleasant surprise in the morning?

A picture of Colt McKendrick in the watery darkness back in Wyoming the week before crystallized in her mind and she smiled softly as she tugged a comb through her wet, tangled hair.

In the four days since she had found him fixing her flat, she couldn't seem to shake the man from her thoughts. He sneaked in whenever she wasn't looking, with that teasing grin, his strong shoulders and those shockingly blue eyes.

How long had it been since she had felt her pulse skitter and hop like that just by a heavy-lidded look from a man like Colt McKendrick? She laughed aloud at the absurdity of her question. When had she ever even *had* a heavy-lidded look from a gorgeous man before that night the weekend before in his camper?

Of all the times for her to develop an attraction for a man, when she was so strung out on nerves. Nothing could possibly come of it, after all. Even if she were the sort of woman who could interest a rough and rugged rodeo cowboy—which she most certainly was not, despite his flirtation the week before—she couldn't spare the energy for this. She needed all her wits about her just to survive.

Besides, her emotional bank balance matched her real

one—completely empty. She didn't have anything left to give any man.

If he showed up and followed through on his invitation to dinner, she would simply have to turn it down. It was the safe, sensible thing to do, she knew it perfectly well. So why did the knowledge leave her with a little ache of regret in her chest?

She sighed. No sense worrying about it now. He'd probably forgotten all about them. On a whim, she decided to leave her hair loose, then gathered her clothing and walked out of the rest room into the early-morning air that smelled tart and fresh, of pine pitch and newly cut grass.

Maybe all this angst was for nothing. Maybe their paths wouldn't cross again. He said he planned to compete in the Butte rodeo, but maybe he had changed his mind. Tonight was the opening round, and she had yet to see his fancy blue truck with the beat-up cab-over camper.

It probably would be for the best if he didn't show up, although it would break Nicky's heart. He had his sights set on riding Colt's horse, and when her stubborn little boy decided he wanted to do something, changing his mind could be a nightmare.

Wondering how she would possibly deter him, she rounded the corner of the little cinder block building housing the rest rooms, but any thought of Nicky was completely wrenched from her mind when she smashed headlong into a solid wall of flesh.

She swayed from the impact and her bag of toiletries tumbled to the ground. Her heart stuttered in sudden fear when hard hands clamped around her forearms, holding her immobile.

She couldn't see who held her, could only focus on the wide male chest in front of her, but her survival instincts immediately kicked in, adrenaline gushing through her in hot, roiling waves.

Escape. She had to escape. Fighting and struggling against the taut grip, she tried fiercely to jerk away.

"Easy. Easy, now, Doc. I'm not gonna hurt you."

Gradually, like water through porous sandstone, reason seeped through her panic and she drew a ragged breath, stilling her frantic scramble to freedom.

She recognized that soft drawl—it belonged to the cowboy she had just been thinking about. Tilting her chin up, she found those startling blue eyes watching her carefully.

He gave her arms a reassuring squeeze then released her. "There now. That's better. Sorry if I scared you, Doc. I was just trying to keep you from falling over after you came barrelin' around the corner."

Her fear ebbed, leaving embarrassment in its wake. Heat soaked her cheeks and she fought the urge to press her hands to them. Okay, so she had overreacted just a tad. What must he think of her, fighting and clawing at him like he was some kind of mad rapist on the loose?

"I…it's not your fault," she mumbled. "You just startled me. I wasn't watching where I was going, and I guess I didn't expect anybody else to be out this early in the morning."

His mouth creased into a smile. "No harm done."

She bent to pick up her scattered toiletries, and he immediately crouched to help. "Here. Let me get this."

"I can do it. Really."

"It's no trouble."

They worked in silence for the few moments it took to pick up her things. It was unnerving, having him help her collect her most intimate belongings: her razor, toothbrush, the scented peach soap she indulged in.

He must have just come from the men's shower himself. His hair was damp, his cheeks and his chin freshly shaved. In the pale, thin hush of the morning she became acutely, painfully, aware of him: the blunt tips of his fingers clutching her delicate things. The scent of his aftershave, a subtle, erotic combination of leather and sagebrush. The layer of crisp dark hair on his arms, the little scar at the corner of his mouth that curved up like an extension of his smile, and those deep blue eyes that reminded her of a clear, pristine mountain lake.

She had no business noticing anything about Colt Mc-Kendrick, let alone the mountain-lake color of his eyes. She yanked in her thoughts sharply and cleared her throat. "When did you arrive?" she asked. "It must have been late—I didn't see you come in before I went to sleep last night."

Those eyes took on a teasing glint. "You weren't watching for me, now, were you, Doc?"

Drat her fair complexion that showed every emotion. She felt her cheeks flood with color again. "Nicky was," she mumbled.

It was the truth, if not the complete truth. Since the moment they arrived at the campground the day before, her son had watched every rig pull in with an eagerness usually reserved for Santa Claus or birthday parties. He had become increasingly dejected as the day wore on when none of the arrivals turned out to be his new pal.

What Maggie didn't add—what she couldn't possibly admit, even to herself, except in her most secret of hearts—was that she had watched each newcomer with the same eagerness as her son. And been just as disappointed when he didn't show up.

Somehow Colt McKendrick had seeped into her subconscious, and she couldn't seem to shake him loose. She would definitely have to do something about it.

When her things were finally collected and stored safely in her rattan bag, they both stood. Colt rested one of those blunt-fingered hands on the cinder block wall of the rest rooms, blocking her way as effectively as if he still held her in those muscled arms. "Now that we've got that settled, Doc, how about you tell me what's got you so jumpy."

Startled, she met his gaze. His eyes held curiosity and a

concern she didn't want to see there. She quickly looked down at the ground. "I don't know what you mean," she lied.

"Come on, Doc. You're more skittish than a broomtail in a nest full of diamondbacks. Is it me?"

Just like that, her nervousness disappeared. She pursed her lips and gave him a quelling look at his arrogance. "Pretty full of yourself, aren't you, McKendrick?"

He grinned, unrepentant. "Just thought I'd ask. Knowing your feelings about us saddle bums and all."

The grin faded and he studied her for a moment, those blue eyes entirely too perceptive. "You know, if you need somebody to talk to, I've been told I can be a pretty good listener."

If only she *could* talk about it. The desire to unload some of her burdens was so powerful she wanted to weep. Maybe if she could share it with someone, this constant fear would ease, would lose its hold over her every waking moment.

He would protect them.

The thought slipped into her mind, more seductive than any physical attraction she could ever feel for him. Somehow she knew Colt McKendrick would do everything in his power to keep them safe.

She opened her mouth, searching for the words to begin, then snapped it shut again. What was she doing? She couldn't tell him, couldn't tell anyone. Her troubles weren't something she could just blurt out to a virtual stranger. *I cowered in the bathroom while two men executed my husband in cold blood and now they're after me and I jump out of my skin any time someone says "boo" to me and I'm ashamed of myself for it but I can't seem to help it. Oh, and thank you for asking.*

Besides, this was not his problem. She couldn't drag him or anybody else into the mess she had made of things. She absolutely refused to put anyone else in harm's way.

No, she wouldn't tell Colt McKendrick anything. "I'll keep that in mind," she said instead, fingers clutching her bag tightly. She couldn't ease her grip any more than she could keep her voice from sounding distant and polite, as if she were refusing tea in the drawing room of one of the society mansions her mother used to drag her to. "I'm sorry, but...I have to go. I left Nicky sleeping back in our trailer, and I wouldn't want him to wake up alone."

He lifted his hand from the wall and straightened to give her room to pass. "I mean it, Doc. If you need to talk, you know where to find me."

She gave a quick nod and began to walk quickly away.

"Hey," he called after her. "If you aren't busy later this morning, I'd be happy to give your little desperado that ride I promised him on Scout. The exercise would be good for him after travelin' all day yesterday."

"For Nicholas or for Scout?"

He grinned again. Despite all her efforts to restrain it, her traitorous heart fluttered in her chest, and she returned his smile with a small one of her own.

"Both, probably," he answered.

"I know you promised, but you really don't have to do that."

"Eleven o'clock work for you?"

She did a quick assessment of her schedule. She had to prepare the exam trailer for any injured riders from tonight's competition, but that wouldn't take her much time. An hour, tops.

And Nicky wanted to ride Colt's horse so badly. How could she refuse her son this one small thing, after she had dragged him away from all that he loved, forced him to give up everything secure in his little life?

"Yes," she finally answered. "I suppose eleven would be fine."

"Meet us at the practice racetrack. You know where that is?"

She nodded. "I think so."

"Good." He smiled that teasing grin she was beginning to find entirely too addictive. "I'll see you then."

He didn't think they'd show up.

Colt kept one eye on the pathway from the campground while he checked Scout's tack and adjusted the stirrups to an appropriate length for an almost-six-year-old.

It wouldn't surprise him if she stayed away. She had been so skittish this morning, avoiding his gaze and hanging on to that bag like it was filled with gold.

Even nearly four hours later, Maggie's tantalizing peach scent still filled his senses. Fresh-scrubbed from the shower, with her skin as dewy as the morning grass and her hair still damp, she'd been damn near irresistible.

When she'd come barreling around the corner and landed in his arms, it had taken every last ounce of his self-control to keep from stealing a little taste.

He wanted her more than he could ever remember wanting a woman. The desire pulsed under his skin and left him itchy and uneasy. It had sure as hell complicated what was supposed to be an easy assignment.

He had to put a lid on it. Simple as that. He wanted DeMarranville too much to let something as insignificant as simple lust screw it up for him. He was bound to make mistakes if he let his hormones do the thinking for him, so the trick would be figuring out a way to keep his distance from the beautiful Dr. Rawlings at the same time try to coax her to open up emotionally.

A warm breeze puffed out of the mountains, ruffling the hair at the base of his neck. It made him think of home and the ranch and the simple joy of working out in the morning sunshine.

To his surprise he felt little more than a passing twinge. He ought to be feeling lousy right about now since he was missing out on his vacation. The idea of spending uninterrupted time at the ranch was all that had kept him going through those last miserable weeks on the Spider Militia case. So why wasn't he feeling worse?

If he didn't know better, he might even make the mistake of thinking he was enjoying himself on this case.

"Colt! Hey, Colt!"

The high-pitched shout dragged him from his thoughts, and he turned to find Nicky peeking through the rails of the fence, his big brown eyes bright with eagerness.

A grin split Colt's face at the sight of the little boy decked out in that Wild West getup again.

"Well, howdy. If it isn't my old amigo, Nicky the Kid."

Maggie's son beamed and stuck out his thin chest. "I'm all ready to ride. Got my chaps on and everything."

"I can see that. You look like a regular bronc buster."

"Mom tried to get me to just wear jeans but I told her I had to wear my chaps or I'd get saddle sore, isn't that right?" the little boy said.

"Smart move." Colt bit down on his smile and turned his attention to Maggie, standing a few paces behind her son. She wore tan jeans and a pale pink T-shirt that made her skin look pearly, almost translucent. Her long hair, loose and unrestrained, swayed like wheat dancing in the wind when she walked forward.

Despite his best intentions, his mouth started to water.

Oblivious to his sudden sharp hunger, she propped her elbows on the top rail of the fence. "What's a mom supposed to say to that kind of argument? I wouldn't want him to get saddle sore, after all."

Her voice was as cool as ice cream in July. Damn. She'd put up those walls between them again. He'd been so close to gaining her trust. This morning he had sensed she was desperate for someone to share her concerns with, that she wanted to tell him what had her running scared. It would make his job so much simpler if she would confide in him. For every inch of progress he made, though, she forced him back another two.

At least the kid was on his side. "Well, partner," he turned to the little boy, "you ready to saddle up?"

Nicky nodded and scrambled through the fence. "You bet-cha." He skidded to a stop near Scout's forelegs and, thumbs hooked in his belt loops, took the big gelding's measure.

Up close the horse must have looked a whole lot bigger than he had from the fence, because Nicky stared at him, gnawing his bottom lip and frowning.

"Uh, Colt…"

"Yeah?"

"I don't think I can climb up there."

"I'll help you." He lifted Nick and swung him onto the saddle. The boy looked incongruously small atop the big horse, but he sat in the saddle like he'd been born to it. He reached forward and patted Scout's neck. "Hi there, Scout. My name's Nicholas."

"Okay now, I'm comin' up. Hang on." Colt grabbed the horn and swung up behind him. The boy settled into his arms and gave a little squeal of excitement when Colt spurred Scout forward.

"Mom!" he yelled to Maggie, watching from the fence. "Look, Mom! I'm ridin' a horse!"

"I can see that," she called back. "Hang on."

They were the only ones using the practice race track, and Nick chattered excitedly as Scout moved along at a steady walk. Colt smiled at one of the boy's funny little observations and was astonished at the pleasure he found in his excitement.

He'd never thought about having a child before. Not that he was consciously opposed to the idea; he'd just never had the opportunity. Cynthia hadn't exactly been the maternal type, and he'd never had strong feelings either way.

Besides, during their two-year marriage he'd been so completely focused on the job he'd never given the idea of bringing children into the world a second thought.

With the soft weight of Maggie's son in his arms pressing

against his chest, though, he couldn't help wondering what it would be like to have a kid of his own, to be teaching his own boy how to ride.

His father had taken him up on a horse just like this before he could walk. It was one of his earliest memories of Jack McKendrick: his father's rough, scarred hands on the reins, his gravelly voice in his ear, telling him how to hold the reins and guide with his knees.

The ache in his throat took him completely by surprise. Jack had been gone nearly fourteen years, after all, since Colt was twenty-two. He thought he'd long ago become accustomed to the realization that he'd never be able to make things right with his father.

"Hi, Mom!" Nicky suddenly yelled. While he was busy woolgathering, Scout had carried them back around the track to where Maggie stood watching. She waved and smiled, and the breeze caught strands of her hair, twisting them around her face.

Lord, she was beautiful. The unique thing about Maggie Rawlings was that she seemed completely oblivious to her appeal. There was a shy kind of innocence about her.

Unless he was a hell of a lot better at concealing it than he thought, she had no idea of the heated little darts of desire that sizzled beneath his skin that would have been obvious to another woman.

He thought again about his vow to contain his growing attraction. He was fairly sure he could handle the physical end of things. It was the emotional tug he felt toward both Maggie and Nick that scared the hell out of him.

"Can we go around again?" Nicky asked.

Colt looked at Maggie for permission. She shrugged. "It's up to you. It's your horse."

"I hate to disappoint a customer. Hang on." He spurred Scout to a trot and was rewarded with a shriek of glee from the boy.

The warm summer sun warmed her back as Maggie leaned

on the fence watching Colt and her son. Nicky was absolutely eating this up. Already, he was imitating everything the cowboy did, from his slow—and she had to admit, very sexy—drawl, to the the way he cocked his dark head when he grinned.

She wasn't exactly sure how that made her feel. Amused, certainly. And maybe a little bereft, too, as if Nicky was pulling away from her.

She *did* know it shouldn't move her so much to see the big, rough cowboy being so gentle with her son. Colt sat with one hand around Nicholas's belly to hold him in place and the other on the reins. As they came around the track again, she could see him dipping his dark head as he talked to Nicky. A few moments later he handed him the reins to let him control the horse for the rest of the ride.

Soon they reined in the horse in front of her again.

"Did you see me, Mom?" Nicky nearly bubbled over with excitement. "I rode Scout, and Colt didn't even help me. Well—" honesty compelled him to admit "—not very much."

"I watched you. You make a good wrangler."

"That's what Colt says. He says maybe I can ride Scout again tomorrow. Can I, Mom?"

"We'll see."

He was still chattering when Colt hefted him down from the saddle and set him on the ground.

Colt glanced up at the sun, now high overhead. "Looks like it's about lunchtime. How would you two like to go somewhere for lunch?"

The invitation took her completely by surprise. "I don't—"

"Please, Mom!" Nicky asked, obviously loath to leave his new hero's side.

Refusing would sound churlish, especially after he had been kind enough to take them riding, but she knew he

couldn't have much money or he wouldn't be desperate
enough to ride on the circuit.

And heaven knew she didn't have much, not even to go
Dutch for fast food.

"Why don't I make us some sandwiches?" she offered,
knowing even as she said it that she would regret it later.
"We could take them over to the park across the way and
have a picnic."

"Sounds great," he replied. "Nick, why don't you help
me take care of Scout, here, and then the two of us can see
if we can rustle up something to drink."

Yes, she was definitely going to regret this, she thought as
she watched Nicky's eyes light up with excitement. How was
she supposed to keep distance between them when her son
obviously adored the man?

Chapter 5

Would two sandwiches be enough for Colt? Knife in hand, Maggie studied the bread laid out in front of her, then pulled two more slices out of the bag. Better safe than sorry. And she hoped he liked turkey, since that was the only lunch meat she had.

While she spread mustard on the bread and added cheese slices and lettuce, she hummed a song she'd heard on the radio, driving to Montana the day before.

It felt nice to be making a meal for a man again. The thought flitted through her mind and she winced. Good grief, don't let anybody from the National Organization for Women hear her. Or the American Medical Association, for that matter. She could almost hear the chorus. *Surely you didn't spend four years in medical school and another four in residency to be content shoving cheese slices on some he-man cowboy's turkey sandwich?*

She didn't mind, she had to admit. She always used to fix Billy Joe's meals when they were on the road, until he married Peg, anyway, when she was ten, and then she and her

new stepmother had shared kitchen duty. No one could ever
call her a gourmet cook, by any wild stretch of the imagination, but she had always enjoyed the process of putting a
meal together, of preparing something nourishing and filling
for her father.

She smiled at the comfort the memory gave her. No matter
what she fixed, he would tell her "thank you kindly" in that
soft drawl of his and pull her into his thick arms for a hug.
He would smell like livestock and Old Spice aftershave, and
she would clutch that feeling close to her through all the
times she lived away from him.

Michael, of course, never wanted her to soil her hands in
the kitchen. Never mind that she spent most of every day up
to her elbows in blood in the clinic. It wasn't at all the same,
he would argue. "That's why we have domestic help," he
used to tell her with that damned superior smile of his.

She used to sneak into the kitchen and help Rosie cook
things for the next day whenever he had to work late—whenever he stayed late to play around with his secretaries, she
amended.

A hollow knock sounded on the aluminum door. Swallow-
ing her sudden, uncomfortable bitterness, she opened the
door to find Colt with one boot resting on the step and the
other on the ground.

She was so busy trying to tell her pulse to settle down at
the sight of that wide grin and those blue eyes that it took
her several seconds to realize he was alone. Without Nicky.
She scanned the area but could see no sign of her son. Panic
suddenly spurted through her like blood from a ruptured artery. "Where is he? Where's Nicky?"

"Relax, he's fine," Colt assured her. "We ran into the girl
who had him last week when you fixed my shoulder—"

"Cheyenne?"

"Right. Cheyenne. She was on her way to the little general
store at the campground office and took Nicky with her to
pick out some pop for our lunch."

Maggie concentrated until her breathing had slowed back to its normal rhythm. She hated this. Absolutely hated it. She used to be so solid, so centered, but now she felt as if she were going crazy, as if everything that had been sane and normal in her life had been forever destroyed.

"Anyway," Colt went on, "they should be here in a few minutes, after he raids the candy counter."

She frowned, although she was relieved to be feeling a normal motherly anxiety instead of raw panic, for a change. "I thought you said he was buying pop."

"I gave him a little extra for a candy bar."

"He'll spoil his appetite."

"Well now, I warned him you'd say exactly that. I told him we'd both be in trouble if he didn't save it until after lunch."

The last of her panic ebbed and she even summoned a smile. "Smart man. Why don't you come in while I finish the sandwiches?"

She held the door open for him, then sucked in a sharp breath when he squeezed past in the small doorway and his forearm brushed the curve of her breasts.

He didn't seem to notice, just ducked his head to enter the trailer. Even inside, he was too tall to stand completely upright so he tucked his chin to avoid bumping his head.

Immediately the little eight-foot-by-fourteen-foot trailer seemed to shrink to half that, every inch of it filled with Colt's broad shoulders and long, rangy legs.

Just as this morning, awareness flooded through her. Flustered and dismayed by the reaction she couldn't seem to control around him, she quickly returned to the counter to finish the sandwiches.

"Can I help you with lunch?" he asked.

"I'm almost finished. It's not much, I'm afraid. Just plain old turkey sandwiches."

"Anything's fine. I'm gettin' pretty sick of chili out of a can."

"Why don't you sit down so you don't have to put a crick in your neck standing like that?"

"Thanks." He settled onto one of the vinyl-padded benches on either side of the table and stretched those long legs out.

She caught herself staring and quickly jerked her attention back to putting the sandwiches in plastic bags. "Thank you again for taking Nicky riding today. You've really made his month."

"I told you before, he's a great kid."

"You're very good with children."

"Never had much to do with them before, if you want the truth."

"You don't have any of your own?" She wondered why it had never occurred to her before. He was such a natural that she could easily imagine him with a whole houseful of children. For some reason the idea didn't sit well with her.

He shook his head. "I was married once but we never had kids. Made it that much easier when the marriage fell apart, I guess."

"I'm sorry."

He shrugged. "Nothing to be sorry about. It was a mistake from the beginning. Neither one of us could be what the other one needed."

"Your wife didn't like ranch life?"

The open friendliness in his face faded and he focused on the floor. "No," he said shortly.

Now why did she have the feeling he was hiding something from her? Before she could decide whether to pursue it, he turned the tables on her.

"What about you?" he asked. "You said the other day that your husband died recently. Was it an accident?"

Only if you call a bullet hole to the head at close range an accident. "No," she said, as shortly as Colt had just a moment before. "He was murdered."

She hadn't meant to tell him that, but somehow the words

came tumbling out before she could gather them up and store them safely away. If she expected him to be shocked, though, she was doomed to disappointment. Other than a tightening around his mouth, Colt seemed remarkably unmoved by what she considered a fairly dramatic revelation.

Maybe he lived in a world much more violent than hers. Again she wondered about his background, about the pieces to the puzzle that didn't quite fit.

"I'm sorry," he said finally. "That must have been traumatic for both you and Nicky."

She concentrated on placing the sandwiches in the basket for their picnic. "I don't really think he understands the implications, other than that his father is gone. Nicky and Michael weren't very close. He was a—a distant sort of father. Still, Nicky tried so hard to please him."

We both did, she added to herself. That was what she was most ashamed of, that she had completely submerged herself in an effort to become the sort of wife Michael had wanted. Except for her work at the clinic, anyway. He had wanted her to quit, but she had steadfastly refused.

Becoming a doctor had been her dream, something she couldn't explain to anyone. It was a seed that had been planted inside her through those summers with her father, when she would see cowboys be carried out of the arena on stretchers only to return to competition the next night. She used to watch with complete fascination as the paramedics worked their healing magic.

It was ironic, really, that the turmoil of the last month should bring her full circle back here, to the rodeo circuit where her dreams began.

"Can I ask why you're workin' rodeos?" he asked, as if he could read the wanderings of her mind.

"What do you mean?"

"Don't take this wrong, but it seems an odd career choice for a woman with a kid. I don't imagine a doctor as skilled as you would have too hard a time finding work somewhere you wouldn't have to travel so much.''

She fumbled for an answer for several seconds, and he must have seen her turmoil because he held a hand up in apology. ''Sorry I asked. It's none of my business. Maybe you like the traveling.''

She used to love it with her father, but now all she wanted was somewhere safe and warm to settle down and raise her son. She couldn't possibly explain that to Colt without going into the details of Michael's death, details she wasn't prepared to share.

''I'm just about done here,'' she said instead, to change the subject. She bagged the last of the sandwiches, then reached into the storage area above the stove where she had placed a few picnic supplies purchased the last time she went shopping. Most of the trailer's compartments were within easy reach, but this was a deep cupboard above her head. She stood on tiptoe and stretched as high as she could, but the paper plates she sought were just out of range of her fingers.

''What did you need?''

She jerked her head around to find Colt standing only inches away. ''How do you do that?'' she muttered, disgruntled.

''What?''

''Sneak up on me so easily.''

He chuckled and she watched in fascination as the sea of wintergreen cotton covering his chest rippled. ''Just a gift, I guess. What did you need up here?''

She lifted her gaze to his face. ''Paper plates,'' she said through a suddenly dry throat. ''They're at the back of the cupboard.''

To her disgust, he barely had to lift his arms above his head to reach into the compartment. He handed the plates to her with another grin. Up close like this, she could see that the little scar at the corner of his mouth wasn't perfectly curved, it zigzagged ever so slightly.

Intrigued, she stared at it, wondering what his lips would taste like, if they would be strong and sure on hers, if his bushy dark mustache would tickle her skin.

"Keep lookin' at me like that, Doc," he said, in a voice so low it vibrated in the little trailer, "and you're gonna get more than you bargained for."

Her gaze flew to his at the soft warning, and she flushed when she realized the direction her thoughts had taken her—and when she realized his blue eyes had darkened with a craving that matched her own.

Suddenly the trailer seemed to shrink several more feet, until there was space only for the two of them and not nearly enough air to go around. She hitched in a quick breath as he stepped forward, knowing what he planned to do just as she knew she should stop him. She opened her mouth, intending to rebuff him, but somehow only a soft, breathless sigh whispered out just as his mouth settled on hers.

She had been kissed by a few rodeo cowboys before, the summer she turned sixteen and had been traveling with Billy Joe and Peg. After years of wishing and hoping and trying every trick she could find to encourage them, she had suddenly sprouted breasts the winter before and she had been foolish enough to wear tight T-shirts every chance she had to show off her new attributes.

It had earned her a bit of attention and a few stolen kisses from some of the rowdier young cowboys before she had gotten a lecture from Peg, of all people, about the dangers of putting out an advertisement for something you're not at all sure you want to deliver.

Judging by the memory of those experiences, she would have expected Colt's kiss to be rough and demanding, an exercise in machismo.

His gentleness, then, took her completely by surprise.

Their lips barely touched, just enough for her to taste some kind of minty toothpaste, but they fit together perfectly.

Her eyes fluttered shut and her hands, trapped between their bodies, came up to rest on his chest, her fingertips absorbing his heat and leashed power. His hands circled her, coming to rest on her back.

She'd been right. His arms offered safety and comfort, all the things she needed so desperately right now. And his mustache didn't tickle at all. It was more like a silky caress.

They stayed like that for several seconds, barely touching, adjusting to each other's scent and taste. She heard a soft, contented sigh and realized with some shock that it came from her. At the sound, Colt made a noise low in his throat and started to deepen the kiss, when small footsteps suddenly clattered up the metal stairs outside.

Footsteps that, if she wasn't mistaken, belonged to a five-year-old boy who would be wearing chaps and a sheepskin vest.

Maggie had only enough time to spring away from Colt before Nicky yanked the door open and charged inside with all his customary energy. Right behind him was Cheyenne, carrying a bag of soda pop. She took in the situation with an amused glance—it was hard to miss, since the air practically snapped with electricity. The girl's attention zinged between Maggie's flaming cheeks and disheveled hair and Colt's obvious tension. To Maggie's overwhelming relief, her step-niece said nothing, just lifted all-too-knowing eyebrows.

"Howdy, Mom," Nicky said, oblivious to the scene he had interrupted. "Look what I bought at the store!"

She tried to make the appropriate admiring remarks about the candy he'd purchased, while she put the finishing touches to their impromptu picnic and tried to still her churning, seething insides.

How stupid could she be? She should never have put herself in this situation. She couldn't blame Colt. He was right, she had all but handed him an engraved invitation to kiss her.

No, the fault rested squarely on her shoulders. She was just going to have to do everything in her power to make sure it didn't happen again—no matter how much she might want it to. She would have to avoid him as much as possible and especially dodge any situation that could put them in this kind of close proximity to each other.

She simply couldn't afford to lower her guard toward him. It left her too off balance, made her too vulnerable.

And where Colt McKendrick was concerned, she was afraid she could be very, very vulnerable, indeed.

As screw-ups go, this assignment was turning into a royal doozie.

In an unused corner of the rodeo grounds, Colt looped the rope over his head and circled the practice iron steer head he'd borrowed from one of the other ropers, trying to find the sweet spot for his throw.

The first round of the Butte Vigilante Rodeo was scheduled to start in less than an hour, and he had all the concentration of a gnat. If he didn't get in a little practice time before the competition, he was going to be laughed out of the arena.

But with each throw, his frustration with himself grew more intense. Damn, he was a complete idiot to kiss her like that. He hadn't been thinking about the job at all. He'd forgotten about Michael Prescott and finding evidence against DeMarranville and all the reasons he was here. He'd forgotten everything but the two of them and her soft, willing mouth and the want in her eyes.

And, of course, the need that had been smoldering in his gut since the day they'd met.

He had totally lost his head, and in the process he appeared to have also lost whatever progress he'd made up to now, trying to gain her trust.

He bit out an oath as his swing went wide. If he needed evidence that he'd completely botched the job, she had given

it to him on their picnic at the little park across the way. She
had been stiff and cool, refusing to meet his gaze and flinch-
ing away if his hand so much as accidentally brushed her
skin. He could see the guilty regret in those cinnamon-
colored eyes every time she looked at him.

Damn it to everlasting hell. He'd spooked his prey just
like a green kid on his first hunt. Now he had to start all over
again. His task would be that much harder now, because he
knew damn well she had spent the whole afternoon recon-
structing the barriers between them.

He coiled the rope again. With a twist of his wrist, he sent
it spinning over his head, then watched it float around the
steer head. Now if he could only have the same kind of aim
when he faced a quick little calf from the back of a horse at
full run in an hour. He might even go home with the calf-
roping purse.

He blew out a disgusted breath. Wouldn't that be a pretty
damn sorry situation, if he found more success with his cover
than he did with the actual assignment?

Several more times he went through the same process, and
each time the loop found its mark. He yanked it tight for the
last time with a grunt of satisfaction, just as he heard the
sound of mocking applause coming from behind him.

Colt whirled, instinctively reaching for the small, efficient
Glock 9mm concealed in the small of his back. His hand
froze when he recognized the figure who had somehow managed to approach without Colt being aware of it while he was
concentrating on his throws.

"Dunbar?" He stared. "What the hell are you doin'
here?"

The agent looked conspicuously out of place. Although he
had shed his usual tailored dark suit, he wore Wranglers still
creased with just-off-the-rack sharpness, shiny new black
boots, a pearl-buttoned shirt and a cowboy hat so white it
put out a glare. He looked exactly like what he was: a city
slicker trying—and failing miserably—to fit in.

"Shouldn't you be working on the case instead of out here playing around with your rope?"

Colt scanned the area quickly, furiously, hoping like hell Maggie didn't see him talking to such an obvious outsider. "What are you doing here?" he repeated in a hissed whisper.

"Checking up on you, since you've been characteristically stingy with information."

"What are you trying to do, blow my whole cover?"

"Of course not." The other agent adjusted his hat. "This job is every bit as important to me as it is to you."

"Did Beckstead send you?"

Dunbar nodded. "He has tried to contact you several times in the last few days but couldn't get through. He finally sent me to try to figure out what you have been up to."

"I told him I'd check in when I had the chance."

"You always say that and you never do."

It was a long-standing bone of contention between him and FBI brass. He liked to work at his own pace without having to run every little decision past a damn committee, which didn't always sit well with his superiors.

"I turned the phone off," he growled. "What would have happened if Beckstead had called sometime when I was with Prescott's widow? I seriously doubt a down-on-his-luck cowboy would own a high-tech cellular phone that cost more than he could reasonably be expected to make in a whole month of rodeos."

"I know you like to think of yourself as some kind of lone wolf, McKendrick, but you have to stay in communication, to keep us apprised of the investigation's progress."

He bit down his frustration. "I'll make contact when I have something significant to report," he said coolly. "And not until."

"Dammit, McKendrick. You know the rules. Agents in the field are obligated to check in with the special agent in charge."

"You don't like the way I'm doing the job, why don't you

do it yourself?'' He held the rope out with a mocking grin. ''Here. You're more than welcome to ride for me tonight.''

His glibness earned him a glare. ''I told Lane you would be difficult,'' Dunbar growled.

''Well now, I wouldn't want to disappoint you. I know how much you hate to be wrong.''

He didn't like Lewis Dunbar. Never had. His unease around him was nothing he could put a finger on, he just didn't trust him. The agent had a good reputation at the Bureau, but in Colt's estimation he was a pompous idiot who did everything by the book, who refused to bend the rules for anything, even when the whole investigation was at stake.

Fortunately, he didn't have to work with him often. Once was more than enough, though, with an attitude like this. ''I don't like you checking up on me like I'm a kid who just got the keys to the car for the first time. I know what I'm doing.''

''Have you found the money and the disk?''

Colt shook his head. ''I've been concentrating on earning the doctor's trust. She wants to talk but she's holding back.''

Thanks to his stupidity in hitting on her this afternoon, now he would have to start all over again. But of course he didn't mention that little tidbit of information to Dunbar.

The weather wasn't all that hot—in fact, a cool breeze drifted down from the mountains—but the Montana sun must have been getting to the agent. He removed his hat and rubbed a handkerchief over his balding head. ''We're on a short clock here, McKendrick. We need to find them.''

''I don't think she knows where they are.''

''Before Carlo wasted him, Prescott plainly implied the doctor had everything. We've combed through every inch of her apartment and can't find the disk or the money. She must have them with her.'' His expression was suddenly intense, almost savage. ''Find them. ''

Colt studied him through narrowed eyes. It wasn't like

Dunbar to get so upset over a case. He was usually cool and unemotional. "Why the sudden urgency?"

"There's nothing sudden about it." Again in control, the agent tucked the handkerchief in his back pocket. "This assignment has always been about finding the records and the money before DeMarranville finds the widow and the kid."

Colt's grip on the rope tightened. "Are his people closing in?"

"Probably." Dunbar shrugged. "With Damian, it's not a question of *if* but *when.*"

A chill that had nothing to do with the temperature blew down his spine with icy breath. What would DeMarranville do to the wife and child of someone who had betrayed him? Especially if he thought they had something that belonged to him or information that could bring him down? Colt didn't even want to think about it.

"Find that money, McKendrick," the other agent said as he started moving toward the arena, already filling up with eager spectators. "I don't care what it takes. Find it."

Chapter 6

"Colt's next! Colt's next!"

Maggie grabbed her son by his belt loop and pulled him back—again—from the metal railing that separated the rodeo spectators from the competitors.

"If you won't settle down, I can't let you watch. You're going to fall over the railing into the arena."

Nicky gave her a disgruntled look. "I'm bein' careful, Mom. I just want to see Scout and Colt."

"You can see them just fine from back here on the bleacher seat. Now park it."

"It's his turn. I'm gonna wave and see if he waves back." He proceeded to shake his arm like a metronome. "Colt! Hey Colt!"

Cheyenne, sitting on his other side, snickered. "I don't think he can see you from way over there, Nicky. Besides, he's probably too busy concentrating on the ride right now."

"Maybe he can." Undeterred, Nicky continued waving.

"Sit!" Maggie said again when he leaned one more time over the railing. Finally he settled back so she could relax and focus on the competition instead of her high-strung little boy.

She didn't have the chance to watch the rodeo events often, but it had been a quiet evening so far. Either these particular circuit cowboys at the Butte Vigilante Rodeo were all in remarkably good condition, or the fates had decided to spare them the usual assortment of bumps and bruises that came with the rough sport.

When Cheyenne and Nicky had stopped by the medical trailer a short time earlier to ask if they could watch Colt ride, she had given in to a sudden, inexplicable impulse to join them.

She just needed a diversion from a slow night at work, she tried to assure herself, a chance to enjoy the pageantry and excitement of the competition. Her presence here was completely unrelated to her growing fascination with Colt McKendrick.

Bull. She winced as her brutally honest conscience pinched at her. That darned fascination was exactly the reason she was here, with the smell of horses in the air and the jostling, colorful crowd surrounding her.

All day she hadn't been able to stop thinking about him, about their soft, devastating kiss in her trailer earlier. Her mind had replayed the scene a thousand times since then— his strong arms around her, his cotton shirt beneath her fingertips, the gentle touch of his lips on hers.

Was she so starved for tenderness after her disaster of a marriage, then, that she completely turned to mush when she found gentle warmth so unexpectedly in a tough and rugged cowboy? It wasn't an idea she was at all comfortable with.

The gravelly voice of the announcer crackled from the loudspeaker, jolting her back to the arena. "Folks, let's give a warm welcome to our next contestant, a cowboy named Colton McKendrick, coming to us from down by Ennis."

Colton? She hadn't realized Colt was an abbreviation. And

he was from here in Montana? How many other things didn't
she know about him?

The crowd applauded politely for him, except for Nicky
who yelled like a banshee when the chute workers released
the gate. A calf with hide the color of sandstone loped
through the dirt. Poor misguided thing probably thinks he's
making a break for freedom, Maggie thought sympatheti-
cally, just as Scout lunged into the arena behind him.

Her heart hammering, her fingers clenched in her lap, she
sat forward on the bench, caught up in the drama.

Calf roping had always been one of her favorite events,
maybe because it didn't have the violence inherent in most
of the sport. Unless you were the calf, she supposed. The
fastest roper won, and the best cowboys could do the whole
thing in less than nine seconds.

And apparently Colt McKendrick was among them. Scout
had just galloped into the arena when Colt threw the rope
with unerring accuracy, jumped from the saddle and raced
with raw grace to the calf. In the time it took her to draw a
breath, he had the calf on its side and whipped his hand
around once, twice and a third time before raising his hands
to signal he was finished.

"Now that's the way it should be done," the announcer
drawled. "A fine showing for Montana cowboy Colton
McKendrick." The crowd applauded with considerably more
enthusiasm now that they recognized he was definitely a con-
tender for the week's purse.

"Did you see that, Mom?" Nicky's eyes widened with
excitement. "Colt was awesome!" He turned back to watch
his hero unhook his rope from the calf.

"He's good," Cheyenne commented quietly. "And not
bad on the eyes, either. Tall, dark and gorgeous. I can sure
see why he makes your heart beat faster."

Maggie sent the teen a swift look. To her embarrassment,
Cheyenne returned it with a knowing gleam in her green
eyes. Maggie's attention shifted from her stepniece to her son

to see if he had overheard her comments. Fortunately, Nicky was too involved watching Colt to pay any mind to the two females.

"I don't know what you're talking about," she finally said, her voice stiff and cool. "We're just friends. Not even that. Casual acquaintances, really."

Cheyenne just grinned and flipped her long red ponytail. "If you say so. I gotta tell you, Aunt Maggie, I wouldn't mind having a few casual acquaintances who looked at me like that."

"Like what?"

The girl's expression softened, her mouth curved with envy. "Like they wanted to carry me away and never let me go."

She rolled her eyes, even as her heart gave a little bump of excitement at the idea. "You're imagining things. I hardly know the man. He and Nicky just struck up a friendship when we camped next to each other last week. There's nothing more to it than that."

Cheyenne shrugged. "You don't have to explain anything to me, Aunt Maggie. I was just making an observation."

"Well, you're way off base."

"It's none of my business, anyway. I was just saying he's one gorgeous piece of work. And if he looked at me like you say he doesn't look at you, I'd grab on with both hands and just enjoy the ride."

Cheyenne was entirely too self-assured for a fifteen-year-old. Maggie opened her mouth to argue with her, then slammed it shut again. Protesting only made her appear more foolish, she realized. She decided to bow out with as much dignity as she had left. "I suppose I'd better return to work. Will you two be all right?"

"Just fine. Maybe we'll watch the rest of the show, just to check out Colt's competition. Is that okay with you?"

"Can we, Mom?" Nicky asked eagerly.

Maggie smoothed a hand across his hair. "I guess so.

Don't give Cheyenne a hard time about bedtime, though, understand? When she says it's time to go, you listen to her.''

Her son gave a distracted nod, engrossed in the next competitor. She gave an exasperated sigh. He was already as addicted to rodeo as his grandfather had been. When they finally settled down, she would have a tough time weaning him away from it.

"Thanks," she said to Cheyenne. "I should be back around the usual time—''

Her voice ground to a scratchy halt as her attention caught and held on a man across the arena. She picked up only random impressions—a neatly clipped mustache, a balding head, a stocky build—but somehow they coalesced into a clear image of one of the men she'd seen that terrible night at Michael's office building.

She quickly, frantically, sorted through her memories of that night after the murder: facing Michael's body; the heart-stopping, excruciatingly slow elevator ride; and finally, that sickening moment when the doors opened and she caught sight of the two men racing into the building.

The first man had been older, handsome and distinguished, like some diplomat out for an evening stroll. But the second had been stocky, balding, mustachioed, exactly like the man across the arena. He had worn a dark, tailored suit that night while this man wore Western clothing like everyone else here, but it had to be the same man.

"Aunt Maggie? Are you all right?"

She blinked, swayed. "I—''

Cheyenne grabbed her arm. "Sit. Right now. You look like you're about to pass out.''

Not daring to take her gaze from the man, she let the teen drag her back down to the bleachers. How could they have found her? Dear God, what was she going to do? She had to protect her son, but where could she run? If they could find her here, at a two-bit rodeo in Montana, they could find her anywhere.

Through the panic swelling inside her, she was vaguely aware of Cheyenne clasping her arm and patting her hand. "Stay with me, Mag. Do you need a drink or something? What happened? Are you sick?"

Her gaze shifted for only an instant at the barrage of questions, but when she turned back, the man had vanished. She blinked rapidly and scanned the entire side of the arena, but could see no sign of the mystery man. The seat in the bleachers was filled now by an adolescent girl with teased blond hair and a black George Strait concert T-shirt.

She rubbed clammy hands on her slacks. The panic gradually subsided, leaving in its place a deep unease. Was she going crazy, conjuring up things that weren't there? Her imagination must just be running on overtime, like an immune system gone amok at the slightest threat to its health. Would she ever stop jumping at shadows, seeing danger where none existed.

"Aunt Maggie? Should I call for a paramedic?"

She gathered her frayed composure around her and turned to face Cheyenne. "I'm fine. I just stood up too quickly," she lied, and tried to give a reassuring smile to the worried girl.

Her attempt must have been convincing. After several beats Cheyenne returned it with a teasing grin of her own. "I think you're just going weak in the knees over Colt McKendrick."

Or weak in the head, anyway. A much more likely explanation. "You're right." She summoned another smile for her niece. "That's exactly what happened. Now I had better get my weak knees—and the rest of me—back to work."

She couldn't do this anymore, she thought as she walked back through the crowd on her way to the medical trailer. She refused to spend the rest of her life looking over her shoulder. That was no way to live, it was just surviving, barely existing.

She was stronger than this. She had to be, for Nicky's sake.

This constant fear accomplished nothing productive, just left her jittery and unsettled.

She wasn't going to give in to it again.

She straightened her shoulders at the internal declaration, suddenly feeling as if a weight the size of one of Peg's prize Angus bulls had been lifted from them. No more. She hid in the bathroom while these men killed Michael, but she would not cower again.

She was done with running scared. If they somehow managed to find her and Nicky, she would fight them with every weapon she had at her disposal.

Or die trying.

Hours later, still thinking about her new vow to stop being so weak and afraid, she sat on the top of the picnic table at their campsite feeling insignificant as she gazed up at a million stars peppering the vast Montana night sky.

Why did the heavens seem so close in the West, she wondered, as if she could simply reach up and tug a few of those pinpricks of light down onto her lap?

The cool night breeze carried the lowing of cattle down at the pens and the smell of woodsmoke from a campfire somewhere nearby. On the breeze also floated a hundred memories of other times she had sat just like this with her father, counting stars and listening to the night.

Billy Joe had known many of the constellations from his stint in the Navy. Orion, Ursa Major, Cassiopeia.

Cassiopeia had been their special symbol, their way of connecting despite the distance between them most of the time. During the school year when she was with her mother, she would go out into the garden whenever Billy Joe called and look for the distinctive W of the constellation.

San Francisco wasn't the best place for stargazing, unfortunately, with the fog and the drizzles and the city lights, but she tried her darnedest. It comforted her on even the bleakest of days to know her father was looking at the same night sky, just from a different perspective.

She smiled softly. She could still pick out Cassiopeia and the Big and Little Dippers but the rest of the sky was a mystery. Shame on her for not retaining more from those summer lessons. She ought to at least buy a stargazing book at one of the tourist traps along the way and try to relearn them so she could pass on the tradition to Nicky. Maybe when all this was over and they were settled somewhere, she could buy a little telescope and they could explore the heavens together.

That seemed to have become her mantra. *When all this is over.* But she was beginning to wonder if it would ever be over, if she would ever feel completely safe again.

As if to test her shaky, newfound courage, the sound of boots striking gravel carried through the night, and she looked away from the stars to find a dark shape walking slowly along the road toward her. Her heart stuttered in panic for just an instant before she quickly regained control. She was done jumping like a damn scared rabbit. Only by being strong and smart could she protect her son.

The midnight rambler was Colt, she realized a few seconds later, with more relief than she cared to admit. She recognized him by that loose-hipped walk and the breadth of his shoulders. He walked toward her trailer, then paused outside it, his hands in the pockets of a denim jacket that had definitely seen better days.

''Evening,'' she called out softly.

This time, she noted with a considerable amount of satisfaction, he was the one startled. His stance became ready, alert, like a mountain lion scenting trouble.

He peered into the darkness to where she perched on the picnic table. ''Doc? Is that you?''

She nodded, then remembered he couldn't see her. ''Yes,'' she answered.

''What are you doing up so late?''

"Watching the stars. Remembering."

He walked closer. "Something pleasant, I hope."

Now why had she said that? The last thing she wanted to do was start a conversation with him. All day she had been telling herself she needed to stay away from the man, and here she was, practically begging him to sit down for a chat.

"My father," she finally said. "On summer nights like this when I was on the road with him, we used to try to see how many constellations we could recognize. I was just sitting here feeling guilty that I can't remember more of them."

"On the road with him? What was he, some kind of rock star?"

She laughed softly at the idea of her gruff father performing in a rock and roll band. "Not even close. In his younger days, he was a bareback rider on the circuit. After he married Peg when I was ten, the two of them started a stock company."

"Rawlings Stock? As in Billy Joe Rawlings?" He gave a long, low whistle. "I should have put the pieces together before."

He looked up at the sky again. "I'm afraid I can't help you with the stars. I can find the Milky Way but that's about it."

"I can go you one better. That's Cassiopeia over there. See the W?"

His gaze followed her finger as it traced the constellation in the sky. "I can see it. Pretty little thing, isn't it?"

"And there you have the extent of my astronomical knowledge."

He chuckled and, without waiting for an invitation, joined her on the picnic table.

Immediately the air smelled of sagebrush and leather and Colt. It's a chemical reaction, she tried to tell herself, when her body instantly went on alert. Pheromones, that's all.

"I watched you ride today," she said.

"You did?" He sent her a quick, pleased look.

"You're good. Very good."

He snorted softly. "I don't know if I'd go that far. I'm competent but that's about it."

"You're second in the standings. I'd say that's a few steps above competent."

"I still have two more rounds to make it through. We'll see where I am in the standings this time Saturday night."

"You ought to be sleeping so you can be rested for tomorrow's competition. What brings you outside so late?"

He paused as if considering his words carefully, then she felt a ripple of movement from him as he shrugged. "I was just checking on things."

"On what?"

"Just wanted to make sure you all were okay over here. I wouldn't want you to have to come out in the middle of the night with your frying pan again to chase down any drunk cowboys."

He didn't add that he had been worried about her and about Nicholas, that he'd already been restless and edgy after their kiss this afternoon, and Dunbar's visit had finished the job, making sleep impossible.

"What makes you think we need protecting?"

That frosty, back-off layer returned to her voice, and for a moment he wanted to pound his head against the picnic table a few hundred times in frustration.

He couldn't remember ever struggling so much with an assignment. Hell, organized-crime bosses were more trusting than Maggie Rawlings.

He was a damn good undercover man. So why couldn't he figure out the best approach to take with her? Everything he said just seemed to rile her.

He sighed with resignation and finally just dived in. "No matter how many times you deny it, something's got you jumpy, Doc. I figure if it's bad enough to put that kind of scare into you, maybe I ought to keep an eye on things, just to be on the safe side. It would sure help if I knew who or what to be watching out for, though.''

Come on, Maggie. He willed silently. *Tell me about the bastards who killed your husband. I can't help you unless you bring me into it. Then we can work together to find whatever Damian wants and be done with this.*

She drew her knees up to her chest and wrapped her arms around them. For a moment he thought she would tell him, but she just rested her chin on her knee and looked out into the night. ''It's kind of you to be so concerned about us, but there's nothing wrong. You're imagining things.''

Damn, damn, damn. She wasn't going to confide in him. ''Doc—''

''Besides, you hardly know us.''

At least she sounded more puzzled than suspicious, he thought with some relief.

''Why would you continue to put yourself through so much trouble for us,'' she went on, ''when we're virtually strangers?''

''For one thing, I owe you.''

At her confused frown, he lifted his shoulder. ''The patch job you did on me last week.''

''If there was a debt there—which there certainly isn't, since I was just doing my job—it would certainly have been settled and then some the night you fixed my flat tire.''

He scowled at the memory of his deception, of piercing her tire. Before this job, lies and subterfuge had been as natural to him as sleeping and eating, but suddenly he hated them with passionate intensity.

''What's the other reason?'' she asked.

''What do you mean?''

''You said, 'for one thing.' That would seem to imply there's another reason you're suddenly acting like a worried older brother.''

He gave a raw laugh. ''My feelings for you are not in the

least brotherly, Maggie. I would have thought that kiss in your trailer earlier proved that.''

At the reminder of that soft, erotic kiss they'd shared, the air seemed to vibrate suddenly with charged tension. She cleared her throat. ''I, ah, I've been meaning to talk to you about that.''

Now, *this* ought to be good. ''What about it?''

''Well, obviously, it was a—a mistake.''

''Was it?'' Never mind that he'd been thinking the same thing all afternoon. For some reason it irritated the hell out of him to hear her agree with him.

''Of course,'' she answered. ''It was purely a—a chemical reaction.''

''A chemical reaction.''

''Right.'' She seemed to warm to her boneheaded theory. ''A chemical reaction, stimulated by the fact that we were in such close proximity, alone there in the trailer.''

''Um, Doc, I hate to point this out, but we're in even closer proximity right now. And we're alone. Feeling any chemical reactions?''

If he hadn't been so frustrated, he would have laughed at the way she inched away almost imperceptibly. ''No,'' she said as primly as a schoolmarm. ''It must have been a one-time occurrence and now it's completely out of our systems.''

This time he did laugh, a low amused laugh that had her sidling away another centimeter. ''A chemical reaction. Right. You keep telling yourself that, Doc,'' he said. ''Maybe sooner or later you'll even believe it.''

''It was,'' she insisted. ''We just have to do everything we can to make sure it doesn't happen again.''

''Like not sit together on a picnic table alone in the dark, under a night sky overflowing with stars?'' he asked quietly.

If she moved away any farther, she was going to fall off the edge of the table into the dirt. She cleared her throat again. ''That would certainly be a good place to start.''

He finally took pity on her nervousness and straightened from the table. "I wouldn't want to blow your theory, so I'll say good night, then."

"I need to turn in, too."

"My rig's just at the end of this row. If you need me for anything in the night, you know where to find me, right?"

Even in the moonlight, he could clearly see the quelling look she aimed at him. "I thought we just established that's not likely to happen."

He laughed. "That's not what I meant, although I sure wouldn't turn you away." His teasing smile faded, and he studied her seriously. "I know you said you don't need protection, Doc, and I can respect that. But if anything spooks you in the night just holler. I can be here before you can say 'Cassiopeia'."

Even in the darkness he could see her eyes soften, her mouth curl up. "I'll remember that, Colt. Thank you."

"You're welcome."

He waited until she was safely in her trailer before walking to his camper and grabbing his bedroll. He sighed, carefully making his way back under the carpet of stars toward the patch of grass under the protective arms of a willow tree near her trailer.

Between his worry over what Damian might do when he found them and the "chemical reactions" still zinging through his blood, he was in for one hell of a long night.

Chapter 7

He hated this.

Colt shoved the pick into the flimsy lock on Maggie's trailer and worked the tension. After only a few twists he heard the last tumbler click and the handle twisted easily in his fingers.

With one more careful look over his shoulder, Colt pushed open the thin door and slipped inside. *Yes, folks,* he thought with no small amount of self-mockery. *There you have it, your tax dollars at work.*

Lock picking was one of the more disreputable skills he'd learned during his training at the academy. It wasn't an official class, but was something he had picked up from other trainees. Throughout the last ten years, his unsavory proficiency had come in handy many times, but he could never remember having this sick feeling in his stomach at using it.

Once safely inside Maggie's trailer, he closed the door behind him and surveyed her temporary home, strangely reluctant to begin.

Intellectually he knew he needed to search the place. If he

could find Damian's money and the records Michael Prescott had kept so carefully—and so stupidly—he knew she would be persuaded to cooperate with the investigation and he could drop this charade that was becoming more uncomfortable by the minute.

Yeah, he knew he needed to do this. But the reality of breaking into her living quarters—of combing through her meager belongings like some kind of thief in the night—seemed like a harsh betrayal. He could just imagine her reaction if she caught him at it, that shocked hurt he knew would bruise her eyes. It left a hollow ache in his gut.

Get on with it, he ordered himself. She wouldn't discover him searching her trailer, she was too busy working. He had left her just moments ago sewing up a cut on one cowboy's forehead while two others waited in line to have joints wrapped.

He frowned. He was almost positive the two rowdy kids with the bad joints had been faking their injuries for a chance to make time with the beautiful lady doc.

He supposed he couldn't get too upset about it. Hell, he would have tried the same thing when he'd competed on the circuit for real when he was their age, so how could he blame them?

Maggie could take care of herself if they tried anything. For all her nervousness about DeMarranville's men, judging by the way she handled herself with the young bucks, she had obviously had plenty of practice dealing with amorous patients.

No, she would probably never know he had searched her temporary home unless he told her himself. Still, eventually she would learn he worked for the FBI, that he had been sent to investigate her. Either he would have to come clean or she would figure it out on her own.

When she did, he knew those eyes would never again look at him with that shy, hesitant interest. Instead, they would be guarded and distrustful, like a puppy that had been kicked once who was waiting for the other boot to strike.

He muttered a low, frustrated curse. He wasn't at all sure he liked having a conscience again. Things were so much simpler when he could go in and do a job cleanly, precisely, without having to worry about a pair of soft brown eyes that could make him ache.

The job. He needed to focus on the job. Instead of thinking about the hurt it would cause Maggie to find out he had lied to her, he forced himself to conjure up an image of Damian behind bars, where he belonged. In prison orange instead of those designer suits he wore so smugly, eating greasy, tasteless prison food instead of the haute cuisine prepared by that French chef he employed with dirty money.

Only a matter of time, he assured himself. The records kept by Maggie's late, unlamented husband would see to that. A grim smile twisted his mouth. He hoped to hell Damian knew he was being hunted like a rabbit. It would give him nothing but satisfaction to know he was giving his former partner a few sleepless nights, that Damian was forced to be a little more watchful, a little more anxious.

He deserved that and much, much more for the havoc the bastard had wreaked in countless lives.

If nothing else, Damian deserved to pay for destroying his illusions about justice and decency, for taking an idealistic young military policeman who was out to prove something to the world and turning Colt into the man he had become. Hard, ruthless.

Despicable.

The reminder was all the impetus he needed. Sharply, brusquely, he buried his hesitation and shoved his fledgling guilt as far down as he could stuff it. No matter what he'd started out as, this was his reality now. This was who he was: a tough, cold-blooded investigator who could submerge his feelings completely for the sake of the job, who could do what had to be done without needless emotion.

Fifteen minutes later, he hungered for a little of that cold-bloodedness while he fought the urge to punch a fist through the aluminum skin of her trailer.

She had to have Damian's merchandise! But where? Not in her trailer, he was sure of at least that much.

After combing through every inch of the place—which didn't take long, since there weren't all that many inches to the little piece-of-junk dwelling—he had found nothing even remotely resembling embezzled money or the computer disk that contained all the evidence needed to bring down De-Marranville.

He *did* have a clearer picture of Maggie Rawlings, but he wasn't sure that was necessarily a good thing. He had discovered she liked books. There were stacks of them scattered around the trailer: medical journals, paperback mysteries, and piles of well-worn children's books for Nick.

She had obviously tried to make the trailer as homey as possible, with patchwork quilts on the loft bed and throw pillows on the bench seats. She'd even stuck a picture Nicky had obviously colored onto the little refrigerator—of a stick-figure cowboy on the back of a misshapen horse, with spindly legs and a huge head. Nicky's scrawl underneath the picture made him smile: "Colt and Scout," with a backward *S*.

Further searching revealed her clothes were plain, practical. Classic button-down oxfords, slacks and skirts, with a few T-shirts and the tan pair of jeans she wore when he took Nicky riding. She even wore practical underwear—white cotton, no frills, no thrills—he'd learned, poking through a drawer like some kind of sick voyeur.

Her clothes weren't in the least what he would have expected from a woman who grew up in the pearls-and-diamonds world of San Francisco society or who had been married to a social-climbing accountant. He would have expected designer labels, expensive fabrics.

She would have been stunning in silk. He did a little mental conjuring. Something short and black and elegant. With that honey-blond hair twisted up into something sleek and graceful and some kind of strappy shoes, she would be nothing short of breathtaking.

He indulged in the possibilities for just a few seconds, then shoved the images away. That kind of thinking would only play hell with his concentration when he could least afford to be distracted. With effort he turned his mind back to the job and what he had discovered about Maggie Sinclair.

He already knew she was into healthy food, and the little pantry cupboard backed that up—low-fat peanut butter, cans of tuna fish, rice, oatmeal. Just what he would have expected except for one renegade bag of Oreos he found in the back of the cupboard, way back where her son couldn't reach. It was shy only a couple of cookies, as if she hoarded them carefully and doled them out to herself just a few at a time. It made him smile, just a little, to discover one of her weaknesses.

Other than that, there were few surprises in the trailer. She had left San Francisco in a hurry but had apparently taken time to grab a few photo albums. They were the only mementos he could find of her life with Michael Prescott.

He leafed through them quickly, finding pictures of Nicky through various stages of childhood. Lying on his stomach on a blanket, naked except for a big toothless grin. In a high chair behind a birthday cake, with frosting smeared all over his face. Riding a tricycle wearing a fierce look of concentration.

He frowned. Maggie was in a few of the pictures, but where was her husband? Flipping pages toward the back of one, he finally found a photograph of Michael Prescott posing stiffly with Nicky on what looked like another birthday celebration. He looked handsome in a well-groomed sort of way but didn't appear at all comfortable with his son.

It made him think of his own father, of Sunday afternoons spent tussling on the living room carpet and midnight fishing trips to Butterfly Lake and learning how to shave by mornings spent watching wide-eyed as Jack McKendrick took an old-fashioned razor to his face.

Guilt crashed into him, painfully familiar, and he slapped Maggie's photo album shut at the same time he slammed the door on his own memories.

Where did he go from here? Beckstead and Dunbar were convinced Maggie had Damian's money and the computer disk. They said Prescott himself said she did the night he was murdered and that they had searched her belongings in San Francisco without success. But if they weren't in the trailer, where else could he possibly look?

He was going to have to tell her he was FBI, and soon. Time was running out. Yeah, it would hurt her, but so what? He was hard, he was ruthless, he was cold-blooded. Right?

Too bad he had such a tough time remembering that when he was dealing with Maggie Rawlings.

Maggie looked through the doorway of Peg's big, plush trailer where Nicky slept on the soft couch inside. "Are you sure you don't mind if he sleeps in here tonight?" she whispered to her stepmother.

"Don't be silly." Peg's voice was brisk. "No sense wakin' him up just to put him to bed again over at your place. We got plenty of room."

Maggie frowned and stepped down from the doorway to talk to Peg outside so she wouldn't wake up Nicky or Cheyenne. "This is the second night this week. At this rate he'll spend more time sleeping in your trailer than in his own bed."

"He's no trouble at all, darlin'. I love havin' him here, you know that. Now why is it so hard for you to accept a little help?"

Maggie jammed her hands into the pockets of her cardigan. She couldn't explain it to Peg until she understood it herself. Maybe her stubbornness had something to do with the fact that she felt she was finally learning to stand on her own.

Maybe subconsciously she was afraid counting on anyone else, even in such a little thing as Nicky sleeping at Peg's trailer overnight, might undermine her new independence.

"Now if I was you," her stepmother went on, "I'd take advantage of not havin' to be a mother for a while and go hook up with that big hunk of cowboy of yours for a little Texas two-step."

Hot color flooded her cheeks at the knowing smile playing around Peg's scarlet-painted lips, especially since the image was more tempting than she cared to admit.

"I don't have a 'big hunk of cowboy,' as you so charmingly put it," she replied.

"Oh, come on. I've been around the block a few times, Miss Maggie. Anybody with a pair of eyes can see the sparks flickerin' between you and that Montana roper of yours."

"What is it with you and Cheyenne? Why is my love life—or lack thereof—so interesting to the two of you?"

Peg's sharp features suddenly, unexpectedly, softened and she reached out and pulled Maggie to her in a quick hug. "It's no secret that no-good husband of yours made your life miserable. We just want to see you happy, darlin'."

She returned the hug with exasperated affection. "What makes you think a 'big hunk of cowboy' is going to be any better for me?"

"I never did like that fella you married. Neither did your dad. Used to say he had shifty eyes. Now McKendrick, on the other hand... I like him. Besides bein' sexy as all get-out, he's real good with that boy of yours. That has to count for something."

It counted for a great deal. She smiled softly, remembering the image of Nicky perched happily in front of Colt on that big buckskin gelding, of his patient answers to a little boy's unending curiosity.

She liked him, too. That was the problem. She could find entirely too many things that were likable about Colton McKendrick. With a sigh, she pulled away from Peg. "I appreciate your concern, really I do, but it's just not a good time for me to be thinking about any kind of romantic involvement right now.''

''Hell, what's there to think about it? For once in your life, don't think. Just feel.''

''I wish it was that easy.''

Peg squeezed her hands. ''It is. Just keep in mind, a man like that one doesn't come around every day.''

Her stepmother's words were still ringing in her ears a few minutes later when she walked to her own trailer and fumbled through her bag for her keys in the darkness. After finding them, she unlocked the door and swung it open, then froze, her fingers still on the cold metal of the doorknob.

Someone had been here.

She stared into the inky blackness, her pulse lurching and bucking. She couldn't say exactly how she recognized the trailer had been invaded, she just *knew*. The moment she opened the door the realization had climbed over her.

Her fingers trembling, she forced herself to go inside and switch on the light above the stove. Its yellow glow warmed her slightly but couldn't completely take the chill from her blood.

Someone had most definitely been here. It wasn't so much a concrete knowledge of something wrong, more like a subtle awareness: a strange scent lingering in the air, a sensation that things were not exactly as she had left them—a book out of place, a drawer slightly ajar.

Her heartbeat continued to stutter wildly. When had the break-in happened? During the rodeo or later? Had they found her, then? Were they out there somewhere, watching, waiting?

With effort, she reined in her gyrating thoughts. It was probably just Cheyenne, she assured herself. She had probably come into the trailer looking for something for Nicky. His pajamas, a stuffed animal, a favorite bedtime storybook.

She had a key, after all, and it didn't appear that the door had been jimmied.

She forced herself to breathe calmly and easily until her panic began to subside. So much for her vow the other night to stop living in fear. The slightest thing seems off-kilter and she completely goes off the deep end. She was only imagining things again.

She had almost managed to soothe her nerves when a rustle sounded through the open window of the trailer, as if the long, draping branches of the weeping willow had been disturbed in the quiet, windless night, pushed aside to let someone through.

Her head jerked up, all her frantic fears returning in force. But she had vowed to face her fears head-on, and face them she would, dammit. Pulse pounding furiously, she picked up the frying pan from its hook by the stove. With the solid weight of the trusty cast iron clenched in her hand, she twisted the knob and pushed open the door.

It was an eerie repeat of the night a week ago—had it only been a week?—when she had found Colt fixing her flat tire. This time it wasn't raining, though. High, wispy clouds floated across the sliver of moon and she heard the distant rumble of trucks on the Interstate.

Most of the campground slept—it was past midnight, after all, and the cowboys put in long hours. She could see a few lights on in trailers here and there and hear the high whinny of a horse hobbled nearby, but other than that, she could have been alone in the night.

She was imagining things again. She had to be. She peered into the shadows under the big willow. There. Did something move? A shadow slightly darker than the night around it? Her eyes strained to see, and she thought she saw the darker spot shift slightly, then move forward.

She gripped the pan tighter, her heartbeat picking up a pace, and she wondered if she really had the fortitude to use it against another human being.

"Doc? Somethin' wrong?"

She nearly collapsed onto the steps. Hot on the heels of her relief was aggravation. Damn that Colt McKendrick anyway, always lurking in the dark waiting to spook her.

"You makin' flapjacks in the middle of the night again?"

Her arm sagged with the weight of the frying pan. "You scared me! What are you doing out here? Don't tell me I have another flat tire."

"Not that I can see. I'd be happy to check it out for you, though."

Her knees shook in delayed reaction and she decided collapsing on the steps wouldn't be such a bad idea. It sure beat toppling over at his feet. She lowered herself to the cold metal and only then saw the sleeping bag he carried over his shoulder.

"Have a hot date, McKendrick?"

"What?"

"Your sleeping bag."

He glanced at the rolled-up bag and then back at her with an almost sheepish look in his face. "Um, something like that."

Jealousy, hot and sharp, pierced her. It came out of nowhere, shocking her with its intensity.

She had no right to be jealous, she reminded herself. No right at all. It wasn't any of her business if he found some ditzy buckle bunny to share a sleeping bag with. Colt was nothing to her but a friend.

"Well don't let me keep you." She heard the tight, prissy tone in her voice and flushed again.

He studied her for a moment, then jerked a thumb toward the willow tree. "I've got a hot date with a patch of grass over there."

"You were going to sleep out here? Why?"

"Maybe I just like sleepin' under the stars."

"How can you see them if you're sleeping under a tree?"

He laughed softly, a low, rough sound that somehow

seemed to score along her nerve endings, raw already with the tumult of her emotions. "Good point."

He gazed up at the moon, then back at her with that sheepish expression on his face again. "Hell, I might as well tell you. You'll figure it out sooner or later. The truth is, I thought it wouldn't hurt to keep an eye on things over here."

She stared up at him. "You were sleeping on the ground to stand guard? Over me?" The idea floored her, completely stunned her.

"It's not so bad. I've slept out during roundups plenty of times and this isn't much different. Warmer, actually. Last night was kind of nice, with a little breeze and the sound of the river in the distance."

His words barely registered through the haze of disbelief that surrounded her.

Once when she was a kid she'd been bucked off an energetic little mare her father had warned her against taking on. She still remembered the way her breath had been punched out of her, the way she had laid on her back and stared up at the sky while her vision dimmed around the edges.

That was exactly the way she felt right now, shocked and breathless and achy.

She had tried to be stoic throughout the last month, had tried hard not to give in to the constant, unrelenting fear. In the process, she had discovered reserves of strength she had no idea she possessed. But the idea of Colt spending a night on the hard ground—of him caring enough to watch over her and her son—somehow reached through her veneer of control and yanked at her heart.

Tears welled up behind her eyelids, in her throat, and she could do nothing but stare at him, speechless.

"Aw, come on Doc. Don't look at me like that," he mumbled.

"I-I'm sorry." She sniffled and blinked and tried to hold her tears back but they finally broke free, chasing each other down her cheeks. Once free, she couldn't do anything to stop them.

She thought she had been touched when he changed her flat tire in the night so she wouldn't have to face it in the morning. That was nothing to this bittersweet warmth welling up inside her.

With a muffled curse, he dropped the sleeping bag and crossed the space between them to where she sat on the trailer step. In one motion, he pulled her to her feet and into his arms. She sagged against his broad, hard chest that smelled like sage and leather, and wanted to stay there forever, just like this, and weep.

She couldn't remember the last time she had cried. When her mother died? Her father? She wasn't the crying sort. Never had been, not even during the worst rigors of med school.

When she was a kid, she had been too busy trying to be a rough-and-tumble tomboy during her summers with Billy Joe to give in to tears often. And Helen had viewed tears as a loss of control, something she simply wouldn't tolerate in her daughter any more than she did in herself.

She could almost hear the litany echoing in her ears. *Margaret, stop that sniveling. Margaret, stiffen your shoulders. Margaret, use a handkerchief.*

Now she felt as if an ocean of tears had been dammed up inside her all these years, capped and contained. It had only taken a sweet, crazy act, like a rough cowboy sleeping out under the stars to protect her, for them to spill free, and now she couldn't seem to stop them.

She felt safe here. The realization only made her sob harder. In his arms, surrounded by his strength and warmth, she felt completely safe for the first time in weeks.

"There now. It's okay." He patted her back with his big hands, and she would have smiled at the awkwardness of the gesture if she hadn't been so completely humiliated at breaking down in front of him. Or so devastated at the knowledge that when he released her, all the fear would come creeping back.

"It's not okay," she mumbled. "It hasn't been for a long time."

"What hasn't been?" His voice sounded hoarse, concerned. "What's going on, Doc?"

"It's not your problem. I don't want to involve you in it," she mumbled against his chest.

He smoothed a gentle hand down her hair in a tender gesture that nearly destroyed her. "Hate to break it to you, darlin', but I'm already involved."

Perhaps it was the tenderness that compelled her to tell him. Maybe it was simply because here, surrounded by his heat and strength, she discovered she could no longer carry this huge weight by herself.

"I'm so tired of being afraid," she managed to sniff out.

"Tell me, Doc. Tell me what's so terrible you don't sleep nights and can't stop looking over your shoulder?"

She pulled away from him then shivered. She was right. Outside of his arms, it was as if she'd been thrust from a sweet, dreamy haven back into the throes of her nightmare.

To fight it—and to combat the overwhelming desire to step back into those arms—she gripped her elbows.

In the thin moonlight, his features seemed blurred, like a photograph left underwater. But still she could see the concern in his vivid blue eyes, see the frown lines radiating from that firm mouth.

Could she tell him? Weeks of keeping silent about what she had seen that night tangled up her tongue. There were a hundred reasons why she knew she shouldn't tell him. He would probably tell her to go to the police. It might put him in danger to know what was going on. He would feel even more obligated to try to protect them.

None of those were the real reason she wanted to stay silent.

The hard, vicious truth was that she was ashamed. Her

shoulders sagged at the bitter knowledge. She didn't want to tell Colt how weak she had been, how timid.

But despite all the reasons she could come up with not to confide in him, there was one overriding argument in favor of it: she trusted him. It had grown slowly over the past days but she had grown to depend on his friendship more than she ever believed possible.

She took a deep breath, filled her lungs with air, then tightened her hold on her elbows until the bony ridges seemed to be imprinted on her fingers.

"I told you my husband was murdered," she finally said in a voice that only wavered a little. "But I didn't tell you I was there, that I watched him die. A man shot my child's father and I did absolutely nothing to stop it."

Chapter 8

At Maggie's quiet confession that she had witnessed the hit on her bastard of a husband, the breath Colt hadn't even been aware he was holding escaped in a rush.

Relief poured through him—relief that she had finally decided to trust him and relief that he could be done with this job soon and put much-needed distance between them again, that he could once more regain perspective and climb back into the careful order of his life.

Tempering it was a sharp ache in his chest. He hurt to hear how her illusions had been shattered so brutally, that she had been exposed so violently to the harshness and ugliness of his world.

She shouldn't have had to watch her husband's murder in the first place and she damn well shouldn't have to relive it, but he knew he needed to hear the story from her own lips before he could help her.

"Aren't you going to say anything?" she asked in a small, tight voice.

His gaze flashed to her face and the expression there

shocked him. In another woman, he would have said she looked guilty, but what would Maggie possibly have to feel guilty about? She had been an innocent witness to her husband's murder.

At his continued silence, her spine stiffened and her chin tilted. "Sorry I troubled you. Forget I said anything." She turned and took a step back toward her trailer but he grabbed her arm.

"Hey, slow down. I'm sorry. You just startled me, that's all. You can't drop a bombshell like that and just expect me to know in an instant exactly how I should react."

"I don't expect anything. I told you, it's my problem and I'm handling it. I should never have dragged you into it."

"And I told you, I'm in it and you didn't drag me anywhere."

Here's where he should tell her he's an FBI agent. It was the perfect opportunity, the ideal opening.

Still, he wavered. The time didn't seem right. He couldn't afford to lose that trust until he heard the whole story about that night, about what she knew of the men who had killed Michael Prescott.

Going with his instincts, he grabbed her hand. "I want to know what happened, Doc. Let's go inside and sit down and you can tell me about it. You've gone this far, you can't back down now."

Shoulders stiff, mouth set, she studied him for a moment, then sighed softly. "You're right. I might as well tell you all of it."

She led the way back to her trailer. He slid onto one of the benches at the table, expecting her to take the other side, but she walked to the little window in the rear of the trailer and looked out at the night.

"Start at the beginning," he said. "What happened?"

She was quiet for so long he thought she wasn't going to answer him, but finally she turned around and in a clipped, expressionless tone, recited the events of the night Michael

Prescott was killed. She told him about their impending divorce, about the bastard's repeated infidelities and about how Prescott had threatened to fight for custody of Nicky to punish her for leaving him.

She had gone to his office that night to try to talk him out of it, she said, and stumbled onto a dark, frightening morass of deception, betrayal and, ultimately, murder.

The more she spoke, the more lifeless her voice became. Her long, elegant fingers were laced together in front of her. They twitched a few times, as if she wanted to fiddle with them, but other than that she remained perfectly still, perfectly composed.

He would have thought she was made of ice until he looked into her cinnamon eyes and saw the stark, raw emotion there.

He wanted to stop her, to gather her into his arms again and tell her she didn't need to tell him anything more, that he already knew the whole story. That he would take care of her. He couldn't, of course. Hell, just the fact he had the impulse in the first place scared the bejeber out of him. Instead, he had to pretend a bemused kind of shock at her story.

"So that's it," she finally said. "This happened nearly six weeks ago, and I've been running ever since."

"Why would they be looking for you? From what you said, they wouldn't know you were even there."

"I don't know why." The fingers definitely twitched this time. "Before the blond one killed him, Michael told them I had something they were looking for."

He felt that little itch between his shoulder blades that usually meant he was close to the crux of a case. "What did he mean?"

"I don't have the faintest idea what he was talking about. I've racked my brains since that night but can't come up with a single thing. I moved out three months before he was killed and took very little with me from our house. Whatever it is must be somewhere in my apartment, I suppose."

"Why didn't you go to the police?" It was one aspect of the case that had bothered him from the beginning.

She didn't look at him, just gazed back out at the night. "You know, before this happened to me, I thought the world was an orderly place that always made sense. Two and two always equaled four, morning inevitably followed night. I thought I knew right from wrong, good from evil."

"But now?"

"Now I don't know who to trust and who to fear. Everything I thought I knew has been jumbled up into a big mess. After I…after I saw the murder, I went to pick up Nicky from the house of the woman who used to be my housekeeper when I lived with Michael. I called the police from there and I would have been desperately grateful to turn this over to someone else, to give a statement, to let them protect me."

Her voice trailed off and she was silent for several moments. Finally, he broke the silence. "What happened?"

"Almost as soon as I hung up the phone, two of the men who were at Michael's building showed up. I have to think they were tipped off by someone at the police station. How else would they have found me so quickly?"

He frowned. Lane hadn't said anything about this in his briefing. He tried to remember what, exactly, the SAC had said. He had mentioned a possible security leak but nothing else. If what Maggie said was true—if DeMarranville's men showed up before the police she had called could even arrive—Beckstead didn't have a leak on his hands, he had a damn gully washer.

She didn't trust the police, with good reason. How could he possibly tell her he was an FBI agent now? He couldn't. But he might be able to lead her in the direction of going to the police.

He paused, choosing his words carefully. "You know, if you decide you want to talk to somebody, that you're prepared to come forward, I know some people who could probably help you.''

''Who?''

''Some friends of mine. Friends who can be trusted.''

She looked undecided, and then pushed away from the window abruptly, clenching her fists at her sides. ''I hate this. I hate being afraid all the time, not being able to relax for even a few minutes. Always terrified to let Nicky out of my sight. You have no idea what I would give for one decent night's rest.''

As he studied her tense posture, a tantalizing idea blew across his mind, then quickly took root. He *could* give her a little peace. It was one of the few things he could offer her. If he packed her and the boy off to the Broken Spur, she could spend at least a few days without fear of Damian's people finding her.

He chewed on the possibilities for a few moments, studying the angles carefully. He was pretty sure it would piss off Beckstead. Agents usually weren't encouraged to invite the subject of an investigation back to their place for a few days.

On the other hand Lane hadn't been completely clean with him. If he was willing to downplay the security leak, what else was his boss keeping from him?

Besides, taking her to his ranch would give him a chance to break the news about being an FBI agent at a time when she might be more receptive. He seized on the thought. ''Where are you heading next week?''

She looked startled at the change of subject. ''Utah, I think. The Pioneer Days rodeo in Ogden. Why?''

He had known it, since Lane provided him an itinerary of all her assignments. Maybe he had subconsciously wanted to take her back to the Broken Spur all along.

He dismissed the thought. She was stressed out and needed a break from the pressure cooker she'd been living in for the past week. That's all there was to it.

''Look, I've got a friend with a little ranch right on the

way there, just south of Bozeman. Why don't you and Nick come with me and spend a few days at his place? The Ogden rodeo doesn't start until Wednesday and that would give you four whole days where you could just relax and let down your guard for a while. Nobody could ever trace you to the Broken Spur.''

She gave a small, scratchy-sounding laugh. ''Are you crazy? You can't just invite a couple of strangers to stay at your friend's ranch without his permission.''

''Joe won't mind.'' He crossed his fingers under the table, wondering just what he would have to do to convince his foreman to pose as a ranch owner during the duration of Maggie's stay. ''He owes me. Besides, you're not strangers to me.''

''Maybe not, but we certainly are to your friend.''

''I promise you, he won't care. Come with me, Doc. There's a great fishing hole and a gentle old pony Nick could ride and all the fresh air and spectacular views anybody could ask for.''

''I don't think—''

''Don't think. For once, don't think. Just come with me.'' Suddenly he wanted her there fiercely, not for the case or for her safety but simply because he wanted her to see the place he was raised, his haven from the ugly world he lived in most of the time.

''You said you were tired of being afraid,'' he went on. ''Just imagine having four days of complete peace, without once having to worry about anybody coming after you.''

It was fascinating to watch the arguments churning in her eyes give way to yearning, like summer storm clouds breaking just long enough to let in tentative sunshine. She opened her mouth as if to try one more time to refuse his offer then closed it softly. ''Are you sure your friend won't mind?'' she finally asked.

''Positive. There's plenty of room in the old ranch house

and he'd be glad to see me. The place can always use an extra pair of hands.''

''In that case, it sounds wonderful.''

He grinned. Now all he had to worry about was convincing Joe Redhawk to participate in the deception, making sure everybody at the ranch kept quiet about him being an FBI agent and convincing Lane that taking Maggie home with him was the best thing for the investigation.

Piece of cake. Right?

''When we gonna be there, Mom?''

She grimaced at the age-old question she'd already heard a dozen times. Aeons ago, some little Neanderthal boy with a jutted brow probably asked his mother the same thing while trekking across the Bering Strait.

''We'll get there when we get there,'' she answered Nicky, sparing just a quick glance across the width of the ancient truck cab to watch her son bouncing eagerly on the seat. He couldn't have been more excited if they were heading to Disneyland.

She smiled at him, then forced her gaze back to the road and Colt's horse trailer up ahead.

The scenery was spectacular, she would give him that much. On one side, huge pine, spruce and quaking aspen towered over the road as it dipped and curved along the terrain. On the other, a fast-moving river cut its way through granite boulders and thick forests. Since turning off the main highway, they had seen deer, elk and even a moose foraging along the side of the road.

Too bad she couldn't enjoy any of it.

She reminded herself to relax her shoulders for the hundredth time since they started out earlier that morning. The twists and turns of the mountain road demanded all her energy and kept her fingers in a white-knuckled grip on the steering wheel, but more than that she had spent the entire two-hour drive stewing and fretting.

What was she doing, traipsing across Montana to a stranger's ranch? This was a mistake. She knew it in her heart, that the more time she and Nicky spent with Colt, the more they would come to care about him, and she couldn't afford to let him in any more than she already had.

He would be out of their lives soon, moving on to the next rodeo. She knew it, had grown up with a rambling rodeo man for a father. Leaving was in their blood, in their bones.

She couldn't have changed her father any more than she could change the course of that river down there. She wasn't entirely sure she *would* have, even if she'd had that power, but she knew what it was to live with the heartbreak of watching him leave over and over again.

She and Nicky had already lost too much: their home, their belongings, the life they had just begun to carve for themselves. They couldn't afford to lose anything else they cared about.

No, she knew perfectly well that she shouldn't be traveling this mountain road on the way to spending four days with Colt. But he had lured her here with something impossible to refuse: the promise of peace; albeit even a fleeting peace that, like the man himself, would be gone all too quickly.

The past weeks of unrelenting fear had left her physically and mentally drained, completely wrung dry, so it made sense that she would find the idea of leaving that behind for a few days so tempting.

What she didn't understand was the equally compelling need she had to spend more time with a big cowboy with thick dark hair and irresistible blue eyes.

She shifted on the seat, uncomfortable with more than the nagging ache in the small of her back from the ancient, springless seat, wondering which appealed to her more, spending a few worry-free days relaxing on a ranch or the idea of spending those days in Colt's company?

Despite her best efforts, he was becoming entirely too important to her, was popping into her thoughts all too frequently. Worse, she could feel herself beginning to slip into old patterns of dependency, of need.

All her life she had allowed others to make decisions for her, had become the person everyone else wanted her to be. The polite, soft-spoken debutante for her mother. The bare-back-riding hellion for her father. The elegant society hostess for Michael.

A psychoanalyst probably would have had a name for someone so desperately eager to please, probably would have blamed it on the tumult of a childhood spent straddling two different worlds without completely belonging to either.

Regardless of the cause, she had vowed not to let herself lapse into that kind of thinking again. She owed it to herself to be her own person, to find her own joy. Not to be dependent on someone else to provide it for her.

"Hey, Mom, guess what?" Her son's voice derailed the train of her thoughts.

"What?"

"Colt says there's a pony at the ranch I can ride all by myself and his name is Star and he's got a white tail that goes clear to the ground. When it rains, Colt says his tail gets all muddy."

She spared one more glance at Nicky, at the little lock of hair hanging into his eyes from the widow's peak, at the freckles scattered across his nose, at the bright excitement glittering in his dark eyes.

Her heart twisted. Here was her joy: her child, who gave her life purpose, who filled it with love and laughter and sloppy kisses. If he had been closer and not belted snugly into the other side of the truck cab, she would have grabbed him close and smothered him with a few of those sloppy kisses. She contented herself with smiling at him. "I'm sure you'll have a great time getting to know him."

"Colt says he can teach me to rope like he does, too. You think maybe I could rope a couple cows while we're there?"

She laughed. "I think you'll probably have to work up to

cows, bud. Maybe he can start you off on something smaller. How about chickens?''

He rolled his eyes, another mannerism he had picked up on the rodeo circuit. ''You don't rope chickens, Mom,'' he said in a disgusted tone of voice that made it sound as if she had just committed the cowboy faux pas of the century.

The left-hand turn signal suddenly blinked on Colt's horse trailer, then the brake lights lit up as he slowed. She pumped the old brakes on her truck, then followed him under a log arch with the words Broken Spur Ranch painted in bright red letters, along with what she assumed was a brand, a simple line drawing of a spur broken in half.

The road was gravel but well maintained, without ruts or washboard bumps to rattle the truck. After only a few hundred yards, the aspen and evergreen forest opened up, revealing wide green meadows that stretched out at least a mile, until they bumped up against the high slopes of a rugged mountain range.

Colt led the way along the road toward a cluster of buildings. She could only see glimpses of them around his horse trailer until he stopped in front of a huge barn that wore a fresh coat of white paint like an old lady in a sparkling new dress.

A hundred yards from the barn was a two-story clapboard ranch house with a wide front porch that looked as if it would be the ideal place for sitting and watching the mountains on rainy afternoons.

Almost before the truck had come to a complete stop, Nicky slipped from his seat belt, shoved open the door and hopped down from the cab. He raced toward Colt's pickup.

She followed him, intent on lecturing him about the rules of vehicle safety when the barn doors opened and a man— her host, she had to assume—walked outside.

He was the most beautiful man she had ever seen, with coppery skin stretched over high cheekbones, dark eyes fringed by long, thick lashes and a sharp, aquiline nose.

She caught herself staring and quickly averted her eyes, feeling a blush heat her cheeks. Instead, she looked for her son, and found him in Colt's arms. The instant she saw the two of them together, she completely forgot about Colt's friend.

Colt was laughing at something Nicky said, and he tilted his head back as he laughed, exposing the corded muscles in his neck.

Her mouth suddenly felt as dry as the dust that coated her truck. Her stomach tumbled and lurched. Some might have said the other man was the more attractive of the two, but there was something powerful, compelling about Colt that made it impossible for her to look away.

Still carrying Nicky, he walked toward her. "You made it."

She gathered her composure around her and, with effort, managed to return his smile. "I was worried there for a while, especially the last five miles. You never warned me about the switchbacks."

"I guess I'm so used to them I don't even think about them anymore."

"Well, I'm still a city girl at heart," she said, just as his friend reached Colt's truck.

"McKendrick. Haven't seen you around these parts in how long has it been again?" Was it her imagination or did his dark eyes gleam with amusement?

"Long enough," Colt answered in what, oddly, sounded like a warning.

Before she could even try to read the currents here, the man turned to her, yanked off a leather glove and shoved a hand out. "How do, ma'am? I'm Joe Redhawk and I'm pleased to have you on the Broken Spur."

The welcome here was genuine, she decided with relief. "Thank you so much for letting us stay here, Mr. Redhawk. I'm Maggie Pr—" She caught herself just in time— "Rawlings. This is my son, Nicholas."

Nicky hopped down from Colt's arms and stared up at the tall rancher, his eyes huge. "Are you a real live Indian?"

"Nicholas!" She felt her blush heat up a notch and vowed to have a little conversation with her son as soon as possible about good manners and political correctness.

Redhawk just chuckled, and she was relieved to see he didn't look as if he had taken offense at the comment. He tilted his hat back and if she hadn't already decided to like him, she would have made up her mind completely when he knelt to her son's level. "Sure am. Of the Shoshone tribe. You ever heard of them?"

Nicky shook his head, still wearing a puzzled expression. "But how can you be an Indian? You look like a cowboy. You got a hat and boots and everything."

"I guess sometimes a fella can be both."

Nicky seemed content with that answer. He smiled back at the rancher. "Colt says there's a pony here named Star, and he said I could ride him all by myself."

"I think we can arrange that. Why don't you all come inside my ranch house," he said, with a strange, amused emphasis on the possessive pronoun, "and I'll show you to your rooms."

"Oh, no," Maggie said. "I just assumed we'd sleep in the trailer."

"Why? There's plenty of room in the ranch house. Come on, let's just get you settled inside."

"I think I can find the way," Colt answered dryly. "We wouldn't want to keep you from all the many things you probably have to do."

The rancher laughed. "Oh, you wouldn't believe how much work there is around here. Finding good help, now that's the secret. Don't you agree, McKendrick?"

"I used to," he muttered.

With another bark of laughter, the rancher adjusted his hat. "If you'll excuse me then, ma'am, I'll get back to work. Colt here can show you to the guest rooms. Feel free to take any of the bedrooms except the master bedroom on the main floor. That, naturally, is my room.''

He sent a glittering, amused look at Colt, then turned to Maggie. ''Again, welcome to the Broken Spur. I don't mind tellin' you, ma'am, I have a strong feeling your visit is really gonna liven things up around the old place.''

Chapter 9

Colt held the cellular phone away from his ear and waited for the dust to settle from Beckstead's explosion about renegade agents and botched investigations. Even with a good foot between the phone and his ear, the SAC's aggravation rang out loud and clear in the evening air.

"You don't check in for days," Beckstead barked, "and then when you finally do, it's to tell me you've taken it upon yourself to haul our witness to your godforsaken hole-in-the-wall ranch in Montana. Not only that, but you haven't even told her you're with the Bureau yet. When were you planning on telling her? Before or after she testifies for us?"

"I'll tell her when the time is right," he said when Lane paused to take a breath. "At this point she still doesn't trust me completely. I wouldn't be surprised if she disappears again if I were to tell her too soon."

He didn't even wince at the lie. If Maggie trusted anybody right now, he was very much afraid she trusted him. She hadn't even blinked when he saddled Scout an hour ago and told her the horse needed exercising after the ride here.

It never would have occurred to her to be suspicious, to guess that he wasn't out for a pleasure ride, but instead planned to go to the northern border of what was his own damn ranch so he could have the privacy he needed to check in with his superiors at the FBI.

He leaned his forearms on the split rail fence and watched a hawk ride the currents looking for prey above the raw mountains bordering the Broken Spur. He had a sudden fierce urge to be there with the hawk among the currents, or at least racing Scout across the high mountain meadows he knew were hidden amid those craggy peaks.

Anywhere but here, where he had begun to feel as if he would choke on all of his lies.

"What's the progress, then? Have you figured out where she hid Damian's money and the disk yet?"

He picked a golfball-size rock from the ground and began to roll it between his fingers. "She didn't hide anything."

"How can you sound so convinced?"

"I can't explain it," he admitted. "She says she doesn't know where they are, and I believe her."

The line was quiet for a few moments. Just when Colt thought he had lost the connection, his boss finally spoke. "I don't know Maggie Rawlings from Elvis but I do know you. You've always had better instincts than any agent I've ever known. If you think the woman is a pawn in this whole thing, I have to trust you."

"The only thing she knows is that her life has been completely torn apart since she watched Carlo Santori murder her husband a month ago."

"You think she'll be willing to testify against him?"

And spend the rest of her life looking over her shoulder in fear of retaliation. Or in a witness protection program someplace where, more than likely, she would never be able to practice medicine again.

He threw the rock as hard as he could and watched it scare

up a couple of rooster pheasants. "I don't know," he said gruffly, then admitted, "Probably."

"Then what are you waiting for?" Lane's tone was brisk. "Tell her you're FBI and let's get her and the kid into protective custody."

It was exactly what he should do, leave her safety in someone else's hands and move on to the next job. But the idea left a sour taste in his mouth. "She's as safe at the Broken Spur as she would be in custody. This is the last place Damian would think to look for her."

Damian hated the place. Colt had brought him here during his first year, hoping to impress the smooth, experienced agent he had come to admire so much. He could still remember the glow of pride he'd felt driving under the arch leading into the ranch. And he could still feel the sting of Damian's ill-concealed disdain for the gravel road, the simple furnishings in the ranch house.

He had been so damn stupid. Stupid and naive, too awed by Damian's stellar reputation in the Bureau to trust those instincts Beckstead was just talking about, too green to question some of his partner's shadier practices. Unwilling to believe what was right in front of his face, he had chosen to turn the other way when cases began to fall apart and witnesses started disappearing.

They were assigned to a team investigating a string of a dozen bank robberies when the truth about Damian's double life had finally become impossible for him to deny.

The Bureau suspected a gang of three men in the bank robberies, two who did the actual robberies and one cunningly elusive mastermind. After months of work, they were close to making an arrest of one of the two bank robbers when he'd received an anonymous call on where to find both of the suspects with some of the stolen marked bills.

Unable to pass up the chance to bring them in, he and Damian had rushed to the scene, a rundown apartment building in a seedy area of San Jose. Colt only planned to snoop around the building a little while they waited for other agents to arrive for the arrest, but then, out of the blue, a bullet whizzed by his ear, fired from one of the apartments.

He remembered running for cover and yelling for Damian to back him up, but his partner seemed to have disappeared. Colt found himself alone, in the midst of a gunfight with suspects he hadn't even seen yet.

As abruptly as it started, the shooting ceased. When the scene had been secured, Colt discovered both of the bank robbery suspects had been killed in the gun battle.

When he had confronted Damian about where the hell he had been during the whole thing, his partner had given him some cock-and-bull story about going back to the car for an extra clip, but he hadn't believed him for a second.

An ugly suspicion had begun to grow and he hadn't been able to uproot it. If Damian had somehow been involved in the bank robberies—if *he* was the cunning mastermind they had been looking for—what better way to cover his tracks than to kill his associates and then set up a phony gunfight with a rookie agent too stupid to know any better?

A few weeks later his partner resigned from the Bureau, but no amount of investigating by Colt could come up with a shred of proof against him.

In the years since, the FBI had become increasingly aware of Damian's other life as one of the most important organized-crime figures in the Bay Area, but they could never find any evidence that would stick, probably because of that damn leak. Damian had an uncanny ability to slip through any trap the Bureau set for him.

Not this time. If they could find the financial records Michael Prescott kept against him that described his illegal empire in detail, they could put Damian away for a long, long time.

This was his chance to redeem himself for not clueing in to Damian's other side when he had the chance.

He blinked away the thought and concentrated on Beckstead's words. "I can't say I'm happy about this, Mc-Kendrick," his boss was saying, "but I suppose I'll have to trust you know what you're doing. I can give you another week."

"A week?" He straightened from the fence. "What if I need more time than that?"

"See that you don't. I want to move on this, get her and the kid into a safe house as soon as possible. One week, McKendrick. I'm afraid that's all we can afford."

When the conversation was over, Colt pressed the end button on the slim cellular, shoved it back into his pocket and then swore, long and viciously.

One lousy week to wrap up the case or he would have to turn it over to Beckstead. And he didn't have the first idea where to go from here.

His mood didn't improve when he rode back to the house and found Joe Redhawk sauntering out of the barn, a bale of hay over one shoulder. He reined in Scout and nodded in greeting. "Where are Maggie and Nick?"

Redhawk jerked his head toward the house but kept walking. "She's inside fixing dinner. I imagine the kid's with her."

He paused in the process of dismounting to stare at his foreman. "She's what?"

Joe hefted the hay over the fence into a feed trough, cut the baling twine holding it together with a pocketknife and started pitchforking it apart. "Hey, don't blame me. It wasn't my idea. I just own the place."

Colt rolled his eyes, knowing he would never hear the end of this one from his foreman. "Knock it off, Joe. Why is she cooking dinner?"

"It's Pablo's week to cook but he wasn't feeling too good so your doctor friend insisted on looking at him. Says he's got the flu and needs to take it easy for a few days. While he's down, she'll take over the cooking, she said. I tried to tell her she was a guest in my house," he said with that same damn mocking grin, ''and she didn't need to work to earn her keep, but she insisted until I didn't have much of a choice but to let her. Pretty strong will on that one.''

''Tell me about it,'' he said glumly.

Redhawk shoved his gloves into his back pocket and leaned his elbows on the top rail of the fence. ''What's her story, anyway? She in trouble?''

''Big time.''

''She kill somebody?''

Colt flashed him a quick look but found only simple curiosity in his expression, instead of the bitterness he might have expected in any other man. Then again, Joe had always been good at putting on a stoic front for the world. Few would suspect his foreman had served three years in prison for killing his father to keep the drunk bastard from slashing his mother to ribbons with a bowie knife.

If they hadn't already been closer than blood, that alone would probably have cemented the bond between them. Joe had chosen a little more direct method than Colt had, but they had both been responsible for their fathers' deaths.

He shoved the grim memories away. ''No, she didn't kill anybody.''

While he uncinched the saddle from Scout, he wondered how much detail he could provide to Joe. On the phone yesterday, he had only told him that he was undercover on an assignment posing as a rodeo cowboy and that he needed to bring someone to stay at the ranch for a few days without blowing his cover.

Joe had balked at first but eventually agreed to cooperate, especially when Colt promised a bonus to all the hands if they could manage to keep quiet about his other life. He deserved at least some background information for his help, Colt decided.

''You've probably figured out Maggie's on the run.''

''Yeah. Who's after her?''

''Damian DeMarranville.''

Joe winced. He was one of the few people Colt had confided in about his former partner. "Nasty business there."

"Right. Her husband cheated DeMarranville out of some serious money. Not only that, but he tried to cover his butt by keeping some very incriminating evidence against him. Before Damian's hired gun killed him last month, Prescott told them the doc knows where to find the money and the evidence."

"Does she?"

"No. Least she says she doesn't, and Maggie Rawlings is not much of a liar."

"She's not bad to look at, either. But I'm sure that's a fact that wouldn't have escaped the eye of a sharp FBI special agent like yourself."

He glared. "It's business, Joe. Strictly business."

His protests must not have been very convincing. His foreman snorted. "Right. If you say so."

"I do."

"Why all the hush-hush undercover stuff? Why does the woman think you're a dirt-poor cowboy instead of a big, hotshot FBI agent?"

He felt a muscle in his jaw twitch. "I'll tell her when the time is right. For now I'm just trying to protect her and figure out what she knows without losing her trust."

"The kid's a little character," Joe said after a few moments of silence. "Reminds me a little of Charlie Junior."

Colt sent another quick look at his friend. Charlie Junior was Joe's nephew, the child of Joe's brother and the girl Colt had always figured would marry Joe. "How is Annie these days?"

Joe gazed at the horses that finally came loping over for dinner and were now milling around the feed trough. "You ought to go see for yourself. Maybe she'd listen to you about kicking him out."

"When did she ever listen to anybody?"

"True enough."

Annie had been the third party in most of their mischief as kids. She lived on the nearest ranch to the Broken Spur and the three of them were always tumbling into one scrape or another when they were kids. Whatever trouble they got into, he had usually been the brains behind it, Joe the muscle, and Annie the guts. That's why neither of them could figure out why she continued to put up with a husband who had spent the last dozen years grinding her into dirt.

Colt frowned. "Things still bad?"

"I talk to her until I'm blue in the face but she won't leave him. It's like he's sucked all the life out of her. Like father, like son, right?" Joe stared at the horses for a minute longer, then shoved away from the fence and yanked on his gloves. "Guess I'd better get my work done if I want to have some of that chicken your friend is cooking in there while it's still hot."

He walked away, leaving Colt watching over him and wondering about the choices people make and the walls they build around themselves to keep out people who want to help them.

She wasn't going to be able to sleep anytime soon.

Maggie would have punched at her pillow in frustration a few times if she wasn't afraid of waking Nicky, sleeping soundly in the other bed in the Broken Spur's guest room. As it was, the bedsprings in the old iron bed creaked every time she rolled over, so for the last half hour she had tried to remain as still as possible.

Instead of finding a comfortable spot, she gazed out the window at the moonlight filtering through the branches of a big catalpa tree and listened to the tree's long, dark seed pods rattle against each other in the breeze like bony fingers.

Her first chance at a real bed in weeks and here she was tossing and turning just as if she were on that awful mattress in the trailer. It was the novelty of being in a strange bed, she tried to tell herself. Her restlessness had nothing to do with Colt and the sparkly heat he ignited in her with simply a look.

An owl hooted somewhere outside, and its cry was answered by another owl farther away. She listened to their conversation for several moments while she tried to force her body to relax, and then finally, exasperated, she slipped from the bed and pulled on a pair of shorts to wear under the long T-shirt she had been trying to sleep in.

She probably shouldn't be wandering around a strange house, especially when she was a guest here. It seemed rude, somehow. Presumptuous. But she would just walk outside for a moment to listen to the night, she promised herself. She was almost positive her host wouldn't mind.

She walked out into the dark hallway, closing the door softly behind her, and she thought about her host, Joe Redhawk, and the strange, subtle undercurrents between him and Colt, undercurrents she couldn't even begin to figure out.

The two men seemed friendly enough, but many of their words to each other seemed to have double meanings, hidden messages. It was almost as if Redhawk was baiting Colt. Taunting him.

It was a puzzle, but obviously one neither man seemed inclined to explain to her.

She quietly made her way down the stairs and through the living room. Despite its obvious masculinity—heavy, oversize furniture, bold colors and the complete lack of anything resembling the kind of knickknacks women tended to surround themselves with—the whole house was comfortable, inviting.

But not as inviting as the cool breeze and that comfortable rocker she knew waited outside on the porch. She walked to the door, then drew back as she realized someone else had had the same idea. A lean figure sprawled casually on the wide porch stairs.

Colt.

For an instant she wondered if she perhaps had expected

to find him here, on some subconscious level. Before she could analyze it further, she caught the expression on his profile as he gazed out at the ranch, and her heart bumped uncomfortably in her chest.

There was longing here, a bittersweet yearning, like he was looking at something he wanted and could never have.

A disturbing suspicion took root just as he sensed her presence and turned. Whatever she thought she might have seen in his eyes faded quickly, replaced only by concern.

"Somethin' wrong, Doc?"

"No," she said softly through the screen. "I just couldn't sleep."

"Join the club. You're welcome to come out here and sit with me if you want. I'm just lookin' for Cassiopeia. You can point her out to me."

"I wouldn't want to disturb you."

"Too late," she thought she heard him mutter, but she must have been mistaken because he gestured to the steps. "Come on out. There's plenty of room."

She opened the screen door and walked outside. The wide wooden planks of the porch felt cool and smooth beneath her bare feet, and the night smelled incongruously of sagebrush and roses. The sage she could understand, since the rolling hills around the ranch wore a thick coat of it, but the roses threw her off until she noticed a climbing bush next to the steps, heavy with lush blossoms.

She settled onto the steps next to him, drawing one knee up and clasping her hands around it. He sat with his elbows propped on the step behind him and his long legs out-stretched, crossed at the ankles.

They sat in silence for several moments, content to let the night breeze eddy around them.

He was the first to break the fragile peace. "So what do you think of the Broken Spur?"

"It's beautiful," she said.

"Prettiest spot in the whole region. A couple filmmakers

came a few years back and wanted to make a movie here but I…uh, Joe wouldn't let 'em. Thought it would spoil the place.''

She hesitated, not wanting to intrude in things that weren't any of her business, but the yearning she had seen in his gaze earlier compelled her to push the matter.

It was the doctor in her, she supposed, the healer who couldn't rest unless she had tried to fix everyone she came in contact with. "Colt, is the Broken Spur your ranch?"

He stiffened, losing his relaxed pose. "What?"

"You told me you used to own a ranch. Was that ranch the Broken Spur?"

He turned away, looking back out into the darkness. "Now why would you think that?"

"It would explain a lot of things. Your familiarity with the place, how you seemed to know where everything was earlier when you showed us to our rooms. The strange looks I'd have to be crazy not to notice between you and your friend."

She paused, hugging her knees tighter against her chest, then added gently, "It also might explain that longing I see in your eyes whenever you look at the mountains. Like this is home."

A muscle in his jaw worked. "Think you're pretty smart, don't you?"

"It's just a guess. I'm right, though, aren't I?"

"Yeah," he said finally. "I grew up here."

She tried to find bitterness in his voice, but couldn't. He spoke as casually as if he were talking about the weather or a sporting event he'd watched on television.

"What was it like?" she asked.

Again he paused, and she thought for a moment he was going to ignore the question, then he grinned suddenly, his teeth flashing white in the dark. "It was a hell of a place to be a kid. You couldn't ask for better. Joe's dad worked for mine, and his family lived in the foreman's quarters. He and

I and little Annie Calhoun over at the Double C did everything together. Fishing or swimming every day in the summer, riding horses all over the mountains, going on roundups
in the fall.''

She sighed wistfully. ''It sounds wonderful. That's the
kind of life I want to give Nicky—the freedom to explore
his world without fear.'' Would the day ever come when she
could let him, or would she always be hovering over him,
afraid to let him stray far out of her sight?

Some of her frustration must have shown in her expression, because Colt reached a hand toward hers and rubbed a
thumb over her knuckles. ''You'll get through this, Doc. I
promise.''

Instead of taking comfort from the gesture, her pulse sped
up a notch at the continued contact, at the heat suddenly
kindling in his gaze. For one crazy instant she completely
forgot about the fear that had become as much a part of her
as her own skin.

The kiss they had shared in her trailer sizzled through her
memory, that gentle, soft kiss that left her aching for more.
She had a sudden, wild urge to flip her hand over and grasp
his rough fingers tightly, to tug him toward her, to press her
lips against that hard, sensuous mouth....

He cleared his throat, and she jerked her gaze from his
mouth to find him staring at her, heat shimmering from his
dazzling blue eyes. Quickly she looked away. What was she
doing? This wasn't what she had come out here for tonight.

Driven only by the need to regain her equilibrium, she
struck on the one topic she knew would erase that sudden
want from his gaze. ''So how did your friend Joe come to
own the ranch?''

As she expected, he stiffened and pulled his hand away.
Instead of relief, she felt strangely bereft as that mouth tightened and he looked out at the night with a face devoid of
expression. ''It doesn't really matter, does it?''

She studied the sharp planes and angles of his face created

by the moonlight, regretting her question. If he didn't want to talk about the ranch, it wasn't her place to push him. He obviously wasn't comfortable with the subject, and, she reminded herself, it was really none of her business.

Still, she couldn't completely suppress the tide of sympathy that washed over her, almost—but not quite—dousing the fierce attraction she didn't want to feel for this man. She forced herself to focus on that compassion, rather than the hard-edged desire.

It must have been terrible for him, leaving the Broken Spur. To have loved and lost such a place would have been heartbreaking. "You didn't have brothers and sisters, then?"

He shook his head. "My folks were older when they met. Dad was a confirmed bachelor until he met my mother on a stock-buying trip. She was waitressing at a truck stop along the way and it was love at first sight. I guess you could call me an afterthought."

"Where are your parents now?"

"My mother died when I was just a kid, five or six. She had breast cancer."

Again, that sympathy crested over her for the little boy he had been, losing his mother when he was just Nicky's age. "I'm sorry," she whispered. "It must have been devastating for you."

"I was too young to know much of what was going on. Just that she was too sick to play for a long time and then she wasn't here anymore and Dad stopped smiling for a long time." He shrugged. "Joe's family moved in not long after that and Mary, his mom, took me under her wing. I guess you could say she sort of adopted me."

"And your father?"

He was silent for a long time, much longer than was comfortable. "He was killed when I was just out of college," he finally said. "He died of a massive heart attack while trying to break up a bar fight at a honky-tonk between here and

Ennis. The drunk cowboy who started the fight just happened to be his only son.''

"Oh Colt. I'm so sorry."

He shrugged again. "It was a long time ago. Doesn't matter anymore."

"Of course it does. It matters to you. You're still hurting, I can tell. You still blame yourself."

He stood abruptly, thrusting a tight fist against the post of the porch. "Hell, yes, I blame myself. All he wanted was for me to settle down on the ranch, but I had my head full of all kinds of stupid dreams. Saving the world. Winning a National Rodeo Finals belt buckle to show him I could be as good a cowboy as he was. Anything but staying on the Broken Spur.''

"Colt—"

He didn't let her finish. "If I hadn't been drinking, trying to act like such a damn hotshot, he wouldn't have had to come lookin' for me. He would have been safe at home, watching TV or reading one of those Westerns he loved so much. Hell, he'd probably still be here today, herding cattle and riding the rest of us into the ground.''

"You don't know that. You can't know." She reached out and touched his hand. "Colt, take it from a physician, heart disease isn't something that develops overnight. If it hadn't happened then, it probably would have happened later that night when he was home in bed.''

"This is something I've had fourteen years to deal with. I was a cocky, restless, immature idiot and my father died as a result of it.''

She followed his gaze to her hand over his, to the contrast of her paler skin against his tanned, weathered skin. His voice deepened, vibrating in the night. "But I do appreciate you trying to make me feel better, Doc. You're a very compassionate woman. I admire that.''

Abruptly the mood shifted. The night sounds seemed to take on a seductive music of their own, and she became intensely aware of the heat of his skin underneath her hand, of the hard strength of his muscles. His gaze met hers and her stomach did a long, slow dive to her toes at the desire flaring in his blue eyes.

She pulled her hand back and folded it carefully with the other one. "Colt—" she began, but whatever she intended to say was snatched completely out of her mind when he reached for her.

Chapter 10

Even as his mouth descended to touch hers, he cursed himself for his weakness. He knew damn well he shouldn't be doing this, that he was compromising the whole investigation. If Beckstead ever discovered he had more than a professional interest in the case—and in the lovely widow who could be their key witness against DeMarranville—he would yank him so fast his head would spin.

He just wanted a kiss, he told himself. One tiny kiss, just one more chance to taste that sweetness. Surely one kiss couldn't blow the whole case, could it?

He didn't give himself a chance to argue. His mouth met hers like a hawk finding its nest and he felt the impact of that single soft connection clear to his toes. She tasted every bit as sweet as he remembered from that day in her trailer—like ripe peaches, bursting with flavor.

Her eyelids fluttered shut at the first touch of his mouth, but he forced his to stay open. He wanted to watch the way her thick lashes fanned her cheeks and the way her skin took on a color like the pale pink of the sky when the sun first sneaked above the mountains.

His fingers caught and tangled in that sleek cascade of hair. The contrast of silk against the roughness of his skin was so sensual, so unbelievably erotic, it ignited fireworks of need in him.

What was it about this woman that affected him so powerfully, that made him feel as if he were on the brink of some mysterious, wonderful discovery?

She had a fragile, innocent kind of beauty, sure. But his attraction to her went far deeper than that.

She was kind, he realized with a jolt. A genuinely good-hearted person. Even when she was in the midst of what was undoubtedly the most terrifying time of her life, she had been moved almost to tears when he told her of his father's death. Hell, he had practically watched her heart smash into tiny little pieces because she thought he had lost the Broken Spur.

He couldn't remember the last time he had come in contact with that kind of goodness. For too many years his life had teemed with hatred and violence, and Maggie's goodness was like a soft, healing rain after years of drought.

He ruthlessly forced the thought away. It wasn't like that. Just as she had said the other night back in Butte, they had some powerful chemistry bubbling between them. That was absolutely all there was to it.

There was no room in his life for goodness, for a soft, vulnerable woman like Maggie. He had to be hard, completely focused, or he would never be able to atone to his father for what he'd done.

He knew he should have stopped the kiss right then, but the feel of her mouth under his was too enticing, too welcoming, and he was dying of thirst. He couldn't resist teasing his tongue ever so gently at the corner of her lips. She drew in a sharp, ragged breath at the soft contact but she didn't pull away. Instead, her lips parted ever so slightly, just wide enough to allow him to slip inside.

With a rough growl, he deepened the kiss. Just a minute longer, he promised himself. One more moment of this forbidden bliss and then he would let her go, would try to block from his mind and his heart this desire pulsing through him.

Her tongue met his shyly, hesitantly, then with growing enthusiasm while her hands trembled between them as if she wasn't quite sure where to put them. Finally they slid up his chest to encircle his neck, holding him even closer.

The movement flattened her breasts against him. The tantalizing, seductive sensation, combined with the hot tangling of their mouths, nearly sent him over the edge.

While her fingers raveled in his hair, he dipped his hands under the hem of her T-shirt, to the silky skin above her hips, wishing his hands weren't so rough against her softness. While her tongue played against his, he slid his thumbs to the undersides of her breasts.

Just before he would have touched her, caressed her, he thundered to his senses. He was crazy—absolutely nuts—to torture himself like this, to start something he knew he couldn't finish without jeopardizing all the slow, painful progress he had fought for on his case.

With vast regret pounding through him, he straightened, wrenching his mouth away. Maggie froze for several beats, her fingers still tangled in his hair, and then she slowly, carefully dropped her hands to her side. She took a step backward, bumping up against the screen door.

Her eyes had darkened to the color of rich cocoa and he could almost see the wheels of regret spinning like some wild, frenzied merry-go-round in her mind.

''Maggie—'' he began, fumbling with an apology, an explanation, anything to break the thick tension suddenly seeping between them.

She lifted one trembling hand. ''Don't say it.''

''What?''

''Whatever you were going to say. We both know this was a mistake that can't happen again.''

He had just been telling himself the same thing. He'd been the one to stop it, after all. But now, perversely, hearing her echo his thoughts annoyed the hell out of him.

He propped a shoulder against the porch support and crossed his arms across his chest. "Why not?"

"Why not?" She stared at him. "A hundred reasons. A thousand."

"Give me one."

She reached behind her with both hands and clenched the doorknob that must be digging into her back. "I have a son."

"Last I checked, that makes you a mother, not some kind of nun."

"A mother who is trying to do everything she can to keep her son safe."

He frowned. "What does that have to do with anything?"

"I can't let myself be distracted by—by what you do to me."

For an instant he felt a fierce satisfaction that she was as affected by their kisses as he had been. Not that he had needed her words to tell him. He had known it in the way her arms had twisted around him, by the way her mouth had gone all soft and gentle under his, by the way he had heard her heart pounding like the hooves of a horse at a full gallop.

He couldn't help his completely masculine sense of triumph that she didn't hide from it, that she was strong enough to admit she had wanted him as much as he still wanted her.

Then the rest of her words suddenly sank through and he straightened from the post. "You and Nick are safer here than anywhere else," he growled. "You know that. No one can get to you while you're on the Broken Spur. I told you I would protect you. Don't you trust me?"

"Yes," she admitted.

"Then why come up with all the excuses? What's the real problem?"

She shifted her gaze down to the old, worn slats of the porch, then finally looked up at him through stricken eyes.

"*You* could hurt me, Colt," she whispered, so softly it might have been the wind sighing under the porch eaves.

He stared at her as an emotion coiled in his gut, so unfamiliar it took him several seconds to recognize it for what it was: shame.

What the hell was he trying to accomplish, pushing and poking at her like this? He knew just as well as she did that it was a huge mistake kissing and touching like this. Sooner or later someone's toes would end up burned. Most likely hers.

She was right. No, he corrected grimly. Not quite. She said he "could" hurt her, when the truth was, there was no "could" about it. He *would* hurt her. He would take her trust and her faith and he would smash them into jagged little pieces.

When he told her he was FBI, she would never forgive him for deceiving her for so long. In the deep dark corners of his heart, he knew that was exactly the reason he hadn't told her yet, when he'd had plenty of opportunities.

All the excuses he had come up with were just that: excuses. The harsh, unvarnished truth was that he was afraid of her reaction, afraid of crushing that goodness he craved even more than her kisses.

Before he could form his thoughts into any kind of coherent answer he could give her, her lips twisted into a tiny smile, so sad it sent stinging shards of guilt into his heart. "I'm sorry," she whispered. "Good night, Colt."

"Doc—" he began, but she had already slipped inside and closed the door softly behind her, leaving him alone with the regret.

"When's Colt gonna come back?" Nicky asked, wiping a milk mustache away with the back of his hand.

"I don't know," Maggie answered for what seemed like the hundredth time since her little caballero woke up. If she had her way, Colt wouldn't return for hours. Maybe with a little more time, she could regain some of the equilibrium she had been seeking so desperately since she had made such a complete fool out of herself with their heated embrace on the porch the night before.

It was just a kiss between two adults who were undeniably attracted to each other. In the cold light of morning, she could see that she had completely blown it out of perspective. *You could hurt me,* she had whispered, and she cringed now, remembering. All he was interested in was a kiss, and she had turned it into a grand love affair that would end with her heart broken and bleeding.

"Why's he been gone so long?"

She scrubbed at an invisible spot on the counter, fervently wishing she could avoid Nicky's questions, all centering on the same male she couldn't seem to shake from her thoughts. "This is a big ranch, Nicky. I'm sure there are plenty of chores to do every morning."

"I could have helped him," he grumbled. "You should've got me up. I wanted to rope a cow this morning."

An image of Nick at the mercy of a steer's powerful hooves and wickedly sharp horns flashed through her mind and she winced. "We'll be here for a few more days. You really don't have to try everything all at once." *And God willing, maybe there are a few things you won't have to try at all,* she added silently.

"Think Colt will take me with him after he comes back and has breakfast?"

"Not if you don't eat a little more of that muffin and drink your milk, young man."

"Cowboys don't drink milk," he grumbled under his breath.

"They do unless they're looking to get into major trouble with their mothers."

Nicky scowled but he knew enough to obey her when she used that tone of voice, and a few minutes later, Maggie heard the unmistakable sound of hard-soled cowboy boots pounding the boards on the back porch.

With a shaky breath she forced herself to tighten the strings on the apron, more to give her fingers something to do than for any other reason, to prevent her from pressing her hands to a face suddenly feverish from more than just the heat pouring from the oven.

Wouldn't that just be a sight? What would Colt think if he walked through the door to find her standing there with her face buried in her hands like some kind of ostrich hoping he would go away if only she couldn't see him?

Her stomach fluttered. She had known this moment was inevitable, that she would eventually have to face him again, but she couldn't help wishing she had a little more time.

No matter how hard she tried, the memory of their embrace had been burned into her mind as surely as the Broken Spur brand in the hide of Joe Redhawk's cattle.

Nor could she forget how she had laid her heart bare to him, as if she were so vulnerable that the few casual kisses they had shared would leave her completely devastated.

Colt probably wouldn't dream of referring to it again. He was too considerate for that. She hoped.

The kitchen seemed to shrink in half when he walked inside, filling the space with his scent, his size, his sheer masculine presence.

''Mornin','' he said, tousling Nicky's hair—for once bare of the too-big hat that usually perched there. Colt turned and sent her a hesitant smile, as if he wasn't quite sure whether she'd smile back or smack him with her weapon of choice, one of the cast-iron frying pans hanging above the stove.

All those fluttery, dangerous feelings from the night before came hurtling back and she was suddenly enormously grateful for Nicky's presence to provide a buffer between them.

''Hey, Colt.'' Nicky grinned widely, with unabashed hero worship in his brown eyes.

''What's for breakfast, partner?''

Nicky's grin faded into a grimace. "Muffins. Again."

Colt sent her a teasing look under long lashes that should have made him look ridiculously feminine but instead only seemed to accentuate his rugged appeal. "Uh, maybe I'll just have some toast."

She swallowed the stray tendrils of desire lingering from the night. If he could act like nothing had happened, she would try her darnedest to do the same. She handed him the tray. "Maybe you'll try a couple of muffins. I made them fresh this morning with bananas and walnuts. They're loaded with potassium and folic acid."

"Mmm. Sounds delicious."

"If you eat them up like a good boy, I might even cook some greasy bacon and artery-clogging eggs to go with it, although it would probably be violating my Hippocratic oath."

"I won't tell if you don't." He grabbed two muffins from the tray and took a bite of one. She waited for him to grimace and spit it out, but to her gratification, his eyes glazed.

He chewed, swallowed, then shook his head at her son with an amazed expression on his face. "Why have you been groaning about having to eat these? They're delicious."

"I'd still rather have cocoa crunch cereal," Nicky muttered darkly.

"And I'd rather have a son who appreciates my cooking. I guess we have to be happy with what we get," she answered, pulling a package of bacon from the refrigerator.

"You know you don't have to do this." Colt gestured to the stove. "Cook, I mean. You're a guest here."

"I don't mind. This way I at least feel as if I'm earning my keep. Your friend was kind enough to open his home to a couple of strangers. Taking over the cooking duties while Pablo recovers is just my way of saying thank you. Besides, I'd rather stay busy."

"It is a big help, but I don't want you to feel like you can't get out and enjoy yourself. That's why you're here."

"I *am* enjoying myself," she answered, lifting her gaze to his. Instantly she knew it was a mistake, that she should have just kept her attention on the stove.

He watched her casually enough, but she thought she could see a flicker of desire there in the depths of his vivid blue eyes. They locked with hers and she hitched in a breath, unable to look away, as the memory of their kiss—of her enthusiastic response, of his tongue tangling with hers—flared between them. Just like that, it was as if they were back on the porch, wrapped in each other's arms while the moonlight washed around them.

Her pulse began to beat a slow, steady rhythm, and she would have stood there all morning, staring at him like some lovesick teenager, but he was the one who broke the contact. He blinked rapidly, then turned one of the ladderback kitchen chairs with a little more force than completely necessary.

Eyes hooded now, he straddled the chair, his forearms crossed along the back.

She took a shaky breath, struggling to rein in the need he unleashed in her with just a look. Hoping the trembling of her fingers wasn't noticeable to anyone but her, she opened the package of bacon and laid several slices in the frying pan. The kitchen was immediately filled with their sharp, pleasing aroma and cheerful spatter and hiss.

Only when she turned again to face the table did she realize her son had turned his own chair around so he could imitate Colt's posture. Nicky's eyes barely topped the highest rung of the chair, but still he thrust his arms above him at an uncomfortable-looking angle to rest his elbows on it just as Colt had done.

It's only one small mannerism, she told herself. It's perfectly normal for a boy his age to do a little hero worshiping, especially when he didn't have any kind of a father figure around. He would easily get over it when they finally found a place to call home, when Colt rode out of their lives as abruptly as he had entered.

Somehow she couldn't quite convince herself. Colt's departure from their lives would be as hard on her little boy as it would be on her.

"Hey, Colt," Nicky said, "will you show me how to rope one of those big cows after breakfast?"

"On a ranch we call those big cows cattle."

"Can you show me how to rope a cattle after breakfast, then?"

Colt laughed. "You bet, partner."

She opened her mouth to protest as visions of that demon steer out for her son's blood flashed through her mind again, but Colt's wink stopped her. "You know, cowboys can't just run right out and rope a steer first thing. You have to practice awhile."

"I've been practicin'."

"I know you have, and you're getting real good at swinging a loop. I have this old iron steer head I practiced on when I was your age. Why don't you help me find it after breakfast and you can work on that for a while? Then later you and I can take on a real steer."

Nicky frowned and started to protest, but Colt headed him off. "In the meantime, how would you and your mom like to ride up with me to my favorite fishing hole today?"

"Yeah!" Nicky gripped the chair in excitement, his brown eyes wide. "Can I ride Star?"

"You bet. Doc, what do you think?"

That I should grab my son and go while I still can, she thought. "I don't know. Shouldn't I be here to fix lunch for the others?" It was a lame excuse, and both of them knew it.

"Maggie, you're a guest here. The whole point of coming to the Broken Spur was to give you a chance to relax for a few days. Remember?"

"Of course I remember."

"Then ride up to the fishing hole with me. Joe and the

rest of the boys can fix sandwiches if they're starving. Isn't that right, Joe?''

She'd been so busy worrying and gearing up for an argument she hadn't noticed her host standing in the doorway. ''That's what we usually do,'' he said.

''Please, Mom?''

She might have been able to resist the entreaty in one pair of eyes. But when both of the males in her life looked at her like that, she really had no choice.

''All right,'' she finally agreed. ''Just don't expect me to fish.''

Chapter 11

Breathtaking. It was absolutely breathtaking.

The three horses had been steadily climbing for an hour, through the fringy, outstretched branches of pine trees and trembling stands of aspen. Now they paused on the crest of a hill, looking down on a small lake whose mirrored surface reflected snow-capped, craggy peaks.

Colt, in the lead of their little procession, reined in Scout, and she and Nicky followed suit with their horses.

"This is beautiful," she exclaimed. "Is it still Broken Spur land?"

He nodded and stretched out a hand. "The ranch border is down there, at the edge of those trees. Beyond that is National Forest land. That's Butterfly Lake there, packed with the best rainbow trout in Montana."

"And it's on your…" she stumbled, then corrected herself "—on Mr. Redhawk's land?"

A muscle in his jaw twitched. "Right," he said tersely.

How could he stand it, knowing this had once been his

and that he had somehow lost it? Her heart twisted with regret for him. "It's a beautiful spot," she said quietly.

He grinned suddenly, unexpectedly, the shadows gone from his eyes. "I practically lived up here at the lake when I was a little kid. I'd hide out up here whenever I wanted to weasel out of ranch work or escape my dad yellin' at me for something or other. Once when Joe and I were about ten or so we snuck away from the bus stop when nobody was looking and grabbed a couple of horses. Spent the whole day up here. Man, that was one great day of fishing."

"You only did it once?"

He chuckled and cast a sidelong look at Nicky, who was too engrossed in his new love affair with the little pony Colt had introduced him to to pay them much mind. "Once was enough. We got busted. My dad caught us trying to sneak the horses back to the pasture. We were stupid enough to bring back a day's catch. Don't know how we planned to explain it to him, but we tried to tell him it was an educational field trip."

She laughed, delighted at the picture of him as a mischievous little boy. "An educational field trip?"

He nodded. "If I remember right, we tried to tell him our class was studying trout habitat and we felt we needed to get an up-close-and-personal look to truly understand what our teacher was talking about. A good story, but he didn't buy it."

"Sounds like a smart man."

His mouth twisted into a bittersweet smile. "About most things."

Not about his son. The words were unspoken, but she sensed them as clearly as if he had said them. Her heart ached for him but she knew he wouldn't welcome her compassion. "Well, do me a favor," she said instead after a few moments, "and don't give Nicky any ideas."

"Ideas about what?" At the sound of his name, her son looked up from patting Star's gray-speckled withers.

"Ideas about catching more fish than me today." Colt gave Nicky a mock scowl, which only earned him giggles from her son.

"How can I catch more than you? I've never even been fishin' before."

"We'll fix that, partner. By the end of the day, you'll be ready to go on the professional trout-catching circuit."

Nicky giggled again. "I'd rather be a cowboy."

"It never hurts for a guy to know how to catch his supper when he's out on the trail." He wheeled Scout around. "Come on. I'll race you down to the lake."

Colt let Nicky and his pony take the lead. She would have been frantic with worry if they were really racing down the hill, but since the pony didn't seem to move any faster than a trot, she just smiled and watched them go, following along at a more sedate pace.

Once on the shore of the lake that couldn't be more than two hundred yards at its widest spot, Colt—with his five-year-old shadow not far behind—led the horses out to hobble them where they could nibble on the fresh meadow grasses.

She carried a colorful old quilt Colt had packed for them to a huge, fragrant pine tree a few feet from the shore. A cool wind, tart from the evergreen trees ringing the little lake, rippled across the sapphire water and teased the edges of the quilt as she tried to spread it. After several attempts, she finally found success and settled down to read.

She had brought along a medical journal to try to catch up on some reading, but for now she let it sit unopened next to her while she enjoyed the view.

The spreading branches of the tree made a cozy little haven, the only sound coming from the wind that sighed above her in the treetops and from a pair of brilliantly colored magpies who loudly protested the invasion of their domain.

She watched them for a few moments, smiling at their antics. It was so peaceful here, even with the angry chattering from the birds. She could feel the the serenity of the place wash over her just like the wind skimming over the water.

The worry that had haunted her for the last month suddenly seemed as distant as those marshmallow clouds overhead.

This is exactly what she needed, she decided, and she made a mental note to thank Colt for having the wisdom to insist she come with them.

A few moments later he and Nicky walked into view carrying what, in her inexperienced opinion, looked like enough fishing equipment for a dozen people.

Her son held out a fishing pole to her. "Here you go, Mom. Colt says this is for you."

She gave the pole a wary look. "No, thank you. I believe I'll leave the fishing to the two of you."

"Come on, Mom. Aren't you even gonna try? It'll be fun."

About as fun as sticking one of those hooks in my eye. She mustered a smile. "How about if I watch you guys for a while to see how it's done? Maybe I'll try later."

"Chicken," Colt said under his breath as he passed the blanket and headed for the trail around the lake.

She smiled sweetly, too content to let him goad her. "Cluck, cluck," she retorted.

He turned back toward her, looking so big and rugged and gorgeous she had to catch her breath. Never far from her thoughts, the memory of their kiss the night before flickered through her mind again, of being held safe and warm in those strong arms. She wanted that again, dammit. It simply wasn't fair that the one man who made her feel alive again should come charging into her life at the worst possible time.

Oblivious to the wayward direction of her thoughts, he grinned at her. "You'll be sorry you missed out when we haul in all the big ones, won't she, partner?"

Nicky giggled. "Yep. You'll be sorry, Mom," he echoed. Somehow she managed to kick start her heart again and forced a smile. ''I guess that's a chance I'll just have to take, isn't it?''

Her reading forgotten now, she watched them dodge rocks and deadfall on the narrow trail until they stopped about a hundred yards away, near two huge boulders that hunkered at the water's edge.

She drew her knees up to her chest, smiling at the solemn expression on Nicky's little face as he listened intently to Colt explain what she could only assume were the rudiments of fishing.

They were too far down the shore for her to hear their conversation, although she caught snatches of it on the wind. Colt, a hip resting against one of the boulders, pointed to something on the fishing pole, and Nicky nodded vigorously. He smiled his gap-toothed grin and said something that resulted in a deep laugh from Colt.

She sucked in a breath. Even from a distance, the man could make her pulse race. He crouched down again and pulled Nicky into the crook of his arms so the boy could watch up close while he baited the hook. Sunlight glinted off their heads, one dark, the other blond, and it looked for all the world as if they belonged together.

Her stomach quivered suddenly, sharply, and she pressed a hand to it, fighting down nausea. Oh, mercy. What had she done?

She had let Colt insinuate his way completely into their lives, even though she knew from the beginning it was a mistake, even though she knew perfectly well he would be just another transitory figure in an already ephemeral existence.

How could she have let down her guard, allowed the two of them to become so vulnerable? She should have been more careful. Nicky already loved Colt, and her son would be nothing short of devastated when the cowboy moved on.

And so would she.

The truth loomed in her mind as huge and forbidding as the mountains around them.

She was falling in love with him.

No, not falling. She was well on her way, had tumbled much too far down to claw her way back up to safer ground.

Where had it come from, this fragile, tender emotion that had taken root and begun to blossom in her? And when had it begun to grow? Last night in his arms or earlier? She tried to pinpoint the exact moment but couldn't. Her feelings had grown steadily over the past few weeks. Maybe she had begun to fall in love with him a little the night she had stumbled on him in the dark, fixing her flat tire.

All this time, she thought she could keep her heart untouched, that a friendship with him would be safe and harmless. It seemed so foolish now, self-delusion at its very worst.

Looking back, she could see that his kindness had tantalized her from the first: the patient, gentle way he talked to her son, the concern he had shown her when the rest of the world seemed a dark, scary place. His misguided efforts to watch over her.

He had made no secret of his attraction to her. And although, the intensity frightened her a little, it had been like a soothing balm to her self-esteem, bruised and broken by her mistake of a marriage.

How stupid could she be? She had known from the first that he would prove dangerous to her soul in ways De-Marranville's men couldn't even begin to touch, but she had ignored her instincts and indulged herself in what could only end in disaster.

She had a sudden, wild urge to weep. What had she done? Hadn't she screwed up her life enough, made enough mistakes for a hundred women? She had married Michael when she was still lost and grieving from her parents' deaths, and look what a gross error in judgment that had been.

Now, when she was even more vulnerable than she had been then, she had buried her common sense, unplugged all her internal alarms, and allowed herself to fall in love with a gorgeous, wandering cowboy with secrets in his eyes.

Nothing could come of it. She knew that perfectly well. Colt was attracted to her, he had made that clear, but he simply wasn't the kind of man a woman settled down with. Even if he was, she couldn't ask him to share the nightmare her life had become. The idea of putting him into danger sent ice racing through her veins.

No, she would just have to get through these next few days here at the ranch by anesthetizing her feelings as best she could. Once they were back into the rhythm of life on the road, she could begin the long, hard process of putting distance between them again.

Chapter 12

"What's wrong?"

At the sharpness in Colt's tone, Maggie whipped her attention from helping Nick dismount from the pony after their ride down from the lake. She followed Colt's gaze to the doorway of the barn, to find her host standing there, his wide shoulders blocking the light.

She could tell by the jut of Joe Redhawk's jaw and the fury in his dark eyes that something was drastically awry, and Colt had obviously recognized the same thing.

"Annie's here." His voice was taut and heavy. "She brought the kids."

Colt started a vicious curse, glanced at Nicky, then bit off the word. "How bad this time?"

"Bad. I think her arm is broken."

"That son of a—" Colt looked as if he wanted to throw the saddle he held through the wall of the barn, but he clamped down on his temper. He sent his friend a critical look. "What are you still doing here?"

"I didn't want to leave her and the kids here alone. Thought I'd wait until you got back."

"Good." Some silent male communication passed between them. "I'll go with you."

The rancher nodded, as if he had expected nothing less. "I'll wait for you inside, then." He turned on his boot heels and headed toward the house, leaving a tense, awkward silence in his wake. Colt didn't seem inclined to break it as he hurried through the motions of removing saddles and tack from the trio of horses.

Finally Maggie couldn't stand it anymore. "Isn't Annie your neighbor? The one you were talking about who used to get into so much trouble with you and Mr. Redhawk?"

He nodded curtly, throwing the saddles over sawhorses set up in the corner of the barn. "Annie Redhawk, used to be Calhoun. She married Joe's older brother."

He glanced at Nicky again but the boy was too busy petting one of the barn cats to pay any attention to them. "Charlie's a real peach of a guy," he went on. "Takes after his father—whenever he drinks too much he likes to pound on his wife."

She murmured a distressed sound. Poor woman. No matter how bad her marriage had been, at least Michael had never struck her.

"Look, I hate to do this to you when you're on vacation and all, but would you mind looking at her injuries, Doc, while Joe and I go take care of a little business?"

She nodded, knowing perfectly well the "little business" he and Joe planned to take care of was Annie Redhawk's abusive husband. "Of course. It will only take me a moment to grab my bag."

When she and Nicky walked into the kitchen, Maggie found two dark-eyed children—a girl who looked about eleven and a boy around Nicky's age—sitting at the kitchen taking tiny, polite nibbles out of a couple of cookies and staring down at the worn gingham tablecloth as if it were the most fascinating thing in the world.

Nicky grabbed a cookie and flipped a chair around as Colt had done earlier that day. "Howdy," he mumbled around the cookie. "My name's Nicholas. Who're you?"

"Leah," the girl said shyly. "My brother's name is C.J."

Maggie left them to make friends in that magical way children have and climbed the stairs for her leather medical bag. When she returned to the kitchen, the children's faces had lost that scared, haunted look and they were chattering away with Nicky about fishing and horses.

Joe Redhawk had returned, as well. "Colt says he asked you to examine her," he said in a low voice so the children didn't hear. "She won't like it. She's ashamed to have anybody know."

"I'm sorry, Mr. Redhawk." She kept her voice brisk, professional. "I don't want to make her uncomfortable, but if she's injured, she needs medical attention."

He gave a curt nod. "You don't have to convince me. I agree with you. I just hope you can do a better job of talking some sense into her than I seem to be able to do. Come on, she's back here in Co—in my room. This way."

He led her down the hall, to an area of the sprawling ranch house she hadn't seen yet and into a large, masculine room, with hunter green walls and oversize furniture.

Despite some clothing folded neatly on one of the chairs and a few books by the bed, the room seemed sterile, unlived in.

The dominant feature in the room was a huge log four-poster bed and dwarfed inside it was a woman who could only be described as elfin. Maggie had a brief impression of a tiny woman with short-cropped red hair, who hardly looked old enough to go on dates, let alone have an eleven-year-old daughter.

She walked closer to the bed then sucked in a breath, her stomach flip-flopping. The woman was probably very pretty under normal circumstances, but right now her eyes sported matching black and purple contusions, an angry-looking abrasion covered one cheek, and her bottom lip was swollen to what was likely twice its normal size.

Maggie had seen plenty of domestic violence cases working at the clinic in the city. Stabbings, shootings, beatings. But it never failed to sicken her what abusers could do to the people they should have taken the most care with. All in the name of love.

Joe walked to the other side of the bed and reached out a rough hand and smoothed it down the woman's hair, with a gentleness that seemed jarring, somehow, coming from such a big, taciturn man.

"Annie?" he whispered.

The woman's eyes fluttered open, and Maggie could see in their unfocused green depths remnants of a nightmare she couldn't begin to imagine. When Annie Redhawk focused on Joe at her side, she relaxed and even tried a smile that turned into a wince as the movement stretched her swollen lip.

"Hi," she said in a hoarse voice, like a rusty swing rattling in the wind, and struggled to sit up.

The rancher dropped his hand and began to fiddle with the rim of his cowboy hat. "This is Maggie Rawlings. She's a doctor and she's here to take a look at you."

Abruptly, that lopsided smile of welcome faded, and Annie's eyes blazed wounded accusation at him. "You promised me you wouldn't call anybody."

"I didn't. She's a guest of the Broken Spur. A friend of Colt's. She just wants to see if anything's broken."

"I don't want her poking at me. I'm fine."

Maggie perched a hip on the edge of the bed and folded her hands together in her lap. From past experience working with domestic abuse cases, she knew she would have to tread carefully if she wanted the woman to agree to an examination. "You have two beautiful children out there, Mrs. Redhawk. What are their names?'' she asked, although she had already heard the answer from them.

The woman frowned at the conversational gambit. "Leah and Charlie. C.J.,'' she answered warily.

"How old are they?"

"Leah will be eleven next month. C.J. just turned five."

"I have a five-year-old myself. Five going on twenty. My Nicholas wants to be a Wild West outlaw. He thinks he can rope and ride with the best of Mr. Redhawk's cowboys."

Some of the suspicion in Annie's expression faded. Encouraged, Maggie reached a hand out and laid it on the other woman's cold fingers, on top of the thick down comforter.

She looked steadily into her mossy green eyes, eyes that had seen too much pain. "Annie, I know you must love your children. What use will you be to Leah and C.J., though, if you're laid up with injuries that don't heal properly?"

Annie's head dropped back against the pillow, and she closed her eyes. For a moment Maggie didn't think she had heard her. When she opened them there was a look of resignation there that seemed oddly familiar to Maggie. It took her several seconds to realize why—it was the same expression she had seen on her own face in the mirror throughout the last few years of her marriage.

"Go away, Joe," the woman finally said.

"Annie—"

"Go on. If I have to do this, I don't want you in here watching. I'll be okay."

"I'll wait outside then." With one last worried look toward the woman on the bed, he slipped from the room.

Annie Redhawk remained stoic and silent while Maggie examined her injuries, mostly scrapes and bruises. She winced only once, when Maggie manipulated her arm.

Maggie's lips tightened and she pulled the only chair in the room—a big Mission rocker—over to the bed. "It's just as Mr. Redhawk suspected. Your arm appears to be fractured.

I really can't know for sure, though, unless you have it X-rayed.''

"I don't want to do that."

"Why not?"

"If I go to a hospital, they'll call the police." The fingers of her good hand tightened on the comforter. "Can't you just set it here?''

"Not without an X-ray to show me exactly where the fracture is, and not without some kind of pain medication for you. If I tried, it would undoubtedly cause more harm than good. At the very least, I likely wouldn't be able to set it correctly. Besides," she asked gently, "why would calling the police be such a bad thing?''

Listen to what a hypocrite she was, giving the woman advice she was unwilling to follow herself. Maggie shifted uncomfortably on the rocking chair. She had valid reasons for not going to the authorities after Michael's death, though, didn't she? She had tried to do the right thing when she called the police from Rosie's house, but instead of calling in the cavalry, somehow she had alerted DeMarranville's men to her presence.

Her heart still picked up a beat when she remembered her fear when the two men she had seen from the elevator had shown up in Rosie's driveway, her frantic flight out the back with Nicky in her arms.

Maybe she had somehow misinterpreted the whole thing. The thought flitted into her head like one of those angry magpies she had seen on the mountain earlier. Maybe the police hadn't tipped DeMarranville off to her whereabouts. Maybe they—or another of DeMarranville's men—had simply seen her leave the building and followed her without her knowledge and had just arrived before detectives could make it.

"I've been through the whole routine with the police," Annie said, wearily closing her eyes, and Maggie jerked her mind from her own problems to the woman's more immediate ones.

"The sheriff arrests Charlie," her patient went on, in the same lifeless voice, "and when he gets out after spending the night in jail, he takes his anger out on me."

"If you press charges, he won't get out." It was the same argument she had made hundreds of times before during her work at the clinic. Like all those times before, Annie Redhawk obviously didn't want to listen.

"Maybe not today and maybe not tomorrow, but he'll eventually post bail and come looking for me," she said.

"What about a restraining order?"

"You probably know as well as I do they're only worth about as much as the paper they're printed on." She rubbed at her arm above the fracture, refusing to meet Maggie's gaze. "Look, Dr. Rawlings, I appreciate you taking a look at me but I don't want to go to the police."

"Mrs. Redhawk—"

The woman didn't seem to hear her. She looked out the window at the Broken Spur and spoke quietly, woodenly, almost as if she was speaking to herself and not to Maggie. "He wouldn't have hit me except I—I pushed his buttons. I just can't seem to learn my lesson. I know what's going to set him off but I can't seem to help myself from doing it, anyway."

"When a man beats his wife, he's the only one to blame. You're not responsible for his actions..." Her voice trailed off. They were words she had said a hundred times before in other similar circumstances but they had never struck her with such force before.

Her situation was not at all the same as Annie Redhawk's. She had never been physically abused, never had to face this kind of ugliness. But Michael had used words as his weapons. He had spent the six years of their marriage relentlessly beating down her spirit.

For the first time she truly accepted that it wasn't her fault, any more than Annie Redhawk was to blame for her husband's abuse.

The realization was liberating, emancipating. A small, guilty part of her had always blamed herself for her husband's actions. If she had been a more enthusiastic lover, maybe he wouldn't have strayed. If she had been less involved with the clinic and more focused on her marriage, maybe he would have spent more time at home instead of at the office. If she hadn't been such a protective mother to Nicky, maybe Michael would have tried harder at being a good father.

She hadn't been the perfect wife, certainly, but neither had she deserved Michael's derision, his belittling little comments that dug away at her self-confidence with sharp claws.

Tears welled up in her eyes—tears of relief to discover she hadn't been the weak, ineffectual woman he had always called her and tears of regret that she had wasted so much time trying to mold herself into the kind of wife he wanted.

Now was not the time for this, though. With new empathy, she took a chance and touched Annie's cold hand again. It trembled underneath hers and Maggie squeezed it firmly. "I realize you don't know me at all and you have no reason to listen to me, but please believe me. This is not your fault. You need to get help."

"It's my problem, and I'm dealing with it."

"You're wrong. It's not just your problem. It affects those beautiful dark-eyed children out there every bit as much. What are you teaching your daughter about how a woman should be treated by a man? And what kind of legacy are you giving your son? That it's okay to beat women, that he'll suffer no repercussions when he does the same thing to his own wife?"

Annie was silent for a long time. Just when Maggie had begun to think the other woman hadn't even heard her, she saw a tear drip into the vivid bruises under one of her eyes.

She closed her eyes before another one could escape.

"Will you send Joe back in here?" she finally asked, her voice low, pained.

Maggie nodded and squeezed Annie's cold hand again, then slipped out of the room.

Hours later Colt let himself into the dark house, feeling restless and unsatisfied. He needed to punch something. Hard. Unfortunately he hadn't been able to go after the source of his fury. Okay, so he and Joe had both used a little more force than necessary shoving Charlie into Colt's pickup so they could take him to jail after Annie agreed to press charges.

Joe had even "accidentally" slammed the door on his brother's fingers. But Charlie had been pathetic, too drunk for them to gain much pleasure out of beating on him like he deserved. By unspoken agreement, they chose to let the sheriff deal with him instead, and Joe had taken Annie to the hospital to have her arm set.

She had insisted on going back to her own ranch to spend the night, and Joe had gone with her to take care of her stock. His absence left Colt to take care of the evening feeding on the Broken Spur, but even two hours of hauling hay hadn't been enough to take the edge off his rage.

It made his stomach clench to think of Annie and the kids living like that. He couldn't understand how the sassy girl he had known—the one who would tear strips off his hide whenever he would tease her about being a little shrimp—would let Charlie get away with treating her like that.

Simmering beneath his fury was no small amount of guilt. She and Joe had been his two closest friends in the world and he had abandoned both of them. While he was running away to join the Marines, Joe had ended up in prison for killing his father, and Annie had ended up in her own kind of grim prison.

If he'd been here at the Broken Spur instead of trying to outrun the ghost of his father, could he have helped either one of them? Could he have protected Annie from Charlie's abuse?

No. If Joe couldn't persuade her to leave his brother—and he knew damn well he had done nothing but try—Colt wouldn't have had any better luck.

He walked into the kitchen and saw that Maggie had left a light on for him, the small one above the stove. The television set buzzed softly in the other room, and he realized she must still be up.

He followed the noise, then stopped abruptly in the doorway. The news was on, the volume turned off, and the TV's flickering blue light cast eerie shadows in the room, illuminating Maggie curled up on the big sofa, sound asleep.

Her hands were tucked under her cheek, just like a sleeping child, and he smiled at the innocence of her posture at the same time a sneaky, fragile tenderness stirred to life inside him.

Without taking his gaze off her, he walked across the room, the thick carpet muffling the sound of his boots. As he sank back into the big plump chair, an odd, easy contentment settled over him, despite the turmoil of the day.

It slowly, steadily washed away the anger and frustration that had been churning inside him since Joe had told him about Annie, leaving only a rare peace in its wake.

Maggie had that way about her, even when she was asleep, he mused. Just her presence was soothing, comforting. Like sitting by the ocean somewhere listening to the waves or in the silence of some still, high-mountain clearing.

She made a little sound in her sleep and shifted. The colorful afghan she had tugged over her against the cool Montana night slipped, but he made no move to lift it again, unwilling to awaken her and destroy the rare peace of the moment.

He wanted this in his life.

Just for an instant a seductive, alluring image crystallized in his mind of what his life would be like if things were different. He could see it clearly: a cold winter night, a fire crackling and popping in the woodstove, and a warm, loving Maggie waiting for him at the end of the day.

It wasn't just this easy contentment he wanted in his life, he realized with a jolt. He wanted Maggie.

The thought came out of nowhere and slammed into him with all the force of a 49ers' linebacker, and he sat back in the chair, reeling. He didn't want her and Nicky just for some imaginary cold winter night, but for always.

The picture shifted and he saw a dozen other scenes. Fishing trips with Nicky up to Butterfly Lake, taking them both along on roundup, making love to Maggie in the big log bed his father had fashioned from lodgepole pine cut on Broken Spur land.

He shook his head to clear the images away. He had no business even *thinking* this kind of nonsense. No business at all. Not only was his timing abysmal—she was on the run for her life, for hell's sake—but she would never forgive him for his deception the past few weeks.

He had a grim feeling that even if she cared for him now, she sure wouldn't after she found out he had lied to her.

Besides, the mistakes he made during his short-lived marriage proved he wasn't a forever kind of guy. He had too many ghosts haunting his psyche, was too restless to ever be content playing house for long.

After a while he would get edgy and have to move on, then where the hell would she be? He couldn't do that to her, not and be able to live with himself after leaving her.

He sat forward, thinking only to leave her sleeping and go somewhere where he could figure out what had just happened to him, but his jeans must have made some sound as they rustled on the upholstery of the chair. She stirred again, and then her eyes fluttered open.

Consciousness returned slowly, like the first gentle flakes of snow on a cold December evening. When she finally awoke enough to sense his presence, her eyes lit up and she gave a soft smile of welcome that seemed to reach right through his chest and yank at his heart, despite his best efforts at keeping it away.

"You're back," she said, her voice rough with sleep.

He nodded, clenching his hands into fists against the need to reach for her, to draw that warmth against him and taste her sweetness, just for a moment.

She sat up, yawning, and clasped her wrists above her head to stretch the muscles of her back. The movement—completely without guile, he knew—thrust out her breasts and threw all his arguments out the window, leaving only white-hot desire.

He wanted her. Right here, right now. Hard and fast, slow and easy, any way he could have her.

He felt his pulse begin to pound, felt the blood begin to pool relentlessly in his groin as he hardened.

Damn. He couldn't do this. He *couldn't.* With more effort than it took to wrestle a four-hundred-pound steer, he managed to clamp down on the desire.

"Everything okay?" she asked.

Not by a long shot, he thought, but he knew she was talking about the ranch chores, not the sudden snarl of his emotions.

He gave a jerky nod. "How about in here? Nick asleep?"

She laughed softly. "He crashed about eight o'clock. It's been quite an eventful day for him. Riding by himself for the first time, catching his first fish, then making two new friends. It wore him right out."

"Looks like it wore you out, too."

She smiled sheepishly. "I wanted to wait up for you, but I'm afraid everything caught up with me. I didn't sleep very well last night."

He thought of the way she had come apart in his arms the night before on the porch, then grimaced as his body responded. He jerked his mind away to safer channels. "I'm sorry about the way the day ended. I promised you a chance to rest, but I'm afraid I haven't been able to deliver.''

"Don't apologize. Our time on the Broken Spur has been exactly what I needed. On several levels,'' she added softly.

"Things were so crazy earlier that I didn't get a chance to tell you thank you. For what you did with Annie.''

She shrugged. "I didn't do anything except give her an examination. I couldn't even set her broken arm without an X-ray.''

"You did more than that. I don't know what you said, but you convinced her to press charges this time. That's more than anyone else has been able to do.''

She was quiet for a long time, fiddling with the fringe on the afghan. "Do you think she'll be okay?'' she finally asked, her voice small and tight. "Will she go through with the prosecution?''

"I don't know.'' Some of the frustration slithered back. "I hope so, but Charlie has some kind of weird hold on her. I don't understand it. She couldn't stand him when we were kids. The truth is, I always thought she and Joe would end up together, but the next thing I know she shacked up with Charlie after I left.''

"I hope she can break away.'' The fervency of her voice startled him, reminding him of the hints she had given about her own marriage.

"Maggie—''

She cut him off. "Nobody deserves to live like that, afraid to say or do anything for fear of the consequences. Nobody.''

An ugly thought sneaked into his mind at her vehemence, a thought so abhorrent he didn't even want to think about it, let alone voice it, but he knew he had to ask. "Doc, did your husband beat you?''

She looked away from him, toward the silent television set. "No. Not like Annie's husband. He was an expert at the kind of jab that always finds its mark. I always blamed myself, thought if I had only been a little bit better at being a wife, our marriage might have been stronger.''

She met his gaze again and there was a new strength there he hadn't seen before. ''I realized something today talking to Annie, though. I couldn't control Michael's behavior, just my own. The one thing I feel responsibility for is that I was willing to put up with it for so long. You know what they say about a fool who spends her time scrubbing the deck while the ship is sinking? That was me, scrubbing away.''

Her voice broke off, and she flushed suddenly and looked down at her hands. ''I'm sorry, Colt. I didn't mean to unload all that on you. It's just been running through my head all evening.''

He shook his head. ''Don't apologize, Doc. I'm just sorry you had to go through that.''

''I survived.'' She smiled then, a radiant smile that took his breath away. ''Besides, if I hadn't married Michael, I never would have had Nicky. Then where would I be?''

He studied her smile and felt something shake loose inside him. His heart, maybe. ''You are one remarkable woman, Maggie Rawlings,'' he said, his voice gruff.

Her cheeks turned a darker shade of pink. ''I'm not.''

''I think you are,'' he said, then, without thinking beyond the need to touch her, he reached out and pulled her from the couch and into his arms.

Chapter 13

She gave a muffled exclamation as he tugged her to him, but lifted her mouth to his with a willingness that seemed to fill a cold, empty spot deep inside him.

The need he thought he had contained came thundering back at the touch of her mouth on his—soft and warm and inviting. It pounded through his veins thickly, urgently.

Her arms slid around his neck, her fingers tangled in his hair, and she sighed against his mouth. The soft sound of arousal was all it took to make him lose control. With a groan he forgot about all the reasons he shouldn't be doing this and deepened the kiss, his tongue teasing hers.

She met him eagerly kiss for kiss, taste for taste, and didn't protest when he pushed her back on the couch, intent only on greater closeness. Her body welcomed him, gentled to accept him.

The heady contrast of her soft curves against his hardness was almost enough to send him over the edge. She moved her hands to his back and clasped him to her more tightly and he pressed into her, stunned by the force of his desire, by the depth of his tenderness toward her.

He trailed kisses down the soft curve of her cheek, down the long, elegant length of her neck, to the neckline of her shirt. He reached for a button, but the jarring feel of the small, hard plastic against his thumb brought reality crashing back.

With a low, heartfelt groan, Colt yanked his hand back as if he'd been stung and wrenched his mouth from hers. He wanted nothing more than to lose himself in her arms, to forget about the job and Damian and everything else.

But how could he possibly make love to her with so many secrets still seething between them?

Simple. He couldn't. He had to tell her the truth, about his assignment, about his real reason for befriending her, about searching her trailer the other night in Butte.

The knowledge congealed in his stomach. He couldn't drag this out any longer—he owed it to her to tell the truth. But damn, he didn't want to hurt her.

Drawing on all his strength, he stiffened his spine and pulled away from her, needing distance for what he had to do. If he risked a glance at her, he knew he wouldn't be able to go through with telling her the truth, so he stood and walked to the window, feeling old and tired and bitter.

"What's wrong? Did I...did I do something wrong?" Her voice sounded low, smoky with need, but the anxiety in it twisted his heart. What had her husband done to her to make her think she wasn't desirable?

He looked out at the mountains he loved so much, seeking strength there. When he turned back, he forced his voice to be calm and emotionless. "No. It's not you. It's me."

She frowned. "I don't understand."

"I'm not the man you think I am, Doc."

For an instant, bewilderment muddied the cinnamon of her

eyes, then it faded, leaving them clear, determined. "You're kind and generous and caring. That's all that matters to me."

It was. She loved him. Even though she knew they would never have more than this moment—that she would be wounded, scarred, forever altered when he moved on—she needed this. She needed something sweet and real and solid to hang on to when their roads separated. She needed to be cherished if only for a moment.

He wanted her, she knew, and although she ached for much, much more from him, it would have to be enough.

Imbued with a confidence she hadn't felt in a long time— if ever—she rose from the couch and crossed the room to his side. The blue light from the muted television she'd forgotten all about flickered over his lean features, giving him odd hollows, unfamiliar planes and angles.

The strange light made him seem like a stranger, someone harsh, forbidding. She replayed his words: *I'm not the man you think I am,* and felt a moment's twinge.

She shook the unsettling thought away. This was Colt, the man who showed such gentleness to her son, who had helped her to laugh again, who made her feel safe.

The man she loved.

"Kiss me again, McKendrick," she ordered softly. She reached out and gripped the fabric of his shirt. His pulse beat strong and fast under her fingertips, and a muscle twitched in his jaw as she reached on tiptoe and pressed her mouth to his.

He stood stiff and unyielding in her arms for just a moment then slowly, subtly, his mouth moved against hers.

Tasting victory, she pressed against him, exulting in the contact of her breasts against his broad chest, even through all the layers of cloth. His hand slid up from her hip under her shirt to the undercurve of her breasts and she held her breath, needing him to touch her more than she remembered needing anything in her life.

His fingers stopped just inches short of touching her heated skin. Abruptly he dropped his hand and she nearly wept in frustration when he stepped away from her. "Maggie. Stop. We can't do this."

All her life people had been telling her what she could and couldn't do. First her mother, then Michael. She was heartily tired of it, so sick she wanted to scream.

She wanted to do this, dammit, and she wasn't going to let him talk her out of it.

"I have to tell you—"

She bridged the distance between them and pressed a finger to his lips. "Not now. Please not now. Tell me later. After, you can tell me anything you want. But not now."

"Maggie—"

"Just let me have this, Colt. Please."

He wavered for just a moment, then with a low oath, he reached for her, kissing her with all the fierce passion she could ever want. With barely restrained violence, he devoured her mouth, his lips and tongue urgent, demanding.

His hands were everywhere, in her hair, on her back, grasping her bottom to yank her against him.

At the feel of his hardness, a thrill of excitement—mingled with a hefty dose of nervous anticipation—shot through her veins like some potent, mind-altering drug, leaving her weak-kneed, shivering with reaction.

Her mouth responded eagerly to his kiss, her hands digging into the skin of his back. She barely recognized herself, this wanton, eager woman who couldn't seem to get enough of him.

Barely aware of anything beyond that devastating kiss, she let him maneuver them both back toward the couch. He lowered her onto it, but before his body could settle over hers, she pushed a hand between them.

"Wait," she murmured, her voice breathless.

He froze, blue eyes blazing when her trembling hands went

to the buttons of her shirt. With a predatory, hawklike gaze, he watched as she slowly, nervously unbuttoned her shirt.

She didn't have much in the way of cleavage. Michael had frequently commented on her deficiencies in that area. He'd even tried to persuade her to have implants. Now she found herself half wishing she had given in, just so she wouldn't have this sense of inadequacy.

It didn't matter, she told herself. Colt wanted her just the way she was. Right? With a last, ragged burst of bravado, she shrugged her shoulders from her shirt and finally forced herself to meet his eyes. Her heart seemed to stutter in her chest at the fierce desire there, and it melted completely when he knelt by the side of the couch.

Her big rough cowboy said nothing, just touched her reverently, gently, with those hard, nicked-up hands she now could admit she had woven so many fantasies about. They looked beautiful, strong and competent, against the whiteness of her skin.

Her head sagged against the back of the couch, her breathing harsh and ragged as first his fingers caressed her then his hot, searching mouth.

While his mouth drove her slowly, steadily crazy, she dipped her hands into his dark hair, pressing him to her breasts, savoring the feel of the thick silk against her fingers and his rugged scent—sage and leather and Colt—that filled her senses.

He trailed soft barely-there kisses from her breasts, across her collarbone and along the length of her neck to her waiting mouth. While their lips and tongues mated, she fumbled with the buttons of his brushed-cotton shirt, needing to feel his skin against hers.

She pushed it off his powerful shoulders and then he pressed her back against the cushions, his chest hard and warm on hers. The erotic friction of skin against skin was almost more than she could stand.

She felt his hardness pushing against the apex of her thighs through the layers of cloth still between them, and a raw, ancient need began to build to a crescendo inside her. She arched against him, her body seeking, craving, entreating.

His touches took on a new urgency, and he reached a hand between them and slipped it beneath the waistband of her jeans. She gasped at the intimate invasion but her wanton body responded instantly, pushing against his clever, clever fingers.

She hovered on the brink of something incredible, some enchanting, magical place just out of reach.

Just before she found it, before she tumbled headlong over the edge, he withdrew his fingers and she couldn't stop her soft whimper of disappointment.

"Not yet," he murmured against her mouth. "Wait for me."

Quickly, he removed the rest of their clothing then pulled a thin foil packet from his wallet. After making sure she was slick and ready for him, he sheathed himself in her. As she felt the heated strength of him inside her—as an avalanche of sensations rumbled over her—she drew a sharp breath. This was everything she wanted. This was real and intense and wonderful.

He kissed her hard at the same time that he sank into her.

All the urgency of before, when he had been touching her so erotically, returned stronger than ever, and she gripped the muscles in his back, feeling as if her world spun and twirled with each thrust. She could feel herself falling, and she gasped his name.

"I'm here, Maggie. Right here."

He held her tightly when the world finally exploded in a sharp burst of vivid light and color, then he thrust into her one last time with a harsh, exultant growl while he found his own pleasure.

After a few moments he shifted his weight from her and

would have risen, but she held him tight and moved to accommodate him on the couch. For a long time they stayed there in a silence broken only by their shallow breathing.

Finally he rose up on one elbow. "Maggie—"

"Don't say it. Don't say you have regrets."

Lord knows, she had enough for both of them. They hovered like a murder of crows in the edges of her thoughts, waiting to sweep in with taunting caws of I-told-you-so's.

She pushed them away. Not now. Now she just wanted to lie right here, with Colt's arms around her and his heart beating strong and sure beneath her ear.

"I shouldn't have…" His voice trailed off and he blew out a breath that stirred her hair. "We need to talk."

"Tomorrow. Can't it wait until tomorrow?" She could hear the pleading note in her voice and despised herself for it, but she couldn't bear for him to shatter what had been the most magical thing she had ever experienced.

He pursed his lips. "Yeah. I guess it can wait one more day."

She gave a tremulous smile of gratitude. *I love you* hovered on her tongue, but she couldn't say it. She knew he wouldn't want it, that it would make him feel uncomfortable, or worse, obligated to say words he didn't mean in reply.

So she contented herself with telling him how she felt with her hands and her mouth and her body.

They made love again, this time slowly, gently, without the fierce urgency of before. For all the softness of the second time, the same torrent of emotions poured through her as she held him and felt him move inside her body. It was still just as overpowering, as devastating.

She tried to store up every touch, every caress, into her memory for the time when he would be gone from her life, but she knew it would never be enough. As sure as she knew she loved him with everything in her, she knew a part of her would mourn forever that this moment was all she would ever have from him.

And when the pearly light of dawn shone through the window, she rose from his arms and stood watching him sleeping. He looked younger in sleep, not so hard, and she tried to burn the picture into her mind, like one of those Broken Spur brands.

Then, with one last kiss against the warm, rough skin of his forehead, she slipped away.

"What do you mean she's gone?" Colt slid from Scout's saddle to the ground, staring at his foreman.

"She left not long after you took off." Joe leaned over to pick a blade of meadow grass and stuck it between his teeth. "She said she had a lot of things to do and wanted to get off to an early start. Oh, yeah, she said to tell you thanks for everything and she'll see you in Utah tomorrow."

Damn. How had she given him the slip like that? He'd only been gone for an hour. One measly hour, just long enough to ride away from the ranch house so he could check in with Beckstead.

He should have known she would try something like this. The shadows he had glimpsed in her eyes the last time they had made love should have warned him.

She must have started packing just as soon as she left him this morning.

He rubbed a hand along the back of his neck. He didn't need this. Not now. He had just spent a half hour on the phone with Lane, avoiding the SAC's pointed questions about the progress of an investigation—or lack thereof. He hadn't had one single concrete thing to tell him.

So much for his plan to tell her he was FBI after breakfast. He grimaced. Could he screw this assignment up any worse?

"Why didn't you stop her?" he growled to Joe.

"Sorry. I didn't realize she was under house arrest."

Colt hefted the saddle from Scout with more force than necessary. "She's not. She hasn't done anything wrong. I told you that. But I still don't like the idea of her heading off to God-knows-where by herself. Why didn't she wait for me?"

Joe shrugged. "Don't ask me. All I know is that she thanked me kindly for my hospitality, said she thought my ranch was the prettiest spot in Montana, then drove that rattletrap pickup down the road in a cloud of dust. Seemed in a real big hurry to be on her way, too."

A big hurry to put distance between them. He didn't need to have it spelled out. When a man spends the night making love to a woman and a few hours later she runs away like her shoes are on fire, he'd have to be crazy not to realize he's the cause.

He blew out a hard breath. He couldn't say he was surprised. She'd had "goodbye" written all over her that last time he'd held her. What *did* shock him was the hurt scratching at his heart.

"You going after her?"

"Have to."

"You going to tell her the truth when you catch up with her?"

He scowled. "Yeah. I'm planning on it. Is that okay with you?"

Joe ignored his sarcasm. "It's about time. It would seem to me, she'd be a pretty hard woman to lie to."

"Tell me about it."

Joe was silent for a moment, and Colt could almost swear that was sympathetic understanding he could read in his friend's normally hard expression.

"For what it's worth, I like her," he finally said. "Not every woman would be willing to pitch in to help around here like she did with the cooking. Especially not some big-city doctor. If you were smart, you'd hang on to that one."

He wanted to. Dammit, he wanted to hang on to her with every ounce of his strength. "I'm going after her because it's my job. That's the only reason. She's the subject of an FBI investigation, our link to DeMarranville, and that's all she'll ever be."

"If you say so." Joe pulled the blade of grass from between his teeth and launched it over the fence.

He glared, knowing he wasn't fooling either of them, then decided the wiser course would be to change the subject. "What are you doing here, anyway? I thought you were staying with Annie."

Joe glanced at the small foothill that marked the boundary between the Broken Spur and Annie's spread, the Double C. "She made me leave this morning. Said she was fine now."

"And you believed her? That son of a bitch brother of yours beat her half to death. Hell, she had a broken arm. She can't get over a beating like that in twelve hours, then just get up and take care of her ranch."

"She never wants me to stay the next day." Joe's voice was expressionless, like his features. Stony and cold, like the top of Coyote Peak. "She's says it's not proper, a bad example to set for the kids. Besides, it just ticks Charlie off more to have me around."

Colt swallowed his words of sympathy, knowing they wouldn't be welcome. It had been no secret to any of them that Joe had been in love with Annie since they were kids. Although he never talked about it, Colt knew how much his friend had grieved for his lost dreams.

"How are we going to get her out of there?" he asked quietly.

"The only way she'll be free is for him to die."

At the determination in his voice, the eerie calm that had come over his expression, Colt shot him a look. "You're not going to do anything crazy are you?"

Joe didn't answer, just continued looking out at the foothill between the two ranches.

"You've already ridden that trail." He stared hard at his friend. "You know what it's like in the system. And as much as I might agree with you that Charlie's a drunk bastard who ought to be rotting six feet under for what he's done to our Annie, I'm sworn to uphold the law. If something happens to your brother, I'm going to have to come looking for you."

"Lucky for you, you'll know right where to find me, right?" Joe shoved away from the fence and headed toward the barn. "You'd better hurry if you're gonna catch up to the doc."

Colt watched him go, the spot between his shoulder blades itching. Trouble was brewing. He could smell it, taste it.

Surely Joe was too smart to follow through with his implied threats, wasn't he?

He couldn't spend any more time fretting about it now, though. One problem at a time. For now he had to concentrate on Maggie and Nicky and keeping them safe from DeMarranville.

With one eye on the small, sparse play area where Nicky worked out his excess energy after the long drive to Utah, Maggie dialed the number to Rosie's house, not far from the little apartment she had moved into after leaving Michael.

The early-evening sun cast long, stretched-out shadows across the campground that was part of the Ogden rodeo grounds. Daylight lasted a long time here in the summer—it probably wouldn't be completely dark until nine or ten, another two or three hours.

"Look at me, Mom!" At Nicky's call, she peered over the side of the phone kiosk and her heart plummeted to her toes. Her little gymnast had shinnied up the monkey bars and was now hanging upside down, his hands flailing several feet above the ground.

"Be careful," she said, fighting her maternal instinct to race over and yank him back to earth. She couldn't protect him from everything. If she tried, she would smother him and would only end up hurting him worse than any tumble from the monkey bars ever could.

"I'm always careful," he responded cheerfully.

Still, she breathed a sigh of relief when he swung forward and grabbed the bars with his hands again. Crisis temporarily averted, she turned her attention back to the call. No answer. After a dozen rings, the answering machine picked up.

"Rosie, it's Maggie," she finally said, after debating what kind of message to leave. "I'm okay. I'll try to call you again."

She hung up and gazed at the phone. She was probably working. After Michael's death, Rosie would have had to find another job somewhere.

What now? She chewed on her bottom lip. She had been so consumed with talking to Rosie about what had happened after her frantic flight—about whether any *real* police officers had showed up that night—that she hadn't given a thought to what she would do if her friend wasn't home.

During the whole endless drive from the Broken Spur, when she had ached with regret, with loss, she distracted herself by concentrating on the thought of putting an end to this nightmare.

She wanted to go the police, but she was afraid they would suspect her in her husband's death if she didn't have all the details from that night, if she couldn't explain why she ran away.

She drummed her fingers on the metal of the phone kiosk. Who would know where Rosie could be reached? Teresa! The name slipped into her consciousness. Teresa, Rosie's daughter, would surely know where Maggie could find her mother.

She fed a few more coins from her precious roll into the

pay phone and dialed information to find Teresa's number, then added a few more to make the call. To her relief, Rosie's daughter answered on the second ring.

There was a long, drawn-out moment of silence on the other end after she identified herself. "Dr. Prescott?" Teresa sounded distraught. "Where are you? Are you all right?"

She glanced at the Wasatch Mountains, hesitant to give her location. "I'm fine." She decided to ignore the first question. The less Teresa knew the better. "Look, I'm trying to reach your mother. Do you know where I could find her?"

Again there was an awkward silence. "She's still in the hospital. I'm hoping to bring her home today."

Cold fingers crawled down Maggie's spine. "In the hospital? What happened?"

"A few days after Mr. Prescott died, she was attacked."

"Attacked? Where?" She didn't have to hear Teresa's answer. She knew. Somehow she *knew*.

The other woman's answer only confirmed her gut instinct. "At your apartment. She was there by herself cleaning up a few things, and somebody broke in. They ripped the place apart and beat her until she was half-dead."

"Dear God." Her knees wobbled and she would have fallen except for the support from the phone booth.

"Dr. Prescott," Teresa said softly, "they were looking for you."

She pressed a trembling hand to her mouth. She should have thought about Rosie, should have realized she might be in danger. If she had thought about anyone but herself, she would have taken steps to protect the woman she loved so dearly.

Later there would be time for this crushing guilt. She forced herself to organize the chaos of her thoughts as the doctor in her rushed to the forefront. "What was the extent of her injuries?"

"Bad." The other woman's voice trembled. "For a while

there, we didn't know if she would make it. She had a couple of broken ribs that punctured a lung.''

Her fault, her fault, her fault. The words seemed to scream in her ear and she pressed a hand to her stomach where nausea suddenly churned. Rosie had been a figure in her life as far back as she could remember, first as her mother's cook, then after Helen died, Maggie had hired her over Michael's objections to be a housekeeper at their house.

She had been like a second mother to Nicky, had watched over him during the days she worked at the clinic and had been a listening ear to Maggie during the worst of her marital troubles.

She thought of her soft arms, her sage advice, and had to struggle to clear the tears suddenly clogging her throat. ''Is—is any of the damage permanent?''

''Too early to say. The doctors think she might have permanent hearing loss on one side, and she'll probably always limp a little. She's made a lot of progress in the past few weeks, though.'' Teresa paused. ''She's wondering what this is all about. I have to tell you, Dr. Prescott, I'm wondering the same thing. First Mr. Prescott is killed, then you take little Nicholas and disappear, then somebody breaks into your apartment and rips it apart. What kind of trouble are you in?''

While she was trying to form an answer, a computerized voice ordered her to deposit more change. She looked in frustration at the empty roll in front of her. She didn't *have* any more change. ''I have to go Teresa,'' she said quickly. ''Tell your mother I love her and I'm sor—''

Before she could complete the inadequate apology, her time ran out and the dial tone buzzed her ear.

She took great care replacing the phone on the receiver, despite the violent urge she suddenly had to take her rage and guilt out on it by smashing it into little pieces.

She had to make this right. No matter what, she had to

stop this DeMarranville person and the men who worked for him.

Because she had let them terrify her and send her running, a sweet, innocent old woman had suffered, but she wouldn't let it go any further. She was going to put a stop to it. She was going to go to the police and tell them everything she knew.

Colt would help her, she thought suddenly. Last week he had said he knew people she could talk to, people who could help her. She would wait for him to arrive in the morning and then she would begin the slow, painful process of re-claiming her life.

No matter what she might have to face, she had to do this, for Rosie's sake and for her own.

Chapter 14

Tired and irritable, Colt pulled his truck and horse trailer next to Maggie's rig.

Damn woman. He'd been driving flat-out for seven hours to catch up with her. Now it was nearly dark, his back ached, and he had a headache that just wouldn't quit, despite a double dose of aspirin and as much caffeine as he could stand.

When he met up with her, he was going to wring her beautiful little neck for running off and leaving him behind. And then he was going to kiss her senseless.

With that tantalizing thought in mind, he eased his sore muscles out of the truck. His boots hit the ground just as the aluminum door to her trailer opened.

Maggie paused in the doorway and stared at him. "Colt!" she exclaimed, and he was gratified to hear a relieved sort of welcome in her voice. "What are you doing here? I didn't expect you until tomorrow morning."

No way was he going to let her get off that easy. A little softness didn't make up for the whole day of stress he had just endured. ''Don't you have more sense than to take off halfway across the West all by yourself?'' he snapped.

''Excuse me?'' Any pleasure he might have heard before in her voice dried up now, leaving it as prickly as a cactus. ''I didn't realize I had to ask your permission.''

''You don't.'' He bit down on his temper. Getting angry at her wasn't going to solve anything. ''You know you don't. I'm sorry I snapped at you, but I was worried. You left without a word. Without even saying goodbye.''

Before she could answer, a familiar little figure burst through the doorway and scampered past her down the steps, nearly knocking her over in his excitement.

''Colt!'' Nicky yelled, jumping into his arms.

''Hey, partner.'' The boy felt so damn right in his arms, like he belonged there. Colt didn't want to let himself think about it, or about how much it would hurt when he wouldn't see the little rascal anymore. ''How was the ride down?''

''Good. I saw some buffaloes and a great big elk and Mom let me get a hamburger Happy Meal for lunch.''

''Wow. Sounds like you two had a real party without me.''

Nicky giggled. ''We did. Me and Cheyenne are makin' cookies. Chocolate chip. You want to help?''

''Mmm. My favorite. I'd love to help, but I need to talk to your mom for a minute. Is that okay with you?''

Nicky nodded and wiggled to the ground. ''Can I go now, Mom?''

''Did you finish your dinner?''

''Yep. Even the yucky peas.''

''All right. Only until this batch is done, though. Then it's bedtime.''

''Save me a cookie, partner,'' Colt said.

''Okay.'' Nicky galloped toward a trailer on the next row, leaving behind a tense, stilted silence that hovered between Maggie and Colt like an angry swarm of bees.

Colt was the first to wade in. ''Why did you run away?'' For several moments, he didn't think she would answer.

She stared out at the mountains, then back at him, her brown eyes murky and troubled. "I needed time, space, to figure out where we go from here," she finally said.

"And?"

"And I think we both know what happened last night was a mistake. A mistake that can't happen again."

"Funny thing about that," he said softly. "My head knows you're right, that we're headin' for trouble. But somehow I'm havin' a hard time convincing the rest of me, especially when all I can think about is taking you in my arms again."

"Colt—" she began, alarm flaring briefly in her eyes when he stepped forward.

"One kiss, Doc. Just one, to see if you taste as sweet as I've been remembering all day."

For all her protests, she came into his arms willingly enough and lifted her face to meet his touch. He kept the kiss easy, nonthreatening, and was rewarded by the softening of her mouth, by her hands fluttering up to rest on his chest.

Just when his body started clamoring for him to deepen the kiss, her hands fell to her sides, though, and she wrenched her mouth away. "Stop. I can't think straight when you do that."

Well, that's something, he thought.

She stepped away a pace from him and folded her fingers together. "Actually, I'm glad you decided to come to the rodeo a day early. I—I need your help."

"With what?"

"I've decided to take my chances and contact the police. I want to give a statement about—about that night, about watching those men murder Michael."

He stared at her in astonishment. It was absolutely the last thing he expected her to say. "Why now?"

Her shoulders tensed, her fingers tightening together until he could see the whites of her knuckles. "I told you about Rosie, didn't I?"

"She's the woman who tended Nicky that night, right? Whose place you went to after the murder."

"Yes. When I…when Michael and I separated, she helped me find an apartment near her house so she could continue helping out with Nicky, even though I couldn't afford to hire a full-time housekeeper. But she's always been much more than that to me. She was…" Her voice wobbled slightly, but she quickly recovered. "She's my friend."

Hearing that wobble, his shoulder blades started up with that damn itching again. "Something wrong with her?"

"I tried to call her a few hours ago to ask what happened after I left her house the night Michael died, if the police officers I contacted ever showed up." Her eyes glittered with unshed tears. "I found out she's been in the hospital almost as long as I've been away. She was attacked, beaten nearly to death, while she was cleaning out my apartment. I'm positive the men who hurt her are the same men who killed Michael."

He swallowed a harsh oath. Why hadn't he heard about the housekeeper being attacked at Maggie's apartment, something with such obvious significance to the case?

"Don't you see?" Maggie went on. "If I had stayed in San Francisco, if I had faced what happened instead of running away, Rosie wouldn't have been hurt."

"You can't blame yourself for this, Doc. You did what you thought was best to protect you and your son."

"Maybe I've been wrong. I can't keep this up. I can't just keep running away for the rest of my life. As long as I do—as long as I let my fear control me—these men will continue hurting people who are completely innocent in all of this."

"Including you and Nicky."

"I have to face this and go to the police. I would have done it earlier tonight, as soon as I talked to Rosie's daughter and found out about her beating, but I didn't know where to go. When I told you what happened, you told me you knew some people who might be able to help me. I want to talk to them. Now. Tonight.''

''Maggie—''

''I need you to help me, Colt. I have to make this right.''

Now was the time to tell her. To whip out his badge and his Bureau identification from his back pocket and be done with the ugly lies. He couldn't put it off anymore. He opened his mouth, searching for the right words, but the ones he chose burned in his throat like bitter acid.

Before he could clear it away, a long, high shriek echoed through the evening air, followed immediately by the slam of a car door and squealing tires. A car's engine rumbled, then began to fade as it left the campground, but the keening wails went on and on.

A chill of foreboding slithered down his spine. He and Maggie shared an alarmed look, then they both raced toward the source of the cries. The chill turned into a downright deep freeze at the sight of Cheyenne, Maggie's niece, standing in front of the trailer she shared with her grandmother.

The girl's eyes were huge and frightened, her hands were pressed against her cheeks, and she rocked back and forth on her heels, staring at the cloud of dust already beginning to settle.

''What is it?'' Maggie asked, grabbing Cheyenne's arms. ''What happened?''

The teenager looked as if she had been seized by some deep, endless horror. She looked at Maggie and didn't seem to recognize her for an instant, then her face seemed to crumple. ''Nicky. They took Nicky.''

Maggie reeled back as if she'd been punched in the gut. She swayed, then her face leached of all color and she started to fall just as Peg rounded the corner.

Colt grabbed her before she could hit the ground and handed her off to her stepmother. ''Take care of her,'' he ordered, already heading for his truck, fiercely praying—as he hadn't done in longer than he could remember—that he wouldn't be too late.

When he reached his truck, he swore, long and violently. Trying to pursue DeMarranville—and he was stupid if he didn't think his old partner was behind this—would be next to impossible with the camper on the bed and the horse trailer still hooked up.

He scanned the campground quickly and raced to the first vehicle he could see that wasn't hooked to a rig, a late-model pickup, souped up with a big chrome rollbar and a wild, psychedelic paint job.

"Hey!" A startled cowboy who had been sitting on the shiny fender flirting with some buckle bunny in tight jeans and caked-on makeup, jumped up when Colt opened the cab.

"Where are the keys?" Colt yelled, conscious that with every passing second, his chances of finding Nicky dwindled.

"Get the hell out of my truck!" The cowboy fumbled with the door.

Colt yanked his badge out and thrust it into the cowboy's face through the open window. "FBI! Give me the friggin' keys."

The kid paused for just an instant, then dug them out of his leather vest pocket and tossed through them in the window. Colt caught them in mid-air, shoved them into the ignition and gunned the engine.

As he roared out of the campground, the last thing he saw view in the rearview mirror was Maggie on her knees in the dirt, clutching her stomach and looking as if her world had just been destroyed.

She was dying.

As a doctor, she dealt with death every day. Sometimes, when she watched her patients cope with the knowledge of their own mortality, she had wondered what it must be like.

Now she knew. It was agony. Sheer, unadulterated agony. Each breath felt like a hundred knives slicing at her lungs, as if two giant hands were squeezing the life out of her heart with every beat.

Nicky was gone and her soul had gone with him.

He had been gone less than an hour, but already she felt as if everything that had meaning in her life had been snatched away from her. She drew in a ragged breath, vaguely surprised that she could even go through even the most basic motions of living when the most important part of her had been excised so viciously.

Colt would bring him back. She clutched the thought like it was her last link to sanity. Colt would find her little boy, and he would bring him back to her. He had to. The alternative was unimaginable.

Without taking her gaze from the road, she rubbed a hand across her heart, trying not to think of her sweet little boy in the hands of the same evil that had killed his father.

In the time since they had stolen Nicky away, the sun had slipped behind the mountains on the west side of Great Salt Lake. Around her, the other rodeo participants went on about their business, unaware of the drama being played out.

The only one who had paid any attention was the cowboy whose truck Colt had appropriated. He had come over babbling some nonsense about cops and robbers and wanting to make damned sure his truck wasn't damaged or the government would pay for it.

She hadn't been able to summon the energy to tell him he must have misunderstood and eventually he had wandered away.

She sensed someone approaching and shifted her gaze from the road only long enough to see that the intruder was Cheyenne, her eyes swollen and red blotches covering her face from weeping.

Her niece stretched a hand out and and touched Maggie's shoulder with icy fingers. She felt as if she were made of fragile, handblown glass, as if she would shatter at even that smallest of touches, but she gathered the pieces of herself together and crossed a hand over her chest to lay it over the girl's.

She squeezed Cheyenne's fingers, feigning a reassurance she was far from feeling.

"I'm sorry, Aunt Maggie," Cheyenne whispered. "So sorry. I just went inside for a moment, I swear. I just needed to check on our cook—"

Her voice broke, and it took a moment for her to compose herself enough to continue. "The timer went off on our cookies. I just went in to take them out of the oven and I heard tires screeching. I thought it was just somebody driving too fast so I looked out the window to make sure Nicky was okay. Next thing I knew, a big dark car pulled up and two men jumped out and they grabbed Nicky and shoved him inside. They—they were gone before I could even make it outside."

"Don't blame yourself, Cheyenne." Her voice sounded bruised, damaged, as if she'd been shouting. Funny, she'd thought all her screaming had been on the inside.

"I should never have left him alone."

"It's not your fault." If anyone was responsible, she was. She was the one who was supposed to be protecting her son. She should have been more alert, more vigilant.

Somehow she had led them here. She didn't know how, but all her efforts to safeguard him had been for nothing. They had found her, anyway, and now held the one sure ace to make certain she cooperated.

They had to know she would do anything, *anything,* if only they wouldn't hurt her little boy.

"Colt will find him. Won't he?"

She met Cheyenne's gaze briefly, and the raw hope there made her ache and look away. It was too similar to what she knew must be burning in her own eyes.

Tempering the hope was a sick, terrible fear that had begun to gnaw at her stomach. Even if Colt somehow managed to catch up with them, what could one man possibly do? He had no weapon, no armor. Nothing to protect himself against the kind of twisted men willing to use a little boy for their own ends.

The pay phone across the road rang suddenly, jangling her already-frayed nerves. Cheyenne forgotten, Maggie stared at it for only an instant, then with grim foreboding, rushed to answer it, instinctively knowing who would be on the other end of the line.

"Dr. Prescott." The voice in her ear was smooth, cultured and had a rolling, hypnotizing cadence. Somehow she knew she was speaking with the devil himself. DeMarranville.

"Where is my son?" she rasped out.

"Your son is fine, I assure you. We're treating him as our honored guest. Right now he's enjoying himself watching a television program and eating ice cream, probably having more fun than he has in weeks."

"I want to speak with him. Let me speak with him."

"I'm hurt, Dr. Prescott. Don't you trust my word?"

She rubbed a fist against her stomach where nausea rolled and pitched. The bastard held her son's life in his hands, and he wanted to play sickening little games with her. Slowly, painfully, she ordered herself to stay calm. Nothing would be accomplished by giving in to the fear and fury roiling around inside her.

"Please." The word whispered between her lips, a prayer to the devil.

DeMarranville must have taken pity on her. "Carlo," she heard him say in the background, "the doctor would like to speak with her son."

A few seconds later she nearly sagged to the ground when she heard his high, sweet voice, sounding as clear and as unhurt as it had less than an hour earlier. "Hi, Mommy."

If she thought she knew death before, hearing his voice so far away from her gave the word a whole new dimension. The knives stabbed into her chest again and again and again, and she bled from a thousand cuts. "Oh, Nicky. Are you all right, sweetheart?"

He sounded remarkably cheerful. "Yeah. I just had a bubblegum ice cream cone and later we're gonna have some pizza and watch a Western movie Mr. Damian got just for me."

"That will be fun," she forced herself to say.

"Mr. Damian says I'm just staying with him for a while because you had some stuff to do. He's pretty nice, I guess, but I'd rather be with Colt or Cheyenne."

"I know. But you'll be back with me soon." Please God, please God, please God.

"Mr. Damian says I have to go now. I love you, Mommy."

How much more could she survive? She managed to keep the tears rolling down her cheeks from coming through in her voice. "Oh, sweetheart. I love you, too."

There was a silence on the line and then DeMarranville returned. "I told you he was fine. You should have trusted me."

"What do you want." The words coming from her throat sounded more harsh than she expected, short and bitter and filled with loathing.

"I think you know the answer to that. Your husband was a very bad boy, Dr. Prescott. Now it's up to you to make it right."

"How?"

"Simple. The money and the disk for the boy."

I don't have them, she wanted to scream at the man, but fear held her tongue. If they thought she wasn't cooperating, what would they do to her child?

At her continuing silence, DeMarranville went on, "We know you must have them. We have painstakingly searched through both your apartment and through your husband's home to no avail. Michael was most clear to my people that you were the one who knew where they were."

"He lied." The words tumbled out before she stop them. She wanted to beg and plead and throw herself on the devil's mercy, anything for Nicholas. "I don't know why, but Michael lied. I don't know anything about any of this. Please, you have to believe me—I have no idea where any disk is, I swear. Or any money, either."

"Then, my dear, I suggest you find it." The calm, matter-of-fact tone chilled her blood more than any threat or angry outburst could have. "You have until tomorrow night, 10:00 p.m. Deliver my merchandise to the rodeo arena entrance and then we'll see about reuniting you with this charming little boy."

He paused, then added in that terrible voice. "At the risk of sounding melodramatic, Dr. Prescott, I really must insist you come alone. If you contact the police or bring McKendrick or anyone else to the exchange, I'm afraid I wouldn't be very happy at all. I might have to take my anger out on both you and your son. You understand, don't you?"

His words struck an odd note of discord beyond the icy terror borne by his threat, but she couldn't think past her fear for her son to analyze what she found jarring about it.

"I—yes," she finally said.

"Splendid. Tomorrow, 10:00 p.m. at the entrance to the arena."

For a long time after DeMarranville hung up, she gripped the phone to her ear and listened to the buzz of the dial tone, reluctant to completely sever the only connection to her son.

She was still standing there several moments later when she heard the rumble of an approaching truck and saw in the moonlight a glimmer of the iridescent paint on the pickup Colt had taken.

Carefully, slowly, she replaced the phone on the receiver and turned to face Colt.

He opened the door and climbed to the ground, looking older, somehow, the sunbaked lines fanning out from his eyes more deeply etched. "I lost them, Doc. I'm so sorry."

''I know,'' she said quietly. She wanted nothing more than to fall into his arms and let him hold her, to take away this pain, but she knew it wouldn't make it better. Nothing would but the return of her child.

''Have you heard from DeMarranville?''

She nodded toward the phone. ''Just now. I have until tomorrow night to find the money and the disk.''

He swore. ''Or what?''

''Or they kill my son,'' she said simply.

''Doc, you know I won't let them hurt your boy, I swear. I have to tell you—''

Barely listening, she turned to go toward her trailer. ''Thank you for your help, but I need to go.''

''Where?''

She didn't look to see if he followed, just continued walking as if in a daze. ''I only have twenty-four hours to save my son's life. If I'm going to find what Michael stole from them, I have to start looking.''

Chapter 15

"It's after three. You need to sleep, Doc."

Without daring to look up for even a moment, she continued digging through Nicky's suitcase again. "We haven't found the disk or the money," she said. Her voice sounded disconnected, as numb as the rest of her. "I can't sleep until we find it."

"It's not here, Maggie," Colt pointed out, so gently she wanted to scream at him. "We've turned this place upside down at least a dozen times and we haven't found it."

She sat back on her heels and surveyed the wreckage of what had once been her haven, the dingy trailer with the peeling wallpaper and the dark paneling that she and Nicky had turned into a home during the past seven weeks.

Now it looked like all the pictures she had ever seen of places hit by natural disasters. The contents of the cupboards were scattered everywhere, on the counter, on the floor, on the table. A jumble of plates and toys and clothing covered every surface, as if her trailer had suffered some violent explosion.

For hours she and Colt had combed through all of her meager belongings again and again, looking for anything out of place. She had even ripped a hole in Nicky's teddy bear and sifted through the stuffing, but they had come up with nothing out of the ordinary.

With every moment that passed without their search yielding whatever it was DeMarranville wanted, Nicky seemed to drift farther and farther away from her. She pictured a helium balloon floating higher and higher until it finally passed out of sight, gone forever, and she vowed with everything inside her to hang on to the thin string connecting them, with all her might.

"Keep looking," she said sharply.

"It's not here."

"It is. It has to be here somewhere."

"Where? We've looked through every inch of your trailer at least a dozen times."

"I don't know, but it has to be here. We'll find it. We *have* to."

"Maggie—"

"What do you want me to do, Colt?" She stood up abruptly, clenching her fists. Her voice climbed to a shout as all her pent-up fear and anger came spurting out. "Do you want me to just give up? They have my son. My little boy. Should I just hand him over, without even fighting? What kind of mother would that make me?"

As quickly as it had come, her anger dissipated, and suddenly she was weeping, huge, wrenching sobs. She clutched her arms to her stomach and rocked back and forth on her heels. "What kind of mother am I to let them take my little boy?"

"Aw, Doc. Hell." Through her grief, she felt his arms go around her, and then he was tugging her toward the vinyl-covered bench that pulled out into her bed. He sat and pulled her onto his lap, cradling her like a child while she cried out all the fear she had been holding inside her.

"You're a good mother," he murmured softly. "The best mother I've ever seen."

She was distantly aware of his strong arms around her, his lips brushing against her hair tenderly, and the contact comforted her as much as she would allow it.

How would she have survived this without Colt here to help her through it? She didn't even want to think about it, and she was suddenly enormously grateful for his presence, for the strength he offered.

"You'll have Nick back, I promise you." His voice was low, rough in her ear.

"I'm so afraid, Colt."

"I know. I know."

"What if I never find what they're looking for? What will they do to Nicky?"

He held her tighter. "Sleep, Doc. In the morning we'll come up with a plan. I'm going to bring in those friends of mine I was telling you about. They'll help us look for him, I promise."

His deep voice lulled her, comforted her. The trauma of the last few hours—added to a seven-hour drive wrestling her truck from the Broken Spur and the sleepless night she had spent in his arms the night before—began to catch up with her.

She had been existing solely on adrenaline since Nicky had been taken. Now that the rush had passed, she felt battered, achy, as if she had just survived some horrific automobile accident.

Through the soft cotton of his shirt she could hear his heart beating strong and steady in her ear. She felt her eyelids begin to droop and couldn't seem to summon the energy to prop them open again. Just for a moment. She only wanted to rest here for a moment, just long enough to regain her strength so she could return to the search....

Colt watched her lose the battle with exhaustion. Her lids

fluttered a few times, her fist clenched the fabric of his shirt, and then she was still.

He studied the fragile beauty of her face in sleep, and his heart seemed to wrench and tug inside him at the dark circles under her eyes, the frown that stayed on her mouth even in sleep.

With his defenses down, the guilt he had been holding at bay all evening crashed over him like a tidal wave he'd seen once in the Marines. This was all his fault. He should have told her he was FBI yesterday—hell, he should have told her weeks ago.

His reasons for withholding the truth had seemed valid at the time, but now they just seemed shallow and selfish, aimed more at protecting himself than in protecting her. If he had come clean she would have been furious, but at least she and the boy would have been in protective custody, out of DeMarranville's reach.

Well, she would find out in the morning. In a few hours Beckstead would arrive to head the investigation into the little boy's kidnapping and the operation to see him safely home.

He rotated his neck to try to relieve the tight ache there. It helped a little but did nothing for the stronger ache in his chest. Nothing would ease that but the return of her son.

With small, careful movements, he stood and gently laid her down on the bench, wishing she had thick, soft down to rest on instead of vinyl that was cold and hard. He tugged a quilt off the loft bed and covered her with it and she snuggled down into the folds of the blanket.

He stood and watched her for several moments, absorbing her features. The pale, soft-blue tracery of veins in her eyelids, the delicate bones in her collarbone, the soft tangles of her hair.

With slow care, he pushed the hair away from her eyes, his fingers lingering on her skin. It wasn't right that she had been through so much already and now the worst possible nightmare had come true. He wanted to take it away, to do everything he could to make things right for her.

He was in love with her.

The knowledge came out of nowhere and slammed into him so violently he had to steady himself against the wall to keep from falling over.

He loved her. Her stubbornness, the deep vein of courage running through her, her gentle compassion that reached out to everyone she met. He loved everything about her.

What in the hell had he done?

He scrubbed his hands over his face. How could he have been so stupid, let their relationship spiral so far out of his control? He knew something had tugged him to her from the very first, that he had grown to care about both her and her son in a way he hadn't cared about anybody or anything in a long, long time.

This fierce emotion choking in his throat went way beyond caring, though, way beyond anything he had ever felt before. It was raw and real and...terrible.

He loved Maggie Rawlings but it wasn't going to do him a hell of a lot of good. Sure as snow on the mountains in January, she would hate him in the morning when she found out about his lies.

Consciousness returned slowly, painfully, like needlepricks of sensation returning to a frostbitten limb.

Her eyes felt gritty and sore, and every muscle in her body ached and pulled. She lay on the hard bench for a moment, disoriented. She could feel the heavy weight of something terrible on her chest, but for long moments she was unable to figure out what it might be.

With effort, she blinked away the lingering tendrils of sleep and tried to sort through what was nightmare and what was reality.

Nicky was gone.

All the helpless agony of the night before rushed back and

she sat up, shoving the covers away. Reality was *worse* than any nightmare. DeMarranville had her little boy and she had nothing—absolutely nothing—to trade for his life.

She hadn't meant to sleep more than a few minutes, but through the little window of her trailer she could see the thin rays of early-morning sunlight filtering through the trees.

The last thing she remembered was Colt holding her in his arms, telling her they would come up with a plan in the morning. Damn. It was morning and her time was running out.

It only took moments for her to change into clean clothes, splash water on her face, then hurry outside to look for him. The air was cool, and silvery drops of dew clung to the grass under her feet.

Most of the rodeo crowd still slept, and the campground was quiet, but as she approached Colt's camper, she could hear the low murmur of male voices on the other side.

The friends he said he was calling in to help search for Nicky must have arrived while she slept. Anger flashed through her, hot and sharp. Colt never should have allowed her to sleep so long. Nicky was her son, and she deserved to be a part of any effort to find him.

Determined to tell him so in no uncertain terms, she round the corner of the camper, then froze, a scream building in her throat and lodging there, choking off her airway.

There, sitting calmly as you please at a picnic table drinking coffee with the man she loved, were two figures from her nightmares. The two men she had seen from the elevator the night of Michael's murder, the two who had found her at Rosie's house.

Her blood pulsed thickly, sluggishly, and she longed for the illusory safety of the camper. Barely aware of the cold aluminum against her back, she tried to swallow her panic while she scrambled to make sense of what she had seen.

What earthly reason could Colt have for talking to them? Didn't he realize they were part of it all? Of course he wouldn't, she realized. He wasn't there that night, and he would have no idea who the men were.

Unless he was one of them.

The thought sneaked into her mind, ugly and dark, and she thought of the secrets she had always sensed in his eyes.

No, she couldn't believe it. Not Colt.

His low drawl pierced the tumult of her thoughts. "Have you figured out how Damian found her yet?"

"He just had to sit back and let her make a move." The older man who looked like a foreign diplomat—or like a clothier at some exclusive men's store—spoke with a clipped Eastern accent. "The doctor made a phone call yesterday to the housekeeper's residence and left a message for her. Damian's people have been watching for it, have been monitoring the phone line. With the phone technology today, a kid could have traced the call."

Her stomach quivered. She had caused this, then. By trying to reach Rosie, she had called down the devil.

The younger of the men, the balding man she thought she had seen that day at the rodeo in Butte, spoke with a derisive sneer in his voice. "If you hadn't completely bungled this assignment, McKendrick, none of this would have happened."

"Back off, Dunbar," Colt growled.

"You should have found the stuff days ago."

"I searched her trailer just like you ordered, and I came up with absolutely nothing."

Searched her trailer? She pressed her eyes tightly shut, trying to make sense of it. That day back in Butte, when she had been so sure someone had been inside the trailer, the invader had been Colt? He had rummaged through her things looking for DeMarranville's money and files?

Under other circumstances, she would have been relieved that she hadn't been imagining things, that she hadn't just been conjuring up threats that didn't exist. But all she could feel now was this sharp ache in her chest and the sick roll and pitch of her stomach.

She had trusted him, kissed him. *Made love to him.* And all the time he was betraying her.

"Maybe you didn't find anything in her trailer because you weren't looking hard enough. Maybe you were too distracted by the beautiful widow to pay much attention to your assignment."

"That's enough, Dunbar."

"No, let him have his say." The fury in Colt's voice vibrated through the morning air.

"Fine. We all know you screwed up," the younger man went on. "If you had done your job, we would have had the disk and the money days ago and all the information we needed to bring down DeMarranville. By now the lovely widow and her kid would have been in protective custody."

Protective custody? Bring down DeMarranville? It sounded like something out of a detective show on television.

Chaotic thoughts whirled around her like leaves in a chill autumn windstorm, but she couldn't seem to grab hold of any of them.

"I carried out this assignment the best way I knew how," Colt said. "If the Bureau didn't like the job I was doing, they should have yanked me and put another agent in my place."

"Nobody's saying that," the older man used a placating tone. "You're a damn good FBI agent and you know it. This case just got away from all of us. We all made mistakes."

Maggie's eyes flew open and she leaned shakily against the bumper of the camper.

Colton McKendrick was a cop. No, an FBI agent. He wasn't a down-on-his-luck cowboy trying to make a few bucks on the rodeo circuit, he was a special agent sent to investigate her.

Everything she knew about him—or thought she knew, anyway—seemed to tilt and slide around like marbles in a shoe box. Without thinking beyond the pain, the bone-deep betrayal, she shoved away from the camper and rounded the corner.

"You lied to me."

All three men looked up at her with varying degrees of surprise. Colt's expression quickly changed to one of wary guilt. "Doc—"

"Don't say a word. Not a word. I don't think I want to hear anything else from you right now."

Inside she felt as if she could hear her heart breaking apart, but she hid it behind a facade of brittle control. She turned to the older man, the one who was obviously in command. "You work for the FBI." It was a statement, not a question.

The man nodded and pulled a black case from the pocket of his jacket. He flipped it open and to reveal the shield. It flashed in the sunlight and she had to blink away the glare.

"Lane Beckstead, special agent in charge of racketeering investigations for the San Francisco regional office. This is Agent Dunbar. And of course you know Agent McKendrick."

She dared one quick, anguished glance at Colt, then turned back to Beckstead. "What are you doing to find my son?"

He cleared his throat. "During the night we contacted every hotel along the Wasatch Front without success, I'm afraid. Our guess is they have your son in a private home somewhere in the area."

And of course they couldn't go knocking door to door at every house in northern Utah. "I suppose you know they think I have money and financial records my hus—Michael Prescott stole from them."

She couldn't call him her husband. Never again, even though technically their divorce hadn't been final at the time of his murder. Because of him—because of his greed, his complete venality—her son was in danger.

"We're aware of that, yes."

She entwined her fingers together tightly. "I don't have

what they want. How can I give them something I don't have?''

''We're working on coming up with an acceptable substitute for the real thing.''

''Don't you think they'll be expecting some kind of trick? They're not just going to hand him over without verifying the authenticity of whatever I give them.''

''No. Probably not.''

''Meantime, my son could be hurt.''

''We'll do everything we possibly can to make sure Nicky is safe. I swear it, Doc.''

She whirled on Colt, and couldn't prevent some of the bitter acid of betrayal from leaking into her voice. ''And I'm supposed to believe you now—trust you, dammit—when every single word you have said to me since I met you has been a lie?''

''Who else can you trust?''

She wanted to scream and rail at him, to lash out, if only to ease some of this pain. But she couldn't argue the truth of these words, at least. She had no one left to trust.

Later, after Nicky was back in her arms, she would have time to grieve for the loss of all the silly, foolish dreams she had been spinning about this man, dreams she hadn't even dared admit to herself.

Later she would have time for anger and regret. Now she had to concentrate on her son, on doing everything she could to see him safe once more.

''We're just trying to come up with a plan.'' Colt slid along the bench to make room for her, and after a brief hesitation she forced herself to join the men at the table, knowing she had no choice.

She sat down, careful to keep as much space as possible between them.

''I have one question before we go any further. Why were you two there that night? At Michael's office and then later at Rosie's house?''

Beckstead and Dunbar exchanged glances, then the older man spoke. "Your husband had been under surveillance for several weeks before his death. We'd been electronically monitoring his office—"

"Bugging it?"

He nodded. "We knew Santori and Franky Kostas planned to pay him a visit and that DeMarranville wanted them to put a scare into him. We were all set to make our move after their meeting, hoping he would be ready to cooperate with us and lead us to someone bigger."

"DeMarranville. The man who has my son."

He nodded again.

"Why? What has he done?"

"What *hasn't* he done?" The antipathy in Colt's voice took her by surprise. "Damian has his fingers in just about every illegal or crooked scheme in the Bay area. Drugs. Prostitution. You name it. Whatever will earn him a buck off other people's misery."

Damian. He had called DeMarranville by his first name. Suddenly she realized what had been niggling at her the night before, after her phone call from DeMarranville. He had mentioned Colt in that slithery voice, had said for her not to bring McKendrick when she made the drop.

Subconsciously she must have noted how odd it was that Damian would know the name of the rough cowboy who had befriended her and her son, but she had been too preoccupied with the idea of Nicky in his hands to register anything else.

"You know each other," she said now.

A muscle twitched along his jawline. "We were partners once. DeMarranville used to be on the job. He was a renegade agent who decided to switch sides."

"This is personal, then."

"For all of us," Beckstead said. "Damian was my protégé."

"That means he knows as much about FBI tactics as the rest of you do," she said.

Colt nodded. ''He was a good agent, which is exactly how he's managed to cover his tracks for the past ten years. By thinking like the FBI.''

Maggie folded her hands together on the table. ''What would you do if this were a normal kidnapping?''

She heard her own words and fought back a sob. ''Listen to me. 'A normal kidnapping,' like there is any such thing. What would you do if your suspect wasn't a former FBI agent?''

''Probably have an agent dress up like you and make the drop surrounded by other undercover operatives, who would jump in and arrest him,'' Special Agent in Charge Beckstead said.

''That's what he'll be expecting, then.''

''Probably,'' Beckstead answered.

She clenched her fingers together so tightly her knuckles turned white. ''So we do what he's *not* expecting. I'll make the drop, just like DeMarranville insisted.''

''No way,'' Colt argued. ''It's too dangerous.''

''He has my son,'' she said vehemently. ''I don't care how dangerous it is. Now let's get on with making a plan.''

Chapter 16

What followed was the longest day of her life. Every minute seemed like hours; the hours like weeks.

She was going crazy from the waiting and the worrying. Finally, in an effort to keep her hands busy at least—if not her mind—she reported to the small cinder block medic office underneath the VIP bleachers and spent a few hours wrapping tender joints for the opening night of the rodeo.

She was winding tape around the bad knee of a hotshot young bull rider from Jackpot, Nevada—and answering in short, distracted monosyllables to his halfhearted attempt at flirting with her—when a knock sounded at the door.

"Yes?" she called, but didn't look up when it opened until the bull rider spoke.

"Hey, McKendrick," her patient said with a nod.

"Rusty." Colt greeted him. "How's the knee?"

"Better. The doc here does one helluva job. If it weren't for her, I would have been sidelined after I got knocked on my butt in Colorado a few weeks ago."

"That's what they pay me for. Patch 'em up so they can

get knocked on their butts all over again the next night.'' Maggie yanked the tape hard enough to earn a wince from Rusty Larsen.

"Hey, watch it," he protested.

"Sorry." She eased up, ashamed that she would take out her storm of emotions on an innocent patient. If she couldn't control herself better than that, she ought to just go back to her trailer and leave someone else to take care of the cowboys.

Colt cleared his throat. "Are you two about done in here?"

"Why?" She didn't bother to keep the icy scorn from her voice.

"I would like to have a word with you."

She spared him a quick look, registering his discomfort in the hard set of his mouth and the Stetson he shifted between his fingers like it was a discus he was ready to hurl, then turned her attention back to Rusty's bad knee. "I don't think I want to talk to you yet."

"Please. Just for a moment."

"Come on, Doc. Talk to the poor guy," Rusty urged, with an enthusiastic grin.

Cowboys always stuck together. It was one of the unwritten rules of the circuit. They could be beating each other to a bloody pulp in a bar fight one minute, but if an outsider stepped in, mortal enemies would join forces against him.

And for all their bluff, cowboys could also be the most romantic souls on earth. She sighed and secured the tape, then straightened. "There you go, Rusty. Be careful tonight and try to put your weight on the other knee when you fall."

"When I fall. Right." He snorted. "When I *jump* off after my bee-yoo-ti-ful eight-second ride, you mean."

"Either way." She returned the tape to the small chest of supplies, careful not to risk another look at Colt.

She'd had all day to think about how he had deceived her. The magnitude of it was only now beginning to hit home. Every word he had said—every gesture, every touch—had been carefully calculated to earn her trust. Nothing had been genuine. She had been an assignment to him and nothing more.

It made her cringe to know how foolish she had been, and how hard he must have been laughing at her willingness to open her life and her heart to him.

"Thanks, Doc," Rusty said after he had yanked on his jeans and his boots. "'Preciate it."

"You're welcome. Good luck tonight." Her smile was forced, her words hollow, but the cowboy didn't seem to mind. He grinned a salute in return and bounded out the door, leaving an awkward silence behind him.

Colt cleared his throat again. It sounded unnaturally loud in the small cinder block enclosure. "I wanted a chance to talk to you before tonight," he said. "To try to clear the air a little."

She remained silent. Nothing he could possibly say would atone for such a betrayal.

"I never wanted to lie to you, Doc."

She didn't want to hear apologies or explanations. She wanted to clutch her anger and shame to her chest like a shield against him. "And yet you did." Her movements were jerky and abrupt as she finished clearing off the exam table for the next patient. "And so well, too. I can certainly see why you're a professional."

"I had no choice."

"In my experience people only say they have no choice when they don't like the alternatives."

"In this case there *were* no alternatives. My assignment was to determine how deeply you were involved in Prescott's dealings. By the time I knew you well enough to figure out you were innocent, it was too late. I couldn't tell you the truth without losing whatever trust you had in me. I thought it was for the best to keep you safe."

"Isn't that convenient for you? Convince yourself you

were doing it all for my good and then you don't have to be bothered by a stupid little thing like scruples.''

''I wanted to tell you a hundred times.''

''But you didn't.''

''Doc—''

She didn't want to hear any more. She wanted to clamp her hands over her ears or, better yet, walk away from him. And yet some masochistic force compelled her on.

''Was anything you told me the truth?'' she asked. ''Did I really have a flat tire that night?''

He shook his head. ''Not until I took a screwdriver to it. I'm sorry, Maggie.''

She felt sick again at her complete gullibility, then stared at him, struck by a sudden thought. ''What about the Broken Spur? Did you really lose it to Joe Redhawk?''

Colt met her accusing gaze with an impassive expression. ''No. It's mine. Joe is my foreman.''

That explained all the currents between them, the strange, amused looks the silent Shoshone wore most of the time while she had been there.

A memory of the bittersweet yearning she had witnessed in Colt surfaced and she frowned. Had even that been a lie? No, she couldn't believe it. The emotion had been too raw, too painful to be feigned.

''Why did you leave it? The ranch, I mean. You obviously love it there. You couldn't have been making that up. Is all this FBI business really worth leaving the home you love?''

He shifted against the wall. How could he possibly explain about the guilt and the shame that had driven him after his father's death. ''No,'' he said gruffly. ''It's not worth it.''

She was quiet for a long time, hands folded together in her lap. When she spoke, her voice sounded small and defeated. ''And what about us? About making love? How did that fit into your lies?''

Her words sliced into him, sharp and brutal. He couldn't blame her for being suspicious. It was no less than he deserved, but it still wounded him. "That was truth, Doc. I swear it."

Her gaze met his and memory flickered for just a moment. But he felt like he was trying to start a fire with wood too wet to burn: the memory died before it could even flare to life.

She looked down at her intertwined fingers. "I wish I could believe you," she murmured.

If you believe nothing else, believe that, he wanted to say, but before he had a chance, the door to the medic office swung open.

Her stepmother, in a glittery scarlet shirt and skintight black jeans, poked her head into the doorway. "Maggie, we need you out in the chutes. One of the wranglers tangled with Corkscrew. Didn't get gored but he was trampled pretty good and took a hard knock to the head. He's still out cold. Paramedics are on their way, but I figured you could get there faster."

After just an instant's hesitation, she grabbed that old leather medical bag never far from her side and rushed out the door, without a backward glance at Colt.

He let out a breath when the door slammed shut behind her. If he was ever going to convince her to forgive him, he was obviously in for a long, hard haul.

And what purpose would it serve to even try, except maybe to make him feel better about what he had done? Even if she did eventually come to understand his motives for living a lie the last few weeks, it couldn't change who he was and what he did.

He was an FBI agent, who would always be waiting for the next assignment. He went undercover, sometimes for months at a time, and when he resurfaced, he was usually so strung out and edgy it took him weeks to decompress.

He couldn't ask her to live with that, even if she would be willing to eventually forget his deception. She would never be happy as the wife of an FBI agent, especially not when she had firsthand knowledge of the kind of violence he faced every day.

She'd be happy living at the Broken Spur.

The thought flickered through his mind, seductive and appealing, and he thought again of those images he'd had the other night when he had come home and found her waiting for him. Of roundups and fishing trips and making love.

Somehow he knew she would love living on the ranch and so would Nicholas. And God knows, the people of rural Montana were always desperate for doctors. She would have plenty of work to keep her busy, if she wanted to hang out a shingle in Ennis and open a practice.

No, that kind of thinking was crazy. He jerked his mind away from the thought. It was crazy and it wouldn't get him anywhere.

Even though it was hard to remember that, when he was looking into those big dark eyes, his role in her life began and ended with this job and that's the way it had to be.

The injured wrangler had already regained consciousness when Maggie arrived at the chutes. Bag held high over her head, she shoved her way through the crowd of people gathered around the cowboy, who was now trying to sit up and was loudly and succinctly swearing a blue streak about Corkscrew and his progenitors.

She had to agree with his sentiments. The brindle bull was one nasty beast. Too bad the ill-tempered ones were always the biggest crowd pleasers.

She set her bag down next to the wrangler and knelt at his side. "I'm Dr. Rawlings. What's your name?"

"Marty," he said through gritted teeth. "Marty O'Sullivan."

"Well, Marty, don't try to get up until I can figure out how badly you're hurt."

The wrangler—just a kid really, with bright red hair and a wild riot of freckles he probably hated—glared at her. "I can tell you exactly how bad I'm hurt, Doc. Damn crazy bull about killed me. Somebody oughta shoot that sumbitch.''

The crowd gathered around seemed to breathe an audible sigh of relief. Maggie did, too. If the wrangler was coherent enough to curse Corkscrew so furiously, he would probably survive.

''It's your hair,'' one of the older cowboys said with a deep, whisky-gruff laugh. ''How many times do I have to tell you to keep your hat on around him?''

The other men laughed, but Maggie barely paid attention to the ribbing as she reached into her bag for her stethoscope. The scope seemed stuck on something. She gave a quick look inside and noticed it had snagged on the brown satin lining. As she tried to twist the earpiece free, she saw that the seam of her bag had begun to fray and the lining had pulled away slightly from the leather.

She caught only a glimpse of something strange and out of place inside the lining. A bandage probably. She concentrated on it only long enough to make a mental note to herself to check it out later, then pulled the stethoscope out and set to work examining the cowboy's injuries.

A few minutes later she finished examining him. ''Everything looks fine, Marty. You might have a slight concussion and a few bruised ribs so they'll probably keep you overnight at the hospital for observation, but it looks like you'll live to bullfight another day.''

She summoned a small smile for him—the best she could do today—just as the paramedics arrived.

After briefing the EMTs on her cursory exam, she left them to transport the wrangler to the local hospital. When she returned to the medic room, Peg was waiting for her, concern in her dark-fringed eyes.

''How you holdin' up, sugar?''

Maggie had been staying in control all day by sheer force of will. Now, at the soft worry in her stepmother's voice, tears formed behind her eyes. She missed her son so acutely it was like a physical ache. *Please, God, let him be safe,* she prayed again.

Ruthlessly she forced the tears back. She had to be strong, for Nicky's sake. "I've had better days," she replied.

"I know." Peg pulled her into her arms for a quick, tight hug. "Only a few more hours and then that little boy will be back with us, safe and sound. You'll see. Colt will get him back for us."

For a few moments Maggie surrendered to the comfort of Peg's maternal embrace and then, when she felt the tears threaten again, she pulled away. "Colt has done enough, don't you think?"

Peg's frown wrinkled the fine network of lines the years and elements had carved on her face. "You're bein' pretty hard on that good-lookin' hunk of cowboy of yours, aren't you?"

"He's an FBI agent, not a cowboy."

"He's a man," Peg corrected. "A man who's hurtin', too."

"It wasn't his son who was kidnapped."

"No, but I have a feelin' he loves that boy as much as he loves the boy's mama."

She opened her mouth to correct her stepmother, then shut it again. She didn't have the energy to argue with Peg when she was in this kind of mood. Maggie knew, though, that Colt didn't love her.

He might want her physically—although she still didn't know for sure whether that just had been part of his deception—but he didn't love her. She had simply been a job to him, just another assignment. As soon as this was over, Colt McKendrick would move on to the next assignment without a backward look.

"I spent six years of my life believing one man's lies. I'm not going to let myself do it again."

Peg snorted on her way out the door. "That cowboy is worth two dozen of that no-good husband of yours. If you're too stubborn to see it, then you don't deserve a man like him.''

Maybe. Twenty-four hours ago she would have agreed completely, but that was before she knew how very stupid she had been, before she had discovered that when it came to things like truth and honesty, Colt McKendrick wasn't so very different from Michael.

Too restless after Peg left to stay in the medic office when no cowboys waited to be treated, she went in search of Agent Beckstead, to find out if he had learned anything more about Nicky's whereabouts.

The familiar weight of her medical bag knocked against her thigh as she walked to the campground and she decided to leave it inside her trailer while she went looking for the agent.

After unlocking the door, she set the bag by the bed, then turned to leave. Just as her hand twisted the doorknob, she remembered the rip she had felt there earlier while tending Marty O'Sullivan.

It wasn't important, she thought. Especially not now when her attention was so completely focused on bringing her son home safely. But some instinct prompted her to investigate it further, anyway. It would only take a moment, after all.

Her fingers felt along the satin lining until she found the slit. Curious. It didn't look large enough for anything to have slipped through, and yet she could plainly see something long and light colored that didn't match the dark underside of the leather.

She pulled it a bit more with her fingernails, careful not to rip the material, just loosen the seam. When she had widened the hole enough for her fingers to slip through, she reached in and grasped the item. It wasn't paper, as she expected, but some kind of soft material. Velvet, maybe, or silk of some kind.

She slid it through width-wise so she didn't have to rip

away more of the lining, then pulled it free and out of the medical bag.

As soon as she saw it, her heart began to pound, and she felt all the blood rush away from her face. Dizzy, she fumbled beside her for the bench seat and sat down hard, staring at her discovery.

It was indeed velvet—a small pouch, really—seven inches long by about five inches wide.

She knew, without even looking at it, what it would contain. Or at least she had a good idea. She hadn't put it there, certainly, and the only other person who would have had access to her bag was Michael.

Had she been carrying it around with her all this time? Packing it from place to place for weeks without ever knowing it was there?

This must be what Damian DeMarranville was looking for, she thought, then frowned. It was large enough to carry a computer disk but certainly not enough money to make it worth DeMarranville's while to kidnap an innocent little boy.

She pulled the silk drawstring on the bag and reached inside. Her fingers first encountered a hard square item and she pulled it out. It was a simple black computer disk with a white lined label that said only "DeM."

There had to be more. There *had* to be. In a frenzied rush, she upended the little velvet pouch, then gasped when a glittery shower of tiny stones rained out.

Diamonds. A veritable fortune in diamonds.

She stared at them, scattered there on the chipped and worn Formica of her humble table, and had to force herself to breathe through the fury suddenly consuming her. *This* was why her son had been kidnapped? Why Michael had died? For a handful of cold little *rocks?*

It was vile. Obscene. Her child was being used as a bargaining chip in a battle for a pile of diamonds.

With an angry sweep of her hand, she shoveled the pile

of stones back into the pouch, thrust the disk in after them, then headed for the door. She had to find Colt.

She didn't stop to consider the irony that Colt would be the first person she wanted to find to show her discovery; she was too consumed with an odd mix of anger and relief.

At least now she would have this in her favor in the grim chess game she played with Damian DeMarranville. She would be able to give him what he wanted and then pray he would play fair and give her back her son.

Since it was right next door, she decided to check Colt's camper first. Instead of Colt, though, the balding Agent Dunbar answered.

"McKendrick's not here," he said when she asked for Colt. "He's over scouting out the drop site with Beckstead."

Ferretlike, his gaze sharpened on the pouch in her hand. "Can I help you with something?"

She started to open her mouth to tell him about her discovery when uneasiness pinched at her and she remembered Colt's animosity toward the agent. She gripped the pouch with suddenly nerveless fingers. "I—no. I believe I'll just go find Colt."

"Does whatever you're holding there have something to do with the case?"

When she didn't answer, he frowned. "As I'm sure you're aware, I'm second in command on this assignment, Dr. Prescott. If whatever you have there is connected to our operation in any way, I really must see it."

His easy tone couldn't completely conceal the layer of steel lurking underneath it.

She weighed her options. She could either ignore his politely worded order, just walk away to find Colt on her own, or she could give in and show Dunbar her discovery.

For some reason she didn't like the agent. He had a shiftiness around his eyes, a hardness around his mouth, that put her off.

But then she hadn't been the best judge of character lately.

The reminder of Colt and the depth of his deception weighed heavily in Dunbar's favor.

After another moment of consideration, she gave a mental shrug. One FBI agent was much the same as another, right? "I think I found what DeMarranville really wants."

She held out the pouch, with it's glittery contents. Dunbar peered inside, then his thin lips stretched into a small, satisfied smile. "You were right to bring this to me," he said.

His fingers covered hers on the bag and a shiver skittered down her spine at their cool pressure. "Thank you, Doctor. I'll take it now."

His high-handedness annoyed her, and that avid gleam in his eyes was beginning to make her uneasy again. She tugged the pouch away. "You know, I think I'd still like to show this to Colt and the other agent. The one in charge. Beckstead, isn't it?"

She started subtly, slowly edging toward the road. "You said they're at the arena? I'll just go look for them there."

She made it only a few steps when she felt those cold, strong fingers clamp around her arm. "I don't think so," Dunbar said. The steel was unsheathed now, hard and cruel. "I've worked too hard to find those diamonds to let you screw things up for me now."

"Don't you mean the disk? The evidence against De-Marranville?" she challenged him.

He lifted a mocking eyebrow. "Right. The disk. I'll take it now. And the diamonds."

She wasn't stupid enough to think he would just turn them over to the other agents. Not with that avarice gleaming in his eyes. He would probably take off as soon as she handed them over, which would leave her right back where she started, without anything to use as a bargaining chip for her son's life.

Not if she could help it. With a great heave, she wrenched her arm away from Dunbar and took off down the road, intent only on finding Colt. She didn't stop to think about his betrayal now. She knew only that he would protect her, would know what to do about the rogue agent.

She only made it a few steps before Dunbar caught her, twisting her arm behind her back so hard tears welled up in her eyes, but she didn't give him the satisfaction of letting them fall.

"Those diamonds should be mine," he growled in her ear, his breath hot and fetid. "I earned them, damn it. I deserve them after all the crap I've done for Damian over the years."

He was working for DeMarranville, too? Just who was she supposed to trust in this whole mess?

Her mind scrambled for an escape plan as he forced her toward her trailer. Only one of them could enter the small enclosure at a time and for the first time she was grateful for the tight quarters.

Once inside, she had a few precious seconds alone before he joined her, but it was enough. Acting completely on instinct, she dropped the pouch and scooped up the first weapon she could find—her trusty cast-iron frying pan.

She didn't give herself time to consider the prudence of her actions or what she would possibly do if she failed. Her son's life was at stake—the only thing that mattered.

Gathering the last vestiges of her courage, she swung the heavy pan over her head and brought it down with a hard thunk. It bounced off Dunbar's temple and he staggered against the door frame, then toppled backward, arms flailing, to the ground.

Maggie grabbed the pouch and ran past him, evading his grasping fingers at her ankles. She rounded the corner of the camp office, only to collide with Colt's hard chest.

His hands reached out to steady her. "What is it, Doc? What's the matter?"

She struggled to catch her breath. "Dunbar—back there—he tried to steal the diamonds—"

"Whoa. Slow down. Start from the beginning. What diamonds?"

She took a deep breath, willing her pulse to slow, her nerves to settle. Finally when the adrenaline rush had ebbed enough to think straight, she shoved the pouch at him. "Look."

He opened the bag, and his eyes widened at its contents. "How did you find them?"

"In my medical case. Michael must have sewn them under the lining somehow."

"What does Dunbar have to do with anything?"

"After I found them, I tried to find you to tell you, but he was at your camper and he said I had to give them to him. When I refused, he tried to take them. He said something about how he'd done enough for DeMarranville over the years that he deserved them."

"That son of a bitch. *He's* the leak."

"Exactly."

Both of them turned at the cultured tones of Colt's superior. He walked around the side of the building, pushing a handcuffed Dunbar ahead of him. A Technicolor bruise bloomed above one eyebrow.

"You have no proof of anything," Dunbar snarled.

"Wrong." The special agent in charge offered a small, satisfied smile. "I have all the proof I need, thanks to the doctor here.

Maggie stared. "What did I do?"

"You offered the right bait. He's been under suspicion for some time but it threw us off when he didn't go to Damian immediately with your whereabouts. But you were looking for the diamonds yourself, weren't you, Dunbar? That's why you didn't want DeMarranville to know where she was until we found them. Until you stole them yourself and had a chance to leave the country, right?"

"You have no proof of anything," the agent repeated.

Again the small smile played around Beckstead's mouth. "I guess it's just your bad luck that I came looking for the doctor when you decided to make your move. I heard every word. And may I say, Dr. Rawlings, you wield that frying pan very well.''

"You hit him with your frying pan?'' Colt stared in disbelief.

She flushed, remembering the times she had almost wielded it against him. "I didn't know what else to do.''

"You did exactly the right thing,'' Beckstead said. "If you can be as cool and quick thinking tonight, the operation should go off without a hitch.''

Chapter 17

Colt checked his watch one more time. Two minutes to ten—120 seconds to zero hour.

He shifted on the hard metal bleachers and pulled the high-powered binoculars back to his eyes, unerringly focusing on Maggie standing a few feet away from the entrance to the arena. The powerful binoculars brought her so close he felt like he could reach out and smooth a hand down her hair or rub a thumb over those pale smudges below her eyes.

Someone who didn't know her would probably never guess at the riot of emotions he knew must be going a hundred miles a minute inside her as she waited for Damian to show up with her son. She appeared outwardly calm, her delicate features composed. But he could see the tension in her tightly clasped hands, in the rigid set of her shoulders, and in the way her beautiful dark eyes never stopped scanning the road.

He hated being so far away from her, that the magnified image was only an illusion. In that moment he would have given anything he owned—*anything*—to be there with her, to hold her close and be able to promise her everything would turn out okay.

Not that she wanted that from him. Or anything else, for that matter, except his help rescuing her son.

He felt as helpless as a damn baby up here on the bleachers, forced to watch everything from three hundred feet away and twenty feet up, but she had been adamant that he stay out of sight.

"DeMarranville said I had to wait alone," she had said, with a firmness that he thought probably surprised her as much as it had him and the rest of the FBI team. "He mentioned you specifically, Colt. If he sees you anywhere in the area, who knows what he'll do?"

He knew she was right, that Damian's unpredictability was one of the things that made him so dangerous—that and his streak of utter ruthlessness. Still, the knowledge didn't take away the impotent frustration churning through him at being sidelined.

She had also refused to wear a wire for the same reason, that if he detected it, Damian might consider it a breach of their agreement for her to show up alone. They had to be content with the audio from the mikes worn by the agents nearby.

Colt *had* insisted, over her objections, that undercover agents be placed just a few feet away from her. One manned the ticket booth, another posed as a vendor selling beer, and two more posed as an amorous couple flirting outside the six-foot-high fence surrounding the grounds.

"How's she doing?"

Beckstead's voice crackled in his ear. The SAC waited with an unlikely team of reinforcements out of view for phase two of their plan, which would go into action after Nicholas was back safely in his mother's arms.

Colt spoke into the tiny, voice-activated microphone pinned to his shirt. "She looks tense. What do you expect? Wouldn't you be, if you knew you'd been set up?"

He knew his anger came out loud and clear to his superior and to everybody else monitoring the voice communications, but he didn't give a damn. He still couldn't believe Beckstead would purposely endanger civilians—a woman and child, no less—to set a trap for a dirty agent.

It made him sick even thinking about it. Beckstead had *known* Dunbar was on Damian's payroll and he'd all but delivered Maggie and Nicky to the bastard on a silver platter.

He wasn't at all appeased by the SAC's explanation that he had people inside Damian's circle ready to move in an instant when DeMarranville found her. This operation was proof that Damian, as always, had been a step ahead of them.

He shoved his fury aside. This wasn't the time for it. Now they had to concentrate on Nicky and bringing him home.

"Any sign of them?" Colt asked.

"Not from this direction. Nuñez, you see anything?"

"Negative, sir." One of the other FBI agents Beckstead had called to join the team from the Salt Lake City office answered. "Wait a minute. Possible suspect vehicle approaching."

"McKendrick. Can you confirm?"

He moved the lenses from Maggie to scan the road, and his pulse hitched up a notch at the sight of a big dark limousine approaching the arena from the west. It had to be Damian. Nobody else would show up to a rodeo in a limousine, especially when the show was just about over, when the only event left was the bullriding.

"Affirmative," he growled. "Suspects in sight." He flipped the binoculars back toward Maggie and inched forward on the bleachers, not taking his gaze off her now for even a second.

Everything else—the buzz of conversation around him, the announcer's crackly voice on the loudspeaker, the cheers and whistles of the crowd—faded as his concentration centered only on Maggie and on the long midnight limousine with tinted windows that pulled up alongside her.

She looked pale, suddenly, and so tired. Through the binoculars he could see her mouth tighten, her lips tremble ever so slightly. Fierce pride washed through him as she stepped forward to face the limousine despite the fear he knew must be pumping through her veins.

The woman had guts. He had always known it, but maybe she would believe it of herself now, too.

The rear door swung out and that son of a bitch Carlo Santori climbed out and greeted her with his usual smirk. His white-blond hair shone in the moonlight and his designer suit looked ridiculously out of place surrounded by jeans and cowboy hats.

If possible, Maggie paled a shade lighter at seeing the man Colt knew had killed Michael Prescott—and probably numerous others they didn't know about—but she took a few deep breaths and seemed to regain control over her emotions.

Santori said something Colt couldn't hear over the agents' microphones and made an obvious gesture for her to get inside the limo but Maggie shook her head in defiance and pointed to the ground where she stood, her hand only trembling a little.

"What's happening?" he said quietly into his mike.

"Damian wanted to talk to her inside the limo but she refused," the agent in the ticket booth murmured.

Good girl, he thought. *Don't get in the car. Make the trade on your own turf.*

She apparently won the first round of their stalemate. After a few tense moments, Damian climbed out of the limousine, as arrogant and cocksure as always.

"DeMarranville's getting out," the man in the ticket booth told those out of visual range.

"He's asking for his merchandise," the agent posing as a beer vendor whispered.

Colt focused in as Maggie produced the pouch from inside the sweater she wore against the night breeze. Damian moved to take it from her, but she quickly snatched her arm back and stuck the pouch behind her with a shake of her head.

Her mouth moved again and Colt growled a frustrated oath that he couldn't make out what she was saying, forgetting that everyone else on the channel could hear it.

"Something wrong?" Beckstead's voice sounded in his earpiece.

"She won't give him the pouch until she sees her son," the beer vendor said.

Colt had guessed as much. He might not be able to hear her from this distance, but he knew Maggie well enough by now to figure what she would do. Exactly what he would have done under the same circumstances.

"Any visual affirmative on the kid?"

A soft chorus of "no" answered Beckstead's question.

"Wait a minute," Colt said. He focused on the limousine door, opening with agonizing slowness. Then a little blond head peeked around. He would have run to his mother's side, but Santori kept a restraining arm on his shoulder. "There. He's out."

"He look okay?"

"As far as I can tell." Colt answered.

His gaze shifted again to Maggie. She reached one hand out as if to touch her son, then she lifted her fingers to her quivering mouth. Abruptly she straightened and pulled the pouch from behind her back and handed it to Damian. Only after he looked inside it did the bastard give a nod to Carlo, who released Nicky.

Maggie crouched and opened her arms and the boy ran into them, eagerly throwing his own little arms around his mother's neck while she touched his back, his hair, his face.

A wave of poignant emotion crashed over him—relief and tenderness and a fierce joy, all wrapped into one.

"She's got him," he said through the thickness suddenly clogging his throat.

"Good. Good," Beckstead replied. "Now on to phase two."

Maggie was supposed to retreat to the medic office with Nicky to wait for Colt while the SAC and his reinforcements—a dozen agents and the Weber County Mounted Posse—would surround DeMarranville and apprehend him as soon as the limousine pulled away from the rodeo arena, where innocent people could be hurt if DeMarranville fought back.

Colt started down the bleacher stairs to meet her. He was halfway down when a low "uh-oh" sounded in his earpiece.

"What?" he growled. "What's wrong?"

The male half of the amorous couple against the fence spoke. "Problems. Santori's not letting her go alone. Damian just said he wants him to escort her back to her trailer."

Colt shoved aside a man coming up the west side of the bleacher stairs and jostled his way to the edge for a better view.

He swore long and viciously when he caught her in his sights again. Maggie, with Nicky holding tight to her hand, was hurrying away from the arena, toward the dark, densely forested banks of the Ogden River on the edge of the rodeo grounds and the maze of pens there that held stock not being used for the night's events.

His blood turned to ice when he focused in on Carlo Santori casually strolling along a few paces behind her. He knew damn well the hand Santori held at a stiff angle in front of him wasn't holding a bouquet of flowers.

"What should we do? Take him down?" the beer vendor asked.

There was no way they could do that without putting Maggie and Nicky directly in the crossfire, exactly what she had been worried about.

"No," he snapped, his mind spinning furiously. If he could get to the pens before them, he might be able to get the edge on Santori. It was a slim chance, but it was the only damn chance they had.

"Everybody stay put. I'm going to head them off."

He raced down the stairs two at a time, barely missing a man carrying a trayful of drinks on his way up the bleachers and a woman with a baby and a diaper bag on her way down.

"McKendrick, wait for back up," Beckstead shouted in his earpiece. "Don't be a damn cowboy on this one."

He reached the ground and started running through the crowd toward the river. "I *am* a damn cowboy. That's why you wanted me on this case, right?"

"Be careful."

He didn't answer the command. "Ending audio communication," he snapped, and yanked out the earpiece as he ran, tossing it to the ground. He couldn't afford to be distracted by voices in his head, by Beckstead yelling commands in his ear. Not when lives were at stake—the lives of the two people he loved more than anything else in the world.

He swung around the pens, sending up a fierce prayer that he wasn't too late, that he could be fast enough and smart enough to save them.

If he couldn't, Carlo Santori might as well kill him, too.

With one eye on the small, dangerous-looking gun almost in her back and one eye on her son, Maggie clasped Nicky's hand tightly and prayed harder than she'd ever done in her life.

She should have *known* DeMarranville wouldn't just allow her to take her son and fade away back into the rodeo crowd once she gave him what he wanted. She should have known the minute she looked into that merciless face that he wasn't the kind to play by rules of honor.

If she had been thinking at all, she would have realized that after he had what he wanted, she and her son would be completely expendable to him. But once the exchange had been made—once Nicky was safe with her once again—she had been so weak with relief she hadn't paid attention to the warning screech of her instincts until DeMarranville had instructed Carlo to escort them back to their trailer.

She had demurred and had told them they were fine, that she could find her own way, but the devil had insisted.

"What kind of gentlemen would we be if we let you wander through a raucous crowd like this alone—a defenseless woman and a small child?" he had asked, his voice tainted with that mocking edge. "No, Carlo, see Dr. Prescott and our young guest to their lodgings."

Alarm shot through her like hot oil at the look exchanged between the two men. Suddenly she knew that the man with the dead eyes who had killed Michael wouldn't be escorting them back to their trailer, but somewhere far more ominous.

Away from the hard glare of the floodlights in the arena, he had produced that sleek, shiny gun, the same one, probably, that had killed Michael, and urged her toward the dark forest of trees near the river with that deadly smirk.

She knew what he intended, that he wanted them away from the crowd for it. She wanted to weep and beg him for her child's life, but she knew she would find no clemency here, and so she had obeyed, searching her mind frantically for a way to escape.

They would get no help from the undercover agents Colt had insisted on, she realized that, too. They were too far away now to do anything.

"I want to see Colt," Nicky said now, a tired whine in his voice. "Where is he?"

Her eyes flashed to the crowd. Had he seen her leave with Santori? Was he watching her now going to her death?

"I don't know, sweetheart," she whispered.

"I missed you, Mommy."

Her heart lurched at the quiet words. She squeezed his fingers, wishing she had even a moment to gather him close, to bury her face in his hair and inhale his sleepy-little-boy scent. "I missed you too, Nicky."

"Don't make me go with them again, please, Mommy?"

"I won't." Her voice broke on the words, but she battled for control. "I promise." She would get him out of this. No matter what she had to do, she would protect her son.

The air had reached dew point and the grass was wet and slick beneath the thin canvas of her sneakers. It smelled of animals and, incongruously, the sticky-sweet scent of cotton candy.

The rodeo-goers suddenly sent up an excited cheer at something happening inside the arena and Santori paused and turned at the sound for just an instant. She should do something now. Think! Before she could come up with a plan, though, he resumed walking.

They were almost past the pens. She could hear the gurgle of the river mingled with the lowing of cattle and the occasional high whinny of a nearby bronco.

This was it. She was running out of time. If they were going to survive, she was going to have to come up with something fast. She could rush him, she supposed, try to take the gun away from him. She dismissed the thought instantly. Not only did he outweigh her by probably sixty pounds, but she was fairly certain Michael wasn't the first man he'd ever killed. He wouldn't be deterred by such a foolish attempt.

It would be suicidal. On the other hand, she was going to die anyway, and if it would give Nicky time to slip away from his father's killer, she had to try.

Just as they passed the last row of pens, she braced her muscles and opened her mouth to order Nicky to run when she heard a flurry of movement behind her, then rough, menacing words. "Move and you die."

She stopped abruptly, her hand tightening on Nicky's, then she realized Santori had stopped as well, that the harshly spoken words hadn't come from him.

"You know the drill, Carlo. Hands up."

That drawl! She recognized it. Finally daring to breathe, she swiveled to look behind her. In the dim moonlight she saw Colt standing so close to Santori, they had both merged into one dark shadow.

He must have slipped through the darkness, she realized, and come around the pen. Relief flooded through her, so intense her knees threatened to give out.

"Okay," Colt said, when Santori obeyed, "now, real nice and easy, drop your weapon."

Santori complied and she heard a whisper of noise as Colt kicked the gun under the wooden fence of the nearest pen, far enough that it couldn't be retrieved without climbing over.

"Doc, you okay?"

Her gaze sharpened on the gun Colt had shoved into Santori's ear. "I'm all right. A little shaky."

"Hi, Colt!" Nicky chirped. He would have launched himself at his hero but Maggie held tight to his hand.

"Hey, partner," Colt said.

He took his gaze off Santori for only an instant, just long enough to give Nicky a reassuring grin, but it was enough for the killer to shove an elbow into his gut. She heard Colt's breath leave him in a whoosh and saw him instinctively step back a pace.

Without blinking those cold, empty eyes, Santori grabbed her, yanking her in front of him, away from her son. She felt brutal fingers digging into her arm then, worse, the cold, sharp metal of a knife at her throat.

Santori's mouth curled into a deadly smirk. "Move and she dies." He parodied Colt's earlier's words. "Then again, you might as well move, FBI. She's going to die either way."

"Mommy!" Nicky cried out. She watched, agonized, as he tried to get at her, but Colt wouldn't let him and shoved the boy behind him.

"Let her go, Santori," he growled, his jaw tight. "Let her go and maybe I won't kill you."

DeMarranville's hired gun just bared his teeth in a smile that didn't come close to reaching his dead eyes. "Big talk,

FBI.'' He gave Maggie a shake that rattled her teeth. ''You're the doctor. Tell your boyfriend here what would happen if I made a nice, neat cut right here.'' He pressed the blade against her carotid artery.

She met his gaze, making no attempt to hide her hatred. ''I'll bleed to death.''

''Exactly. You must have been first in your class.'' He sneered at Colt. ''If you don't want the kid here to watch his mama bleed to death like a stuck pig, I suggest you drop your weapon. Real nice and easy,'' he added, in that same mocking voice.

''Don't do it, Colt,'' she said. ''It doesn't matter. Just take Nicky and get out of here.'' She knew Carlo Santori would take Colt's gun and kill them all. She didn't want to die, but she would if it would save them.

''Shut up,'' Carlo said, giving her another hard shake. ''Drop it, McKendrick.''

After another moment's indecision, Colt glanced at Nicky out of the corner of his gaze. He must have decided Carlo wouldn't do away with his one advantage—her—while Colt was still holding the gun.

''Nick,'' he said urgently, ''I need you to run as fast as you can and find your Grandma Peg or Cheyenne over at the rodeo, all right? Don't come back, just stay there until I come get you. Hurry.''

''No!''

''Yes. You have to. I'll take care of your mama, I promise.''

With one last scared look at her, Nicky obeyed, slipping through the damp grass as he ran. She closed her eyes and said a silent prayer of gratitude. At least Nicky would be safe.

Carlo hissed between his teeth and pressed the knife harder against her throat. ''Why did you do that?'' He asked Colt. For the first time, she heard emotion in his voice—fury. An instant later she felt a hot prick against her skin and knew he must have drawn blood.

Colt's gaze focused on the burning spot and something wild and furious flared in his eyes. "You wanted my weapon. Here you go." He pushed a lever on the gun—the safety, she assumed—and dropped the handgun into the grass.

Maggie drew in a sharp breath as she watched it fall. He had to know that the moment Santori picked up the gun, he would kill Colt. Why would he do such a crazy, suicidal thing?

In that single instant she realized the truth, the truth she had known all along. Colt was nothing like Michael. Even though they had both lied to her, everything Colt had done had been for her own good. He had only been trying to protect her, to watch over her. That's all he had ever done. Even now, he was willing to put his life on the line for hers.

"Good," Santori said. "Now slide it over here."

"Let her go first."

"And have you pick up your Glock and kill me as soon as I do? What do you take me for, FBI? Slide your weapon over here first, and then I'll let the doctor go."

After a tense moment Colt nudged the gun with his foot and sent it scooting slowly across the five or six feet that separated them.

She couldn't just watch him die. She had stood by and done nothing while Michael was killed, but she refused to the same thing while Santori killed Colt. Not this time. She loved him too much.

If she could provide a diversion, it might give Colt enough time to step forward and beat Santori to the gun.

Santori returned the knife to the sheath under his suit coat then stepped away from her to reach down for the handgun. Here was her chance, possibly her only one.

When he was bent over and slightly off balance, she took a deep breath, drawing on the last reserve of courage inside her, and shoved against him with all her strength, sending both of them careening into the wooden slats of the fence.

He must not have had a steady hold on the weapon. At the surprise attack, it slipped out of his hand and went spiraling into the air, falling not far from Santori's own weapon inside the pen.

"Bitch. You stupid bitch." He pushed her away and drew back his fist. She had less than an instant to prepare, when the world exploded into jagged shards of agony.

She reeled and fell, clutching the cheek he had struck. He pulled his fist back, prepared to hit her again, but before the fist could connect, Colt was on him. He shoved him away and back against the fence, pummeling him over and over, fury in his eyes.

The wood fence groaned and shuddered with the impact of each punch, but after a moment of shocked stillness, Santori began to fight back. He brought his hands up to deflect Colt's blows, then started returning the punches with lethal force.

Maggie scrambled to her feet, her bruised face forgotten, and watched helplessly while the two men pounded each other. Their grunts and curses filled the air, and the constant shaking of the fence, as first one man was shoved against it than the next, seemed to be riling the animals inside the warren of pens. Loud, anxious whinnies sounded from the broncs, and the cattle joined in with upset snorts.

After several moments of tussling, Colt seemed to be getting the upper hand. With one powerful heave, he shoved Santori facedown to the ground and thrust a knee in his back, yanking one arm behind his back while he reached for a set of handcuffs she now saw dangled from one of his belt loops. "You're under arrest," he panted out, "for the murder of Michael Prescott and the attempted murder of Maggie and Nicholas Prescott."

Even with his cheek pressed against the grass and a knee in his back, Santori's eyes held no expression as Colt started to handcuff one hand. It was eerie, she thought, looking into those dead eyes. Then to her horror, she realized Santori was reaching with the other hand for the knife at his side.

"Colt," she yelled. "The knife."

The words were barely out of her mouth when Santori grunted and swung the knife at Colt's stomach. At the last instant, Colt stumbled back, avoiding the blade, but his movement also freed Santori from the knee hold. The handcuffs swung from one hand as Michael's killer lunged for the FBI agent with the knife.

"Maggie, get the hell out of here while you can," Colt growled.

Not a chance. She wasn't going to leave him here alone, even if she couldn't do anything but watch. The two men moved in a savage ballet, one parrying, the other backing away, then to her horror, Colt reached in to try to grab the weapon away.

The two wrestled for a few moments, then she heard a low, muffled groan and both men froze. Who had been stabbed? She couldn't tell amid the tangle of arms and legs. Finally, with excruciating slowness, they separated. Santori backed away, leaving Colt clutching his rib cage, where a crimson stain began to soak the blue cotton of his shirt.

"Colt!" she screamed.

He looked at her, his eyes glazed with pain. "Get out of here," he growled again.

"Stupid FBI bastard," Santori muttered, shoving Colt to the ground, then she heard an ominous crack as he viciously stomped a boot hard on his left temple.

Santori straightened his jacket, sent her that mocking smirk and began to climb the wooden fence into the pen to retrieve the handguns inside.

She saw him go, but barely registered it, concerned only for Colt. Rushing to his side, she felt for a pulse. It was there, weaker than normal, but still there. Santori's violent kick must have knocked him out. He didn't even move when she yanked at his shirt, sending buttons popping off in her rush to examine the stab wound.

She probed at the gaping hole, then saw his eyes flutter open. They were disoriented at first, then they focused on something behind her.

"Just take it easy," she murmured. "You'll be—"

Her breath left in whoosh as Colt yanked her down to his chest, then with a grunt, he rolled over, pinning her beneath him.

She could barely see over his shoulder, but now she realized Santori stood inside the pen, holding both his weapon and Colt's and aiming one right at them.

Maggie braced herself for the impact. She was going to die, but at least she would die in the arms of the man she loved.

She should tell him, she thought. She couldn't die without letting him know how she felt.

"Colt," she began, but stopped when she felt a strange vibration against the ear that was smashed to the ground.

She tried to see over Colt's shoulder again and looked up just in time to see a massive shape thunder toward Santori. Corkscrew! Peg's bull must have been upset by the commotion around his pen!

Santori must have finally heard the animal. He turned at the last minute and fired the gun, but the shot went wild and the bull kept coming, fury blazing from his small black eyes.

DeMarranville's hitman didn't have time to squeeze off another shot. With the speed that made the brindle bull a favorite on the circuit, Corkscrew reached him just seconds later with an angry bellow, and then Maggie heard a terrible, agonized cry and then the rending of flesh and the crunch of bones as his sharp horns found their target.

And then there was only silence, broken by the ragged sound of their breathing.

Chapter 18

Hours later, too keyed up to sleep despite the exhaustion that made her feel jittery and off balance, Maggie sat at the table inside her trailer and watched her son sleeping in his loft bed, safe and sound once more.

He was so beautiful, with those little freckles dusting his nose and that blond widow's peak. A world full of miracles wrapped up in a little bundle of energy with a gap-toothed grin and mischief in his eyes.

She smiled gently now as he rolled over in his sleep, facing away from her. Even as her mouth twisted into a smile, she felt the tears of reaction build in her throat again, as they had done repeatedly in the hours since their ordeal had ended with Carlo Santori being gored to death by Peg's meanest bull.

How would she have survived if something had happened to her son? If Colt hadn't been there, if he hadn't risked his life for both of them?

Colt. There was the other reason she sat here in the dark

predawn hours, unable to close her eyes and succumb to the sleep her body needed so desperately.

She had called McKay-Dee Hospital, where the paramedics had taken him, just an hour ago, and the duty nurse told her he was sleeping comfortably and would probably be released in just a few days.

She knew from earlier phone calls to the hospital's emergency room that the knife had miraculously missed all of his major organs, although it had nicked a rib and come dangerously close to his spleen. She hated getting the information secondhand and had wanted to go to the hospital with him to take care of his stab wound herself, but he wouldn't let her.

"Your boy needs you right now," he had said, with that soft drawl. "He's had a big scare, and right now he needs his mama to hold him and tell him everything's going to be all right."

He was right. She had known it, that Nicky had to be her priority. She had stayed for her son's sake, but also because it was obvious Colt didn't want her at the hospital.

Even while she worked to stop the bleeding before the paramedics arrived, he had avoided her gaze and made it a point to keep from touching her as much as he could.

He couldn't have made it more plain: now his job was over, he just wanted to move on, wanted them out of his life. And how could she blame him? She had made it just as plain that she preferred it that way, that she and Nicky would be just fine without him.

She sighed softly and rubbed her fist at the sudden ache in her heart. She was such a liar. She missed him already, his laughter and his teasing gentleness with Nicholas and the vibrant, sensuous energy that infused her whenever he was around.

What would she ever do without him?

She would go on. *That's* what she would do. She had become an expert at rebuilding her life since she had first gathered her courage and walked out on her husband six months ago. She had done it before and she could do it again.

She would just load up this broken-down trailer and head her battered old pickup down the highway until she and Nicky found a nice little town to settle in. Somewhere out here in the rural West, a town in need of a good family doctor. She would open a practice and buy Nicky a horse and try to live with this aching hole in her heart where a blue-eyed cowboy with a teasing grin and work-worn hands used to live.

She sighed again. It sounded abnormally loud in the otherwise quiet trailer, but not loud enough to mask the rustle of sound from outside.

Probably just the wind, she thought, but pushed aside the curtain, anyway, to make sure. The full moon sneaked out from behind a cloud just then, and she thought she saw movement next to the big pine tree across the street.

Someone stood there watching her trailer. And by the width of the shoulders and that long-legged stance, she knew exactly who it was. For just an instant, fierce joy spilled over her—that he was here and that he was all right—then common sense intervened.

Was the man completely crazy? Her mouth tightened. He had just sustained a major abdominal injury and a possible concussion. He shouldn't even be out of the hospital, let alone walking around in the middle of the night.

Her professional instincts inflamed, she shoved open the door and hurried down the steps to confront him. "What are you doing here?" she demanded. "Why aren't you in the hospital?"

His mouth stretched into that characteristic grin, but she saw with concern that it looked a little ragged around the edges. "Nice to see you, too, Doc. I released myself on my own recognizance. Figured I could recuperate on my own at the ranch as well as I can at any hospital."

"You are absolutely nuts. You need to be under the care of a qualified physician."

"Are you applying for the job?" He tried to grin again, but she could see the pain there.

"Sit down," she ordered, leading him toward the picnic table at her campsite. When he followed her docilely, she knew he must be hurting. "You're going to tear out your stitches with this kind of nonsense. What were you thinking?"

"Do you know that when you go into doctor mode, your voice gets all prim and crisp around the edges? It's very sexy."

She flushed but refused to let him distract her. "What are you doing here, Colt?"

"I hate hospitals. Don't take it personally, Doc, but they give me the willies. All those nurses with their needles and their quiet voices and their sensible shoes." He shuddered. "Makes me itchy just thinking about it."

Good grief. The man was a hardened FBI agent who could face down a cold-blooded killer without even blinking, but a bunch of nurses made him nervous?

"Get over it," she snapped. "You need to be in the hospital."

"I'm fine, I swear. I just stopped by to check on you and Nicky, make sure you're both okay after what happened earlier. In a couple of hours, when it gets light, I figured I'd get somebody to help me load Scout so I can pull out."

She had known it, of course, that he would be moving on as soon as he could, but hearing him say the words made her feel as if she was the one who had taken a knife to the gut. "Where are you going?"

He shrugged, a ripple of movement in the darkness. "I have some vacation coming to me. A lot of vacation, actually—Beckstead promised me two months once this investigation was done. I figure in a week or so I'll be as good as new. That should still give me about seven weeks to help out at the Broken Spur.''

''Will you be able to stay that long?'' she asked quietly.

He shot her a quick look, then gazed up at the night sky. ''I don't know. Maybe.''

She was suddenly sick to death of all the secrets between them. There were still so many things she didn't understand.

Like how he could make love to her with such tenderness when she was just another assignment to him. She quickly pushed the stray thought away. That wasn't what she meant at all.

She forced herself to concentrate on one of the mysteries she might just have a chance of solving. ''Why just 'maybe'? What keeps you away from the Broken Spur? I know you love the ranch, I could see it in your eyes when we were there.''

''It's hard to explain.''

''Your father?'' It was just a guess, but she knew she was right when his gaze flashed to hers. All teasing was gone now. There was guilt there and those deep, deep shadows.

She expected him to deny it, to offer some glib comment, but he shrugged again.

''All he ever wanted was for me to stay on the Broken Spur and take over for him. When he was alive, I was so busy trying to prove I could be better than just some dirt-poor Montana rancher, first in college, then on the circuit. I was so afraid of turning into him, old before my time, with nothing to talk about but beef prices and feed ratios.''

She ached to reach a hand out and comfort him. To fight it, she pressed her fingers tightly together. ''And after he died?''

He shrugged. ''I tried to stay for a while, but it felt wrong. I wrestled with it for a couple of months, but then I couldn't do it anymore. Here I was living his dream but he wasn't there to see it. Because of me.''

''Oh, Colt. Your father's death wasn't your fault.''

"Intellectually, I know that. But in here," he tapped his chest with his fingertips, "that's another story. If he hadn't come looking for me, if I hadn't been drinking and fighting with anything that moved, he wouldn't have had to come get me and he probably wouldn't have died. That's a pretty hard thing to face."

He paused for a moment, then looked at her. "Everything at the ranch reminds me of it. I can usually stand it for a while, but eventually I get too antsy and I have to move on."

They sat in silence for a while as the campground slept around them. She yearned to help him. He had given her back her son, and for that she owed him everything. If she could make him see things from a different perspective, perhaps it would repay her debt. At least a little.

"Do you blame me or Nicky because you were stabbed tonight?" she finally asked.

He stared at her. "Of course not."

"But Santori never would have stabbed you if you hadn't come after us, if you had stayed in the arena where you were out of harm's way."

"It was my job to come after you."

Would you have come after us if it hadn't *been your job?* she wanted to ask, but knew she never could. He had made no promises, offered no false declarations of love.

Maybe she had even imagined that soft tenderness lurking in the depths of those blue eyes when he held her and caressed her.

This wasn't about her, anyway, she reminded herself. This was about Colt and trying to exorcise the ghosts that haunted him in the one place where he should have been able to find peace in the hard world he lived in.

"So why do you blame yourself because your father did what any good father would have done? He came looking for his son to protect him, because he didn't want you to be hurt. I didn't know him, of course, but from what you've said about him, I can't believe he's the kind of man who would ever hold you responsible for what happened or who would ever blame you for his own choices.''

Wasn't that just like his Maggie? If he hadn't been aching so bad at the idea of never seeing her again—not to mention the fiery hole in his gut—he would have laughed.

She had been through hell just a few hours before, something that would have traumatized most men he knew. In the last two months she had seen her husband murdered right in front of her, had been terrorized and hunted by a group of ruthless killers and had been duped by one of the government's best liars.

But here she was trying to comfort him because she didn't want him feeling guilty over Jack McKendrick's heart attack.

Lord, he loved her. It was like a hot, heavy ache inside him, worse than a hundred knife wounds, especially when he knew he could never tell her how he felt.

If he did, she might feel obligated to say things she didn't mean, out of gratitude or some stupid sense of obligation.

She deserved so much more than what he could offer. She deserved somebody who could be there at night instead of off on some assignment God knows where.

Nick deserved a father he could count on, somebody who could show up at his baseball games and help him with his homework and do more at his birthday parties than show up and sit there like a mannequin.

They sure as hell deserved better than a burned-out lawman with a whole damn semi full of baggage.

What did it matter, anyway? He had just spent three weeks living a lie, completely deceiving her. He didn't exactly have the best kind of track record with her when it came to the truth—what made him think she would even believe him if he told her how he felt? Why should she believe anything he said, after what he had done?

He blew out a breath and deliberately turned the conversation away from the Broken Spur. ''What about you? What are your plans?''

With Damian in custody and the disk—and his myriad financial records—as evidence, the FBI had enough on him to see that he was put away for a long time. He doubted that her testimony would even be needed, especially with Santori dead.

He knew he should have been elated that Damian wouldn't see the light of day for a long, long time. But all he felt was this hollow ache.

She gave a soft, sad smile. "I have another month left on my contract with the rodeo sponsors, but after that I'm not sure what we'll do. I suppose I could go back to San Francisco, back to the clinic, but I'm not sure I want to do that now."

She shrugged. "Maybe I'll start over. I was just thinking that I would try to find a small town to settle in. Somewhere out here in the West, where I could make a difference. Wyoming, maybe. Or Idaho."

What about Montana? The words hovered on his tongue but, of course, he could never ask her, especially when he didn't know how long he would even be staying.

"I guess I can go anywhere now," she continued. "Have trailer, will travel."

The clouds parted for a moment, giving him a better glimpse of her in the moonlight, and he was shocked by the shadows under her eyes and the wobble in her smile.

She must be exhausted. And here he was keeping her up even later. "You need to rest, Doc. What were you doing awake at this hour, anyway? Especially after everything that's happened in the last two days?"

"I didn't want to take my eyes off Nicky for even a moment."

"How's he doing?"

"He's fine. Children can be amazingly resilient. He was more worried about you being hurt than anything else." She paused. "You know, he's really going to miss you."

What about you? Will you miss me, too? He cleared his

throat. "Let me know where you eventually settle and I'll come visit. Just call the Broken Spur, and Joe can give me a message if I'm not there."

She stood up from the picnic table. "I don't think that's such a good idea, Colt."

The ache in his gut intensified. Walking away from her was so hard, the hardest thing he'd ever done. "Okay. Sure. You're probably right. If you think that's best, I understand."

"Do you?"

"I lied to you. I can't expect you to just forgive me for that, to act like it never happened. Besides, it was a job and now that it's over, we should probably just go our separate ways."

If anything, her smile became even more wobbly. "That's right. It was just a job to you, wasn't it."

"Doc—"

"I need to go back inside, Colt. Nicky might wake up."

He had hurt her. He could see the pain in her eyes. "I'm sorry, Maggie. I'm so sorry." For everything, for the lies and the betrayal and for not being the sort of man who could give her promises.

"You have nothing to be sorry about." She folded her hands together. "Nothing at all. You saved our lives, gave me back my son, and I can never repay you for that."

"You don't owe me anything."

She was silent for several moments, then she smiled that sad smile again. "Goodbye, Colt. I— Goodbye. And thank you. For everything."

With that, she turned around and walked to her trailer, without ever knowing that she took his heart with her.

Notepad in hand, Maggie took inventory of the supplies she might need for the remaining two weeks of her rodeo contract. She was getting a little low on suture kits. And she could probably use another couple bottles of antiseptic.

She studied the one remaining bottle and it brought into

sharp focus a memory of the night she sat at Colt's table and cleaned his hand after he cut it fixing her flat tire, the first time she had felt that wild, fluttery attraction toward him.

She sighed. It had been two weeks since she walked away from him in Utah, and she couldn't seem to go five minutes without him filling her thoughts.

Everything seemed to remind her of him: turkey sandwiches and Wrangler jeans and a night sky overflowing with constellations. She had just about made a fool of herself earlier in the day when she had spied a dark-haired cowboy riding a buckskin horse toward her, but it had turned out to be somebody else.

The nights were the worst, when she would lie there on her uncomfortable bed in the trailer and replay in vivid detail the time she had spent in his arms at the Broken Spur. The memories would leave her aching and restless and feeling more alone than she ever had in her life.

She pushed the thought away. She was doing okay. Better than okay. Wasn't she? Finally free of the fear of De-Marranville's men that had been her constant companion for so long, she was finally able to relax and enjoy her work again. She was keeping busy, she was sending out feelers to find out what communities might be in need of a doctor with her skills, she was taking time to play with Nicky.

Who was she kidding? She blew out a breath and shoved the antiseptic to the back of the supply cupboard, way back where she couldn't see it anymore. She *wasn't* okay. She was lonely and miserable and missed Colt like crazy.

Nicky missed him, too. Her son asked a hundred times a day when Colt was coming back or when they would be going to the ranch again to see Colt and Star. No matter how many times she tried to explain to him that Colt had been sent to protect them—and that now they were safe, he had other people to protect—Nicky couldn't understand how his friend would abandon him.

Just the other night he had asked her what was wrong with

him that made Colt not like him anymore, just like his father hadn't liked him. It broke her heart into jagged little pieces, but she had tried her best through the tears to reassure her son that Colt hadn't left because of anything he had said or done.

The door to the medical trailer suddenly swung open and Peg stuck her bleached-blond frizz inside. "Hey, Maggie, heads up. You got another one comin' in. A real good-lookin' son of a gun, too."

Well, here was one for the record books, Peg hinting that there could be another man on God's green earth who might interest her besides Colt McKendrick. Her stepmother hadn't let a day go by in the last two weeks without reminding Maggie she thought she was a dozen kinds of fool for letting him slip away.

She didn't like that mischievous little smile denting the wrinkles around the older woman's mouth, though. "What kind of injury?" she asked suspiciously.

"I'm not sure. Why don't you ask him yourself?" she asked, and slipped back out.

The door swung open wider and a tall, dark cowboy filled the space.

There was no mistaking this one. Her heartbeat suddenly sounded unnaturally loud in her ears, and a wild, urgent hope soared through her. She had to sit down. And quickly. She felt behind her for the rolling stool she used for exams and carefully lowered herself onto it. "Colt! I don't... What are you doing in Missoula?"

He took his hat off so he could duck inside, leaving his hair flattened. It made him seem younger, somehow. Vulnerable. She wanted to reach out and smooth it back, to touch that warm skin so she could assure herself he was really there and not some delusional fantasy.

He stood in the doorway, holding his hat and looking uncomfortable. "I was in the neighborhood and thought I'd get these stitches out by somebody I could trust."

"Oh." His stitches from the stab wound. Of course. That soaring hope plummeted to earth, and she chided herself for letting those foolish dreams get away from her.

"You mind taking a look at it?"

"I... No, of course not. Sit down." She gestured behind her to the exam table, and after a few awkward beats he went to the table and leaned against it, his long legs out in front of him.

She cleared her suddenly parched throat. "Um, you'll have to take off your shirt."

His hands went to the buttons of his shirt and she watched, hypnotized, while he worked them free and pulled the shirt off, baring the hard, smooth expanse of his chest.

She felt hot, suddenly. Feverish. Whatever happened to the damn air-conditioning in here?

Removing his shirt also exposed a white bandage the size of a dollar bill, just under his rib cage, looking stark against the rest of his tanned skin. The sight jerked her attention back to his injuries and to her professional responsibilities, and she flushed.

"I, uh...I'll need you to lie down."

He complied, swinging his legs to the end of the table and resting back on his elbows so he could see what was going on. Despite her best efforts to control them, her hands trembled as she removed the bandage, revealing ten neat black stitches.

"The wound looks like it's healed well." Despite her best attempts at being professional about this, her voice came out thin and scratchy. "How does it feel?"

He shrugged. "Most of the time I forget it's there."

"That's a good sign." She reached a hand out to probe the wound for any abnormal swelling. His skin was warm— so warm—and she wanted to press against that chest, to have those arms go around her and hold her as tightly as he could.

At the first touch of her hand on his skin, though, his tight stomach muscles contracted, and he hissed in a sharp breath.

She snatched her hand back as if she had touched hot coals and stared at him, stricken. Oh, Lord. She couldn't do this. She couldn't stand here casually and treat him as if he were simply any other patient. Not when she couldn't think past the emotions churning through her that just being near him again stirred up.

She backed away from the table and turned to gaze out the window at nothing. "I'm sorry, Colt. I—I think maybe you'd better find somebody else to help you." *Just go away. Please, just leave before I break down and make a complete fool of myself.*

"Doc." His voice trailed off. "Doc, I didn't really come here to have you take my stitches out. Anybody could do that. Hell, I could probably do it myself."

Her gaze flew to his. He watched her with an unreadable light in those blue eyes. He shrugged into his shirt, then swung his legs over the side of the exam table and put his weight on the floor.

"Why did you come, then?"

He started to button his shirt back up. "To see you," he said.

"Okay. You've seen me. I'm just fine," she lied. *Now go.*

"Well, I'm not."

At his words she looked into his eyes again and something in the intensity there made her heart beat faster and that wild hope return. "Are you...are you sick?"

He picked up his Stetson off the table and twirled it around his fingers. He only did that when he was nervous, she realized. What could he possibly have to be nervous about?

"No," he answered. "Not sick. Just stupid."

"I don't understand."

He sighed and scratched at his ear, looking more uncomfortable than she had ever seen him. "Neither do I, Doc. Neither do I. See, I had everything worked out when I left you back there in Utah. I figured it would be best for you if we went our separate ways."

He concentrated on a spot above her head. "I also knew when I left," he continued in that strangled voice, "that I didn't have a single thing to offer you, that I couldn't be the kind of man you and Nicky needed."

Did that mean he had *wanted* to be that man? Why was he here, telling her this, if he didn't? She thrust her hands into the pockets of her lab coat to still their sudden trembling. "And now?"

"And now I'm willing to try to be any kind of man you want."

At his low declaration, she gazed at him, her thoughts racing, that stubborn wild hope doing aerial acrobatics. To keep it from spiraling completely out of control, she forced herself to concentrate on the first part of his words.

"Let me get this straight. You walked out of our lives because you made the decision—the completely unilateral decision—that you weren't the kind of man I needed or wanted. Is that right?"

"Something like that."

"How do you know what kind of man I need? Or want, for that matter. Maybe," she added quietly, "what I want *and* need is an FBI agent who can rope and ride with the best of them."

He seemed to have become inordinately fascinated with his hat. "I'm afraid you'll have to do a little searching, then. The only cowboy I know in the Bureau quit this afternoon."

She stared at him, shocked. "Why?"

"A lot of reasons." He looked at her again. "I've been burned out for a long time. The weeks I spent with you made me realize how much I'd come to hate it."

He paused and his fingers clenched on the brim of his hat. "No, *hate* is too strong a word. Somewhere along the line I just stopped feeling. I built this shell around me, so thick and hard that nothing could break through. Then I met you and Nick, and you made me realize how how long it's been since I really cared about anything."

"Oh, Colt." She felt tears, hot and thick, behind her eyelids. One sneaked out before she could stop it, and if she hadn't been so affected by his words, she would have laughed at the sudden horror that came over Colt's expression when his eyes focused on its trickling path down her cheek.

"Aw, Maggie. Hell. Don't cry."

At last—at long, long last—he stepped forward and gathered her into his arms. She closed her eyes against the torrent of feelings that threatened to overwhelm her as his sage-and-leather scent surrounded her, as his strength encircled her.

It felt *right* here, she thought. Exactly right. Like home.

"I'm sorry." She sniffled against his shirt. "I don't know what's gotten into me."

"I didn't mean to make you cry, Doc. I'll just go away again, if that's what you want."

"No!" She tilted her head to face him and lost her breath at the fierce emotion blazing from those beautiful blue eyes. "I don't want you to go away. Never again."

Those eyes searched her face, and then, with a low groan, he lowered his mouth to hers. It was a gentle kiss, full of gratitude and healing and tenderness, and it moved her as nothing ever had before.

They stayed that way for several moments, his mouth cherishing hers, and then he pulled away. With his hands cupping her face, he met her gaze with fierce intensity. "I love you, Maggie. Lord, I love you."

Her knees felt weak again, and she was glad for the support of his arms as joy exploded inside her. Her hands wrapped around his neck tightly. "I love you, too," she murmured against his mouth. "So much. I have for what seems like forever."

"Does this mean you've forgiven me for lying to you? For not telling you I was with the FBI?"

"Oh, Colt. I realized that night in Ogden there was nothing to forgive. Everything you did was to protect us. I can never thank you enough for that." She pressed her lips to his, trying to show him with her mouth everything she felt, all the love she thought he would ever want.

There was only one other chair in the trailer besides the rolling stool and the exam table, and he guided her over to it, then sat down and tugged her down onto his lap.

"What made you come find me?" she asked, when she was safe and warm in his arms again.

"I've been miserable without you. Snarling and snapping and picking fights with everybody. Joe finally told me if I didn't come after you, he was going to come find you himself and drag you back to the ranch until we worked things out. I realized he was right, that I needed to see you one more time, if only to tell you how I feel. If you shoved me out the door, I would just have to live with it, but at least I would know I tried."

Her cheek resting against his chest where his heartbeat sounded strong and solid against her ear, she smiled softly. "Remind me to thank him the next time I see him."

"You'll have to go over to the Double C to do it. I fired him."

She stiffened and jerked away. "You didn't! Colton McKendrick! What kind of thing is that to do to your friend, just because he was looking out for your best interests?"

"Easy, Doc." He grinned at her. "It's your fault."

"My fault? What did I do?"

"Well, I don't know what you said to Annie Redhawk that day you treated her, but she filed for divorce last week."

"Good for her!"

"Yeah, it's about damn time. Her son of a bitch husband disappeared, though, so now she needs a good foreman to help her run the place. Since I plan to be on the Broken Spur full-time now, I figured Annie could use Joe's help more than I could."

She studied his features. "Do you think you'll be able to stay?"

His arms around her tightened. "I've had two weeks to

think about what you said that night in Ogden, and I realized you were right. I'll probably never completely forgive myself, but I need to move on. I belong on the ranch. It's the only place I've ever really belonged and maybe I just needed someone to make me see that.''

He took one of her hands and brought it to his mouth, his brushy outlaw's mustache tickling her skin. ''I love you, Maggie Rawlings,'' he murmured. ''And Nick, too. I want to marry you, to spend the rest of my life showing you just how much. I don't want to live at the Broken Spur—or anywhere else, for that matter—without you and Nick there, too.''

Nicky! What on earth was he going to say to the idea of having Colt for a father? He would be elated, she realized. And Colt would be a wonderful father to him, caring and involved and committed. Exactly what her son needed. And what *she* needed.

Another tear slipped down her cheek, but he didn't seem to notice. ''I know the ranch house isn't what you're used to,'' he went on. ''There hasn't been a woman living there since my mom died years ago. But you could fix it up any way you want. Gut the whole thing if you want and start over.''

Did he really think she cared where she lived? She had spent the last two months living in an eight-by-fourteen-foot aluminum box, for heaven's sake!

''And I know it wouldn't be very glamorous or exciting, but the ranching families around the Broken Spur are always needing a good doctor, if you wanted to open a practice.''

Glamorous or exciting? Is that what he thought she wanted? She couldn't help it. She started to laugh.

''What's so funny?'' he asked.

''You can save your sales pitch, Colt. I'm already convinced.''

Already gearing up for more arguments, he closed his mouth with a snap and searched her features. All he saw was joy and a deep, pure love he thought he would never find. "Is that a yes?" he asked in a voice suddenly gruff.

She smiled softly and brought his mouth to hers again. "I can't think of anything more wonderful than marrying you and living on your ranch with you and Nicky for the rest of my life."

A vast relief poured through him, and he tangled his fingers in her hair and kissed her hard. Finally, when they were both breathless and the need between them had begun to build into something he knew they couldn't finish here, where any minute they might be interrupted, he dragged his mouth away.

"Are you sure you're willing to take on a disillusioned ex-FBI agent with more than his share of baggage?" He knew he had to ask, even though he wasn't sure he wanted to hear her answer.

But her lips just twisted into that soft, healing smile. "No," she answered, and there was a world of promise and hope and love in her voice. "But I'm willing to take on you."

It was all he needed to hear.

* * * * *

If you enjoyed what you just read,
then we've got an offer you can't resist!

Take 2 bestselling love stories FREE!

Plus get a FREE surprise gift!

▰▰▰▰▰▰▰▰▰▰▰▰▰▰▰▰

Clip this page and mail it to Silhouette Reader Service™

IN U.S.A.	IN CANADA
3010 Walden Ave.	P.O. Box 609
P.O. Box 1867	Fort Erie, Ontario
Buffalo, N.Y. 14240-1867	L2A 5X3

YES! Please send me 2 free Silhouette Intimate Moments® novels and my free surprise gift. Then send me 6 brand-new novels every month, which I will receive months before they're available in stores. In the U.S.A., bill me at the bargain price of $3.57 plus 25¢ delivery per book and applicable sales tax, if any*. In Canada, bill me at the bargain price of $3.96 plus 25¢ delivery per book and applicable taxes**. That's the complete price and a savings of over 10% off the cover prices—what a great deal! I understand that accepting the 2 free books and gift places me under no obligation ever to buy any books. I can always return a shipment and cancel at any time. Even if I never buy another book from Silhouette, the 2 free books and gift are mine to keep forever. So why not take us up on our invitation. You'll be glad you did!

245 SEN CNFF
345 SEN CNFG

Name	(PLEASE PRINT)	
Address	Apt.#	
City	State/Prov.	Zip/Postal Code

* Terms and prices subject to change without notice. Sales tax applicable in N.Y.
** Canadian residents will be charged applicable provincial taxes and GST.
   All orders subject to approval. Offer limited to one per household.
   ® are registered trademarks of Harlequin Enterprises Limited.

INMOM99   ©1998 Harlequin Enterprises Limited

*Membership in this family has
its privileges…and its price.
But what a fortune can't buy,
a true-bred Texas love is sure to bring!*

Coming in November 1999…

Expecting…
In Texas
by

MARIE
FERRARELLA

Wrangler Cruz Perez's night of passion with Savannah Clark
had left the beauty pregnant with his child. Cruz's cowboy
code of honor demanded he do right by the expectant
mother, but could he convince Savannah—and himself—
that his offer of marriage was inspired by true love?

THE FORTUNES OF TEXAS continues with
A Willing Wife by Jackie Merritt,
available in December 1999 from
Silhouette Books.

Available at your favorite retail outlet.

Silhouette ®

Visit us at www.romance.net

PSFOT3

Don't miss Silhouette's newest cross-line promotion,

Four royal sisters find their own Prince Charmings as they embark on separate journeys to find their missing brother, the Crown Prince!

The search begins in October 1999 and continues through February 2000:

On sale October 1999: **A ROYAL BABY ON THE WAY** by award-winning author **Susan Mallery** (Special Edition)

On sale November 1999: **UNDERCOVER PRINCESS** by bestselling author **Suzanne Brockmann** (Intimate Moments)

On sale December 1999: **THE PRINCESS'S WHITE KNIGHT** by popular author **Carla Cassidy** (Romance)

On sale January 2000: **THE PREGNANT PRINCESS** by rising star **Anne Marie Winston** (Desire)

On sale February 2000: **MAN...MERCENARY...MONARCH** by top-notch talent **Joan Elliott Pickart** (Special Edition)

ROYALLY WED
Only in—
SILHOUETTE BOOKS

Available at your favorite retail outlet.

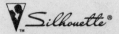

Visit us at www.romance.net

SSERW